Blood Rain

Michael John Dibdin was born in Wolverhampton in 1947. His mother was a nurse and his father a Cambridge-educated physicist with a passionate enthusiasm for folk music. The family travelled extensively around Britain until Michael turned seven, when they settled in Northern Ireland.

After graduating with an English degree from Sussex University he took a Master's Degree at the University of Alberta, Canada. Dibdin's first published novel, *The Last Sherlock Holmes Story*, his self-proclaimed 'pastiche', appeared in 1978. Shortly afterwards he moved to Italy to teach for a number of years at the University of Perugia where he was inspired to write a second novel, *A Rich Full Death*, set in Victorian Florence. In 1988 he wrote *Ratking*, the first of the famous crime series featuring the Italian detective Aurelio Zen. The novel won the Crime Writers' Association Gold Dagger award. Other books in this series include three of his best received titles, *Cabal* (1992), which was awarded the French Grand Prix du Roman Policier, *Dead Lagoon* (1994), and finally *End*

Games, published posthumously in 2007. Amongst his best-received non-Zen novels were *The Dying of the Light*, an Agatha Christie pastiche, and the darkly comic *Dirty Tricks*.

While Dibdin travelled frequently to Italy, he lived in Seattle with his wife the novelist Kathrine Beck, from where he wrote all but the first three Zen novels. The city also provided a new location for his other detective novels, including *Dark Spectre* (1995) and *Thanksgiving* (2000), the story of a British journalist's obsession with his recently dead American wife.

Michael Dibdin died in 2007 at the age of 60.

MICHAEL DIBDIN

Blood Rain

faber and faber

First published in 1999
by Faber and Faber Limited
Bloomsbury House
74–77 Great Russell Street, London WC1B 3DA
First published in paperback in 2000
This paperback edition first published in 2011

Typeset by RefineCatch Limited, Bungay, Suffolk
Printed and bound by CPI Group (UK) Ltd, Croydon, CR0 4YY

The right of Michael Dibdin to be identified as author of this work
has been asserted in accordance with Section 77 of the Copyright,
Designs and Patents Act 1988

A CIP record for this book
is available from the British Library

ISBN 978-0-571-27083-5

Without Sicily, Italy leaves no clear and lasting impression; this place is the key to everything.
Goethe, *Italian Journey: Palermo*, 13 April 1787

to Paolo Bartoli

Tannu lu veru amicu chiancirai
Quannu lu perdi e nun lu vidi cchiui

PART ONE

What it all seemed to come down to, in those early days when everything looked as clear as the sea at sunrise, was the question of exactly where, how and when the train had been 'made up'. It was only much later that Aurelio Zen came to realize that the train had been made up in a quite different sense, that it had never really existed in the first place.

At the time, the issues had seemed as solid as the train itself: a set of fourteen freight wagons currently quarantined on a siding in the complex of tracks surrounding the engine sheds at Piazza delle Americhe, on the coast to the north of central Catania. The site where the body had been found was within the territory of the *provincia di Catania*, and hence under the jurisdiction of the authorities of that city. So far, so good. From a bureaucratic point of view, however, the crucial factor was where and when the crime – if indeed it was a crime – had occurred. As all those concerned were soon to learn, none of these points was susceptible of a quick or easy answer.

Even assuming that the records provided by the State Railway authorities had been complete and credible, and no one in his right mind would have been prepared to make such an assumption, only a few unequivocal facts emerged. The first was that the train had originally left Palermo at 2.47 p.m. on 23 July. At this point it consisted of seven wagons, three of them empties commencing a long journey back to their depot in Catania, the others loaded with an assortment of goods ranging from empty wine bottles to drums of fertilizer. It was not clear whether or not the 'death chamber', as it was later dubbed by the media, had been one of these.

Having trundled along the north coast as far as the junction of Castello, the train turned inland, following a river valley up into the remote and largely depopulated centre of the island. Here, always assuming that the scanty records of the *Ferrovie dello Stato* were to be trusted, it had disappeared from official view for the best part of a week.

When it re-emerged on 29 July, at the junction of Caltanissetta-Xirbi, the convoy consisted of twelve wagons, including some – or possibly all – of the seven which had originally started from the island's capital. There had apparently been a lot of starting and stopping, of shunting and dropping, during the long, slow trip along the single-track line through the desolate interior of Sicily. No one was in any great hurry to get anywhere, and the staff in charge tended to make on-the-spot decisions about the composition and scheduling of such freight trains on a pragmatic basis, without bothering their superiors about every last detail. If the odd empty wagon got uncoupled or hitched up at some point, to keep the load down to what the ancient diesel locomotive could handle on the steep inland gradients, that was not regarded as a matter that needed to be brought to the attention of the officials in Palermo. Nor would the latter have been pleased to be informed about such minutiae, it being notorious that they had better things to do than their jobs.

At all events, the resulting train – whatever its exact composition – had continued via Caltanissetta and Canicattì to the coast and then headed east, picking up three (or possibly four) more wagons and losing one (or possibly two) to form the set now reposing on a secluded siding in Catania, its intended destination all along.

According to the subsequent deposition of the driver and his assistant, however, it had been stopped by a flagman near the unmanned station of Passo Martino, just south of Catania, and diverted into a siding there for several hours. This, they claimed to have been told, was due to emergency repair work on a bridge to the north. At length the flagman gave them the all-clear, and the freight train completed its journey without further incident, arriving on 1 August towards eight o'clock in the evening.

It was two days later that the State Railway offices in Catania received the phone call. The speaker had a smooth, educated voice, but his accent was unfamiliar to the official on duty. Apparently he wanted to report a public nuisance in the form of a wagonload of rotting goods parked on a siding at Passo Martino. The smell, he claimed, was dreadful, and what with the heat and the usual stench from the swampland all around, it was driving everyone out of their minds. Something should be done, and soon.

The railway official duly passed the message on to his superintendent. Maria Riesi would normally have dismissed the matter as just another crank call from some disgruntled eccentric, but under the circumstances she was only too happy to have an excuse to leave her stifling office and drive – all windows open, and the new Carmen Consuela album blasting from the speakers – down the *autostrada* to Piano d'Arci, and then along the country road which zigzagged across the river and the railway tracks to the lane leading down to the isolated station. She didn't believe for a moment that there would be anything there, but that didn't matter. The call had been duly logged and noted, so by going out to investigate she was merely doing her job.

Much to her surprise, there *was* a wagon there, parked on a set of rusted rails almost invisible beneath a scented mass of wild thyme punctuated by some scrubby cacti. There were other, less pleasant smells in the air too, and a lot of flies about. The sun was a strident scream, the heat reflected from every ambient surface its sonorous echo. Maria Riesi walked along the crumbling platform towards the rust-red bulk of the boxcar.

As a matter of routine, the first thing she checked was the waybill clipped into its holder beside the doors. This document listed Palermo as the origin of the wagon, and its destination as Catania. The writing was a mere scrawl, but the contents appeared to be listed as 'lemons', and the bill had been over-stamped in red with the word PERISHABLE. Judging by the swarms of flies and the nauseating stench, whatever the wagon contained was not only perishable, but had in fact perished. This came as no surprise to Maria, who knew very well that perishable goods did not travel in this type of wagon. It only remained to find out their nature, and if possible their provenance, and then write an anodyne report handing the whole matter over to Central Headquarters in Palermo. Let them decide whose head should roll.

Even standing on tiptoe, Maria Riesi could not reach the handle to open the wagon. But although short, she was both resourceful and strong. The station had been abandoned for years, but one of the large-wheeled baggage carts used to unload goods and luggage was still parked in a weed-infested corner of the platform, its handle propped up against the wall of a shed. Maria marched over and, grunting from the effort, managed to get it moving and to haul it over to the stalled wagon. She clambered up on to the slatted wooden floor of the cart, her silk blouse stained with sweat, and, by dint of putting her whole weight on the lever which secured the sliding door, eventually forced it open.

Everyone subsequently agreed that she had done more than could have been expected under the circumstances, and that it was not her fault that she vomited all over herself and the baggage cart. The post-mortem was conducted that evening, in an army tent hastily erected at the end of the platform, well away from the assembled group of policemen, magistrates and reporters. The remains had been removed from the wagon earlier by hospital personnel clad in plastic body suiting equipped with breathing apparatus. If the results of the examination were not very informative, this was due more to the condition of the corpse than to the pathologist's understandable desire to conclude the proceedings as soon as possible. The most he could say, based on a preliminary visual examination of the fly larvae present, was that the victim had been dead for at least a week.

Although the body had been discovered in the province of Catania, the ensuing investigation was technically speaking the responsibility of the police force having jurisdiction in the province where death had taken place. In the present case, this was an extremely moot point. In its peregrinations across Sicily, the train had passed through the provinces of Palermo, Caltanissetta, Palermo once again, Agrigento, Caltanissetta *bis*, Ragusa, Siracusa, and finally Catania. Six jurisdictions could thus assert a claim to investigate 'the Limina atrocity', to use another journalistic label soon attached to the affair. The wagon in which the corpse was found could not be traced with certainty to any of the many and only partially documented stops which the train had made, and even if it had, its original provenance as a 'death chamber' remained unknown.

None of this would have much mattered, of course, if it hadn't been for the provisional identification of the victim. On the contrary, everyone would have been only too happy to hand such a messy, unpromising case to their provincial neighbours on either side. Some vagrant had jumped a freight train somewhere down the line. He may have had a specific goal in mind, or just wanted to move on. Yet a further possibility was that he was on the run from someone or something, and needed to resort to clandestine forms of transport.

Unfortunately for him, the loading door on the wagon he selected had closed at some point after his entry. Perhaps he had even shut it himself, for greater security, not realizing that it could not be opened from the inside. Or maybe some jolting application of the brakes had done it, or simply the force of gravity acting on one of the gradients the train had climbed during its journey through the mountains.

At all events, the door had closed, locking the intruder inside. At that time of year, daytime temperatures reached well over thirty degrees, even on the coast. Inside the sealed metal freight wagon, standing for days at a time on isolated sidings in the full glare of the sun, a hypothetical thermometer might well have recorded temperatures in the mid-forties.

Trapped inside that slow oven, the victim had recourse to nothing but his bare hands. His feet were also bare, and both were even barer by the time the body was discovered – stripped to the bone, in fact. The flesh had been abraded and pulped and the nails ripped off in the man's attempts to attract attention by hammering on the walls of the wagon and, when that failed, to prise open the door. No fingerprints, obviously. There wasn't much left of the face, either, which he had smashed repeatedly against a metal reinforcing beam, a frenzied effort at self-destruction indicating the intensity of the ordeal which he had sought to bring to a swift end.

The victim's pockets were completely empty, his clothing unmarked. In the absence of any other information it would have been almost impossible to identify him, except for that mysterious scribble in the Contents box on the wagon's waybill, which was eventually deciphered as being not '*limoni*' – 'lemons' – but 'Limina'. It was this which ultimately led to the authorities in Catania being allotted jurisdiction in the case, for the Limina family ran one of the principal Mafia clans in that city, and Tonino, the eldest son and presumptive heir, had been rumoured to be missing for over a week.

The woman was standing at the corner of the bar, below a cabinet displaying various gilt and silverplate soccer cups, photographs of the shrine of Saint Agatha, and a mirror reading, in English: 'Delicious Coca-Cola in the World the Most Refreshing Drink'. She was drinking a *cappuccino* and taking small, precise bites out of a pastry stuffed with sweetened ricotta cheese. In her early twenties, she was wearing a pale green linen dress and expensive sandals with heels. Her brown hair, streaked with blonde highlights, ran smoothly across her skull, secured by a white ribbon, then poured forth in a luxurious mane falling to her shoulders.

Nowhere else in Italy would this scene have rated a second of anyone's attention, but here it was seemingly a matter of some general concern, if not indeed scandal. For although the bar was crowded with traders and customers from the market taking place in the piazza outside, this woman was the sole representative of her sex present.

Not that anyone drew attention to her anomalous presence by any pointed comments, hard looks or tardy service. On the contrary, she was treated to an almost suffocating degree of respect and courtesy, in stark contrast to the rough-and-ready treatment handed out to the regulars. While they jammed as equals in the jazzy rhythms of male talk, fighting for the opportunity to take a solo, she was deferred to in an outwardly respectful but in practice exclusionary way. A request that her tepid coffee be reheated was met with a cry of '*Subito, signorina!*' When she produced a cigarette, an outstretched lighter materialized before she had a chance to find her own, like a parody of a seduction scene in some old film.

But although the atmosphere was almost oppressively deferential, it could not have been said to be cordial. The other customers all clustered at the opposite end of the bar, or backed away towards the window and the door, creating a virtual exclusion zone around this lone female. Their voices were uncharacteristically low, too, and their mouths often casually covered by a hand holding a cigarette or obsessively brushing a moustache. For some reason, this unexceptionable woman appeared to be regarded as the social equivalent of an unexploded bomb.

When the man arrived, the palpable but undefined tension relaxed somewhat. It was as if one of the problems which the woman's presence represented had now been neutralized, although others perhaps remained.

The newcomer was clearly not a local, even though his prominent, prow-like nose might have suggested some atavistic input from the Greek gene pool which still surfaced here from time to time, like the lava flows from the snow-covered volcano which dominated the city. But his accent, the pallor of his complexion, his stiff bearing and above all his height – a good head above everyone else in the room – clearly ruled him out as a Sicilian.

To look at, he and the woman might have been professional acquaintances or rivals meeting by chance over their morning coffee, but that hypothesis was abruptly dispelled by a gesture so quick and casual it could easily have passed unnoticed: the man reached over and turned down the label of the woman's dress, which was sticking up at the nape of her neck.

'*A lei, Dottor Zen!*' the barman announced at a volume which might or might not have been intended to undercut the politeness of the phrase. With a triumphant yet nonchalant gesture, he set down a double espresso and a pastry stuffed with sultanas, pine nuts and almond paste. Zen took a sip of the scalding coffee, which jolted his head back briefly, then pulled over the copy of the newspaper which the woman had been reading. DEATH CHAMBER WAGON TRACED TO PALERMO, read the headline. Aurelio Zen tapped the paper three times with the index finger of his left hand.

'So?' he asked, catching his companion's eyes.

The woman made a gesture with both hands, as though weighing a sack of some loose but heavy substance such as flour or salt.

'Not here,' she said.

And in fact the bar had suddenly become amazingly quiet, as though every single one of the adversarial conversations previously competing for territorial advantage had just happened to end at the same moment. Aurelio Zen turned to face the assembled customers, eyeing them in turn with an air which seemed to remind each of the company that he had urgent and pressing matters to discuss with his neighbours. Once the former hubbub was reestablished, Zen turned back to start his breakfast.

'You're going native,' he said through a bite of the pastry.

'It's just common sense,' the woman replied, a little snappily. 'They know all about us, but we haven't the first idea about them.'

Zen finished his coffee and called for a glass of mineral water to wash down the sticky pastry.

'If you start thinking like that, you'll go mad.'

'And if you don't, you'll get killed.'

Zen snorted.

'Don't flatter yourself, Carla. Neither of us is going to get killed. We're not important enough.'

'Not to be a threat, no. But we're important enough to be a message.'

She pointed to the newspaper.

'Like him.'

'How do you mean?'

The woman did not answer. Zen finished his pastry and wiped his lips on a paper napkin tugged from its metal dispenser.

'Shall we?' he said, dropping a couple of banknotes on the counter.

Outside in Piazza Carlo Alberto, the *Fera o Luni* market was in full swing. Zen and his adopted daughter, Carla Arduini, had made this their meeting point from the moment that she had arrived in Sicily a month earlier, on a contract from her Turin computer firm to install a computer system for the Catania branch of the *Direzione Investigativa Anti-Mafia*. It was roughly half-way between the central police station, where Zen worked, and the *Palazzo di Giustizia* where Carla was battling with the complexities of setting up a network designed to be both totally secure and interactive with other DIA branches in Sicily and elsewhere.

Since arriving in the city, Zen had taken to leaving the window of his bedroom open so that he was awakened about five o'clock by the first birds and the barking of the local dogs, in time to watch the astonishing spectacle of sunrise over the Bay of Catania: an intense, distant glow, as though the sea itself had caught fire like a pan of oil. Then he showered, dressed, had a cup of homemade coffee and left the building, walking north beneath hanging gardens whose lemon trees, giant cacti and palms were teasingly visible above.

At about seven o'clock, he strode up to one of the conical-roofed booths in the Piazza Carlo Alberto which sold soft drinks, and ordered a *spremuta d'arancia*. In fact, he didn't need to order. The owner, who had spotted Zen's tall figure striding across the piazza, was already slicing blood-red oranges, dumping them in his ancient bronze press, and filling a glass with the pale orange-pink juice. Zen drank it down, then walked over to the café where he knew that Carla would be waiting for him. It was all very reassuring, like the rituals of the family he had never had.

When he and Carla emerged from the café, the sky above was delivering an impartial, implacable glare which merely hinted at the inferno to come later in the day, when every surface would add its note to the seamless cacophony of heat, radiating back the energy it had absorbed during hours of exposure to the midday sun.

A woman who looked about a hundred years old was roasting red and yellow peppers on a charcoal brazier, muttering some imprecation or curse to herself the while. Behind their wooden stalls drawn up in ranks in the square, under their faded acrylic parasols, traders with faces contorted into ritual masks either muttered a sales pitch in the form of a continual litany, as if reciting the Rosary, or barked their wares in harsh, rhetorical outbursts like the Messenger in some ancient play announcing a catastrophe unspeakable in normal language. This speech duly delivered, they surrendered the stage to one of their neighbours and reverted to being the unremarkable middle-aged men they were, gazing sadly at the goods whose praises they had just been singing, until the time came to don the tragic mask again and announce in a series of blood-curdling shrieks that plump young artichokes were to be had for seven hundred and fifty lire a kilo.

And not only artichokes. Just about every form of produce and merchandise known to man was on sale somewhere in the piazza, and those that were not on display – such as women, or AK-47s in their original packing cases – were available more discreetly in the surrounding streets. Zen and Carla walked through the meat section of the market, a shameless display which said, in effect, 'These are dead animals. We raise them, we kill them, then we eat them. If they're furry or have nice skin, we also wear them, but that's at the other end of the piazza.'

And it was this end that they had now entered, away from the specialist sellers of olives and peppers, fennel and cauliflowers, tomatoes and lettuce. Here it was all clothing, household goods and general kitsch and bric-à-brac, and a significant number of the traders were illegal *extracommunitari* immigrants from Libya, Tunisia and Algeria. An understood and accepted form of racism was in force: the locals wouldn't accept food from black hands, but they were perfectly happy to buy socks and tin-openers and screwdrivers from them, as long as the price was right.

'What were you saying about the body in the train?' asked Aurelio Zen as he and his companion passed the fringes of the market and emerged into the startlingly empty street beyond.

Carla glanced around before replying.

'The buzz in the women's toilet is that it wasn't the Limina boy at all.'

They walked in silence until they came to Via Umberto, their traditional parting place.

'Which judge is handling the case?' asked Zen.

'A woman called Nunziatella. First name Corinna.'

'Do you know her?'

'We've met a few times, and she seems to like me, but obviously I try to keep out of her way. A humble technician like me is not supposed to interfere with the work of the judges any more than is strictly necessary.'

Zen smiled, then kissed the woman briefly on both cheeks.

'*Buon lavoro, Carla.*'

'You too, Dad.'

Zen walked down Via Umberto to the corner, then turned into Via Etnea, the town's main street. As he crossed, he glanced as always at the snow-capped mass of Etna to the right, looming up over the city like a nightmare acne pimple. After that, it was a short and pleasant walk along a hushed back-street to the little piazza where the Questura was situated.

With a nod to the armed guard in his bullet-proof booth at the door, Zen entered the building and went upstairs to his office: a cool, spacious room on the second floor of the elegant eighteenth-century *palazzo*, formerly a bank, which now housed the Catania police headquarters. Floor-length windows gave on to a balcony commanding a view of the street below. The walls were adorned with photographs of Carla Arduini and Signora Zen, as well as a framed poster entitled *Venezia forma urbis*, a large collage of aerial photographs forming a precise and evocative map of Zen's native city.

He had never bothered to personalize his temporary quarters like this before, and if he had now, it was because he had reluctantly accepted that these were not temporary. On the contrary, Zen had every reason to suppose that he would be stuck in Catania for the rest of his career.

The proposition which had been made to him in Rome by the famous film director known as Giulio, prior to Zen's visit to Piedmont, had turned out to be as false as it was flattering. Zen had been privately advised that an élite corps was being put together to smash the Mafia once and for all, and that following Zen's 'anti-terrorist triumph' in Naples he had been chosen to join this select group, despite the notorious inconveniences and risks, occasionally fatal, of a posting to Sicily. The deal had been that in return for Zen's assistance in the Aldo Vincenzo affair, Giulio's contacts at the Interior Ministry would arrange for him to be sent not to one of the island's hot spots but to an attractive backwater on the fringes of the real action. Syracuse had been mentioned as one possibility: a city 'possessing all the charm and beauty of Sicily without being tiresomely Sicilian', as Giulio had so invitingly put it.

Almost every aspect of this cover story had turned out to be untrue. For a start, the new 'élite corps' did not exist, or rather it existed already in the form of the *Direzione Investigativa AntiMafia*, set up in 1995 by Judge Giovanni Falcone with the collaboration of the then Minister of Justice, Claudio Martelli. Aurelio Zen had not been invited to join this group, and not surprisingly, since it consisted of young, keen, energetic volunteers from the country's three separate police forces. Nevertheless, he *was* being posted to Sicily, he had learned shortly after his return to Rome following the false close he had achieved in the Vincenzo affair. In what role, however, remained for the moment ambiguous.

'Essentially, you're to act as a facilitator,' Zen's immediate superior had told him before his departure from Rome. 'Needless to say, the DIA are doing admirable work, on the whole. Nevertheless, there is a growing feeling abroad that, like every élite division, they sometimes exhibit a regrettable and perhaps potentially perilous tendency towards a . . . How shall I put it? A degree of professional myopia. There have been instances, some quite recently, when they have regretfully been perceived to be acting without due consultation, and in apparent ignorance of the wider issues involved.'

The official paused, awaiting Zen's response. At length, realizing that it would not be forthcoming, he continued.

'With the aforesaid factors in mind, a decision has been made at ministerial level to deploy a pool of mature and experienced officials such as yourself to liaise directly with members of the *Polizia Statale* seconded to the DIA. Your role will be firstly to report to us here at the Viminale on the nature and scope of DIA initiatives, both current and planned, secondly to monitor the response of all local personnel to ensuing governmental directives, and thirdly to communicate these in turn to Rome, all with a view to expediting an efficient and unproblematic implementation of official policy. Do you understand?'

Zen understood only too well: he was being asked to act as a spy. The position of Head of Post in each DIA office was allocated in turn to a representative of one of the police forces involved, each responsible to a different ministry in Rome: Defence, Finance, or Interior. The novelty of the DIA was that it had been set up from the first as a cooperative venture involving all three forces, and had been specifically designed to function independently of any ministerial interference.

At the time, in the wake of the bloodbath initiated by the Corleone clan, and the killings of General Dalla Chiesa and the judges Falcone and Borsellino, it would have been politically unthinkable for any interested party to try to limit or control that independence. But times had changed. The Mafia had apparently been broken, with all but a few of its top *capi* jailed or in hiding, and there had been no large-scale outbreaks of violence for several years. Clearly someone in Rome, possibly several people, felt that the moment was now propitious to rein in this too-efficient and semi-autonomous organization. Even the public seemed to be starting to feel that enough was enough. Where would it all end? Were we to bring back the Inquisition?

It was in this new climate of covert consensus that Aurelio Zen had been sent south, and not to Syracuse but to Catania, the island's second-largest city and a stronghold of various Mafia clans who had long resented the power, fame and influence of their rivals – and sometimes uneasy allies – in Palermo. The office of the DIA responsible for the *provincia di Catania* was presently commanded by a colonel of the paramilitary Carabinieri, whose ultimate loyalties – in the event of any inter-ministerial disputes – lay with his superiors at the Ministry of Defence. The new political appointees at the rival Interior Ministry wanted their own man on the spot, and Aurelio Zen – unambitious and deeply compromised – had been their choice.

Superficially, Zen had to admit, it was not a bad job. Every week, each DIA office submitted a strictly confidential report on its current activities to headquarters in Rome. Thanks to a highly placed contact there, copies of these were passed to the Interior Ministry on the Viminale hill – as well, no doubt, as to the other two interested ministries. On the following Monday, a transcript of that portion of the report pertaining to the province of Catania turned up on Zen's desk. His official title was Liaison Officer, and he supposedly functioned as a sort of surrogate uncle dispatched by the new, 'caring' ministry in Rome. His real job was to amplify and amend the extract from the DIA's bare-bones document in the course of casual conversation with the seven officers of the *Polizia Statale* on the local DIA roster.

He took them out for a coffee, a beer, even a meal, ostensibly to discuss their personal problems and keep them informed about pension plans, medical benefits, alternative career openings and the like. Then, at a certain point, he would let drop one of the facts garnered from his perusal of the previous week's DIA report, in a manner which suggested that he respected his younger colleagues for doing such important and dangerous work and would be interested in knowing further details. These were generally forthcoming. Like anyone else, Zen's contacts loved to chat, bitch and gossip about their work, except that in their case this was impossible, stuck as they were deep in enemy territory. But here was a senior officer in their own force, a man of wisdom and discretion hand-picked by the authorities in Rome to look after their personal and professional well-being. If they couldn't trust him, whom could they trust?

Today, Zen was lunching with Baccio Sinico, an inspector in his early thirties who had been in Sicily for almost three years, first in Trapani and then Catania, and now wanted to be transferred back to his native Bologna. This put Zen in an even more awkward position than usual. Sinico's request was perfectly in order, and would already have been approved if it had not been for Zen's intervention. Of all his contacts inside the DIA, Sinico had turned out to be by far the most informative and uninhibited, and Zen didn't want to lose him. At the same time, he completely understood and sympathized with the man's wish to return home.

It wasn't so much a question of the physical danger, he had realized, although this was real enough. But in the course of their conversations Zen had sensed that Sinico was afflicted by another complaint, at once vaguer and more disturbing. Although Sicily was part of Italy and therefore of Europe, it didn't feel like it. In everything one did, saw and heard, there was a sense of being cut off from the mainstream, from *il continente*, as Sicilians termed the mainland. The result was a peculiarly insular arrogance, a natural reaction to centuries of being either ignored or exploited by whoever happened to be in power in the places that mattered.

Baccio Sinico was suffering from a reaction to this mentality, as perhaps was Zen himself, on those not infrequent mornings when he woke at three or four in his darkened apartment for no apparent reason and found it impossible to seduce sleep again. This will end badly, he thought, standing at the open window, the smoke from his cigarette wafting gently away on the sea breeze which came by night to mitigate the rigours of the southern sun. All was balmy, all was calm, but an ancient instinct buried deep within his cortex refused to be fooled. This will end badly, it told him, with all the authority of a source at once disinterested and well-informed. This will end badly.

Her journey to work seemed, as always, a crude parody of her entire existence: a cartoon-strip version, at once focusing and parodying the life she now lived.

At five to eight the sirens were already audible in the distance, throated along on the morning breeze off the Ionian Sea, growing in strength all the time, nearing, homing in on their target. Precisely as the hour struck from a nearby church, they peaked and then wound down in front of the apartment building where she lived. 'One, two, three, four, five . . .' she counted under her breath. When she reached ten, the phone rang.

'*Tu proverai sì come sa di sale lo pane altrui,*' a voice announced.

'*E com'è duro calle lo scendere e'l salir per l'altrui scale,*' Corinna Nunziatella replied, and hung up.

As always, she asked herself which ironic genius had selected Dante's famous lines on the bitterness of exile as that week's coded phrase announcing her body-guards' arrival: 'You'll find out just how salty other people's bread tastes, and how hard a road it is to climb up and down other people's stairs.'

Prior to her present appointment, Corinna had spent a year working in Florence and realized that the poet had meant this quite literally: Tuscan bread was made without salt and was, to her taste, insipid. Poor Dante, on the other hand, in exile north of the Apennines, had evidently been appalled by the daily discovery that the most basic human foodstuff was different there. Although without a trace of self-pity, Corinna could not help reflecting on the still greater bitterness of her own situation: a Sicilian born and bred, yet now an exile in her native land, unable to go up and down her *own* stairs without an armed guard.

A knock at the door announced the latter's arrival. Corinna checked by looking through the spyglass inset in the armoured panel, then opened the door with a sigh. Her personal escort that morning was Beppe, a gangling, semi-handsome son of a bitch who, as always, tried to get familiar as they walked downstairs together, she in her dark tailored suit and sensible shoes, he in camouflaged battledress accessorized with a machine-gun suspended on a leather belt strung over his shoulder.

'Beautiful day!' was his opening line.

'Yes.'

'But not as beautiful as you, Signorina Nunziatella.'

'That'll do, Beppe.'

'I'm sorry, *dottoressa*, but what do you expect? Here I am five hundred kilometres from home, stuck in a squalid barracks with a bunch of other jerks doing their military service, and risking my life every day to protect the most beautiful woman I've ever seen! Have you ever heard of what they call "the Stockholm syndrome", where the victims fall for their kidnappers? This is a similar thing. Because if you think about it, I've been kidnapped by the system, which you represent, *dottoressa*, so it's not surprising that I've fallen for you like a ton of . . .'

But by now they had reached the front door, and Beppe had to attend to his duties. He activated the radio strapped into a pouch on his belt and exchanged cryptic and static-garbled phrases with his companions. Then he counted slowly to five, swung open the door and ushered Corinna urgently outside. The two other guards had taken up point positions to either side of the three Fiat saloons which had drawn up in front of the building – where no other vehicle was allowed to park, even momentarily – and were anxiously scanning the street in every direction, their automatic weapons at the ready. Corinna ran the short distance to the second of the cars, whose rear door stood open, ready to receive her. Beppe, who had followed her, slammed the door shut and slapped the roof with his palm. Instantly the convoy containing Judge Nunziatella and her heavily armed escort moved off at speed, sirens screaming and blue lights flashing to alert the citizenry to the fact that yet another government functionary under sentence of death was passing by, panoplied in all the impotent might of the Italian state.

The Palace of Justice in Piazza Verga was an impressive work dating from the Fascist era, occupying an entire city block. Just outside the main entrance stood an enormous statue of a crowned female representing the justice supposedly dispensed within. One of her outstretched palms supported a jubilant male nude, while on the other a similar figure hid his head in shame or fear. Both these figures were more or less life-size, while Justice herself was at least ten metres tall, her vaguely Roman vestments overflowing on to the stone plinth below.

Classical allusions continued in the form of twenty-four rectangular pillars supporting a decorative portico, which in the present political climate gave the impression that the building itself had been imprisoned, and was gazing out at the city through the bars of its cage. But the most disturbing effect was that, apart from an hour or so around midday, the pillars to either side of the statue cast strong vertical shadows across it, turning the image of Justice into an obscure, faceless icon of some pagan deity, utterly indifferent to the joy or the misery of the paltry human figures it held in the palms of its hands.

The perimeter was impressively guarded, with canvas-covered trucks full of soldiers in battledress and an armoured car sporting a 4·5 cm cannon mounted in a swivelling turret. The army had been deployed on the streets of Catania and other Sicilian cities when it became apparent that the burden of protecting prefects, judges, magistrates and other functionaries was putting such a strain on the police forces that there weren't enough officers left to carry out the investigations and arrests ordered by those members of the judiciary who had survived the assassinations planned by Totò Riina and carried out by his Corleone clan.

Now, though, the political pendulum seemed to be on the point of swinging back again. Voices had been heard in parliament claiming that such a massive show of force was undermining the democratic culture of Italy and shaming the country in the eyes of its part-ners in the European Union. One deputy had gone so far as to compare it to the brutal repression instituted by Cesare Mori, Mussolini's 'Iron Prefect', who virtu-ally eradicated the Mafia in the 1920s, only for the invading Allies to release the jailed *capi* and their fol-lowers just in time for them to get rich on the easy money and unregulated growth of post-war Italy. No one in the government had expressed such views as yet, but Corinna Nunziatella was by no means alone in feeling that it was only a matter of time before Beppe and his fellow recruits were reunited with their girlfriends and families, and the situation in Sicily returned to what had always passed for 'normal'.

The convoy of cars drove round to the rear of the Palace of Justice, past the armed guards in their bullet-proof vests, and down a ramp leading into the bowels of the building. Corinna thanked the members of her escort – whose lives, of course, were as much at risk as hers – and took the lift to the third floor, where the offices of the *Procura della Repubblica* were located, and then walked along a corridor ending at yet another checkpoint. Here she not only had to present her iden-tification to the guard on duty – despite the fact that they both knew each other by sight – but also to pro-nounce the codeword, changed daily, which permitted access to the offices of the so-called 'pool' of AntiMafia magistrates. The security precautions protecting this high-risk group were undeniably impressive, but Corinna knew better than to assume that they would be effective in the event that an order was given to elimi-nate her. The Mafia was traditionally compared to an octopus concealed in a rocky crevice, its tentacles reach-ing everywhere. Corinna thought that a pack of invasive rats provided a more accurate analogy: if you blocked up one entrance, they would find or make another.

Despite the élite status of the AntiMafia pool, or perhaps because of the widespread resentment which this exclusive club attracted from colleagues in other branches of the police and judiciary who had not been invited to join, Corinna Nunziatella had as yet been unable to obtain an office more suited to her requirements than the dingy, dark cubicle at the north-east corner of the building which she had originally been assigned. The pointless and oppressive height of its ceiling merely served to emphasize the meagre proportions of the floor space dictated by the newly installed wall panels: 3.5 square metres, to be exact.

Since she could not expand laterally, Corinna had followed the Manhattan model, stacking files in precarious piles propped up one against the other like exhausted drunks. Retrieving any given file was a work of considerable dexterity, requiring the skills of those conjurors who can remove a tablecloth while leaving the dinner setting intact. Relief was promised shortly in the form of a computer network linking all members of the Catania DIA pool both to each other and to their colleagues in the other provincial capitals, but despite a month of installation work, it was still not up and running. In the meantime, the massive terminal squatted idly on her desk, taking up yet more precious space.

'*E se tutto ciò non bastasse . . .*,' she murmured under her breath.

Yes, indeed. As if all this were not enough, Corinna Nunziatella was beginning to suspect that she was falling in love.

She was not left long to brood on these incidental problems, for within a few minutes the phone rang, summoning her to the director's office for a 'progress report'. Corinna hastily grabbed an impressive-looking dossier of papers, some of which were actually related to her current cases, checked that her appearance was at once professional and uninviting, and proceeded up to the fifth floor.

The arrival of Sergio Tondo, the recently appointed director of the AntiMafia pool, had proved a source of much mirth to his subordinates, since in appearance he resembled the classic, slightly racist stereotype of the typical *mafioso*: short, broad, sallow and intense, with a moustache of which he was excessively proud, black voided eyes, and an air of undefined but potentially threatening distinction. The punchline of the joke was that, far from being Sicilian, or even a southerner, Tondo – originally, no doubt, Tondeau – was in fact a native of the Valle d'Aosta, the French-speaking mountain region in the extreme north-west corner of the country, well over a thousand kilometres from Catania as the crow flew, had there been any crows ambitious enough to attempt such a trip.

As though to confirm the initial impression he had created, Sergio Tondo seemed to go out of his way to act as well as look like a caricature Sicilian, to the extent of having made explicit sexual advances to all the female magistrates on his team. Corinna Nunziatella had already been obliged to remove one or other of his hands from her hip, her knee, her shoulder and just below her left breast, and to do so in such a way as to make it seem that she hadn't really been aware that it had been there in the first place.

It was a delicate operation, calling for exquisite timing, adroitness and tact. Corinna would have been the first to admit that she was ambitious, and it was hard to overemphasize the importance of her promotion to the AntiMafia pool at the age of only thirty-four. To be eased out now would not just mean a return to her previous, uninspiring postings; it would mean being marked for the rest of her life as someone who had been given a rare chance to succeed at the highest level, but who had failed. No one would ever know why, still less bother to find out. And if she started retailing stories about sexual harassment, everyone would just assume that she was trying to lay the blame elsewhere in a feeble attempt to excuse her own incompetence.

Her tactics at present were to try to make herself look drably forbidding. Not so much impregnable, which might put the director on his macho mettle, as unworthy of the effort involved. The image she strove for was that of a walled mountain village at which the invading hordes in the valley below cast a brief glance, then shook their heads, shouldered their weapons and moved on to easier pickings elsewhere. The trick was to make Tondo feel that he had rejected her, thus leaving his pride and self-esteem intact – and, above all, to do so before he pushed matters to a point she could already sense somewhere close ahead, where she would ram her knee into his bulging crotch and rake her clawed nails across his piggy little eyes.

The moment she opened the door to the director's absurdly spacious office, Corinna Nunziatella knew that something had happened, and that it was not good news. Having dreaded being overwhelmed by unwanted attentions, she found herself treated to an almost brutal absence of elementary politeness, never mind charm, which she found threatening in a quite different way. So far from rushing over to 'drink in your perfume', as he had once said, Sergio Tondo did not even bother to get to his feet. His greeting was perfunctory and barely audible. In short, his manner was everything she had wished it would be – cool, distant, and totally professional – and it scared the hell out of her. Because if the director was finally treating her as a colleague rather than a woman, it could only mean that something was very badly wrong indeed.

Corinna Nunziatella sat down in one of the two armchairs facing the desk, the antique leather creaking beneath her. Apart from a crucifix, a portrait of the president, a map of the province of Catania and a couple of shelves of law books apparently selected on the basis of format and size rather than content, the director's office was strikingly, indeed significantly, empty. No piles of files here, no unsorted notes, no computer terminal. All this austerity made the three telephones on the desk – red, blue and yellow, respectively – loom even larger. One would be for internal calls within the building, another an 'open' external line.

And the third? Corinna Nunziatella found herself irresistibly reminded of the so-called *terzo livello* of the Mafia, whose existence had often been postulated but never proved; the fabled Third Level, far above mundane criminal activities and inter-clan rivalries, on which the most powerful and influential bosses met with their political patrons and protectors in Rome to discuss kickbacks, mutual interests, and the delivery of votes come election time.

'So?' the director remarked, as though Corinna had requested a meeting with *him*.

'I understood you to say that you wanted a progress report,' she replied stiffly.

Sergio Tondo smiled superficially and made a throwaway gesture with his left hand.

'That was just a manner of speaking. I really want to have a chat, hear what you're working on at present, that sort of thing. As you know, I try to foster a team spirit here, and I feel very strongly that face-to-face meetings like this, informal and off the record, without the inevitable stresses of peer pressure, can genuinely promote a sense of individual empowerment in each and every member of the department, resulting in an enhanced professional dynamic and group cohesion.'

Corinna kept her mouth shut.

'How's the Maresi case going?' the director continued at length.

'It isn't going anywhere. It's been deadlocked for months, and looks likely to stay that way.'

'And the Cucuzza business?'

'That looked promising, until the Supreme Court released my principal witness, who promptly disappeared and is now probably in hiding abroad or dead.'

'The court was merely upholding the law,' Sergio Tondo remarked in a tone of light reprimand. 'The procedural irregularities which had evidently occurred – through no fault of yours, *dottoressa*, I dare say – unfortunately made it impossible for them to act in any other way.'

Corinna Nunziatella nodded sagely.

'I'm sure the citizens of Italy will sleep more soundly in their beds at night, knowing that the legal rights of convicted *mafiosi* are being protected with such rigour.'

The director gave a sympathetic sigh.

'I know how frustrating these setbacks can be, but try not to feel too bitter. It's quite pointless, and might ultimately have a negative effect on your performance as a valued member of our team.'

Again Corinna chose not to respond.

'Those two files are currently inactive, then,' Tondo went on. 'So what *have* you been working on?'

'The Tonino Limina case has been occupying almost all my time in the past weeks.'

'With what results?'

Corinna took a deep breath and counted silently to five.

'As I explained at the general briefing last week, *direttore*, I have been working on two main fronts. Firstly, I have tried to trace the provenance and movements of the wagon in which the body was found. As you know, the waybill attached to the so-called "death chamber" indicated that it formed part of a stopping goods train, schedule number 46703, which left Palermo on 23 July. However, despite lengthy interviews with the various crews who worked this train, I have as yet been unable to determine conclusively whether the said wagon originated in Palermo or was attached to the train at some later point. It is also unclear how and when it came to be abandoned on the siding where it was later discovered. The train crew explicitly deny that they detached any wagons during their layover at the station of Passo Martino. On the other hand, they admit that they remained in the cab of the locomotive during this time. It is therefore possible that some third party detached the wagon without them noticing. What we *do* know is that the signalman who brought the train to a halt was not a railway employee, and that the repair work which he used to justify the manoeuvre was not in fact taking place.'

The director nodded in a slightly bored, dismissive way.

'And your second line of enquiry?'

'To try to contact the Limina family with a view to making a positive identification of the victim.'

The director smiled yet again, more intensely, but he did not speak.

'Needless to say, this has also proved extremely problematic,' Corinna went on. 'The Limina family are not given to communicating with the authorities at the best of times, still less with a magistrate participating in the AntiMafia pool. Nevertheless, I have been able to establish a tentative initial contact, using an associate of the family with whom I have had dealings in the past.'

'Who's that?' Sergio Tondo demanded, suddenly alert.

'He is referred to in my files under the code name "Spada".'

The director frowned at her.

' "Swordfish"? And what is Signor Spada's real name?'

Corinna Nunziatella's face hardened.

'I have no idea. Nor do I wish to know. This is an extremely sensitive and covert contact, and in my view one which the Limina family deliberately keeps active in order to facilitate communications with us and with other clans when this suits their purposes. If Spada's real name became known, the contact might well be seriously compromised or even terminated.'

Corinna Nunziatella had spoken in a deliberately measured tone, weighing her words. The director considered her statement for a moment.

'And what did your Swordfish have to say?' he asked with a markedly ironic inflection.

'It's been inconclusive so far. He's intimated that the family will have a statement to make, but that they want to make sure that all members of the "family" have been informed before they make any public pronouncement. With luck, I hope to have some definite news in a week or so.'

'Oh, before that, I think!'

Sergio Tondo stood up and walked over to the window. He paused there for just long enough to make Corinna wonder if the interview was over, then turned on her abruptly.

'The Liminas have already been in contact. With me. Through other channels.'

Corinna felt her spine tense up.

'What do you mean, "other channels"?' she demanded. 'What kind of . . .?'

'The family lawyer,' Tondo replied evenly. 'Dottor Nunzio Lo Forte, a highly respectable figure specializing in civil and commercial law. He phoned me yesterday to arrange a meeting, at which he presented this document.'

He walked back to the desk and handed Corinna a typed sheet of paper. It was a sworn declaration by Anna Limina, mother of Tonino, to the effect that her son was at present on holiday in Costa Rica, and that she knew him to be alive and well. In evidence, she appended a set of his dental records for forensic comparison with the body found on the train.

'I sent the records over to the morgue immediately,' the director went on. 'The pathologist assures me that the dental details do not match those of the victim in any way. This has quite clearly been a case of mistaken identity.'

'But what about the waybill with "Limina" written on it?' Corinna protested.

The director raised an admonitory forefinger.

'It wasn't written, but scrawled, and further examination by a noted graphologist at the University of Catania suggests that the word was in fact *limoni*, as the railway official Maria Riesi originally thought. In other words, the perishable contents of the wagon in question were simply lemons, which were no doubt off-loaded further down the line. In short, whoever the unfortunate victim of this tragedy may have been, he was not Tonino Limina, and there is absolutely no reason to suppose that there is any Mafia connection at all. That being so, the matter is of no further interest to this department. The file can therefore be closed and the whole business turned over to the normal authorities for routine investigation, leaving you free to pursue your own work on such matters as the Maresi and Cucuzza cases, which by your own account appear to have been languishing of late.'

He sat down again behind his desk and made a note in his diary. Corinna Nunziatella got up and walked over to the door.

'Did I tell you how lovely you're looking this morning?' Sergio Tondo said suddenly. 'That outfit really suits you, and haven't you done something to your hair?'

The words emerged in a rapid murmur, at once acknowledging and dismissing the existence of the director's former persona, much as one might a twin who had died in infancy. Sad business, of course, but no longer really . . . *relevant*.

There was a draught about, faint but perceptible, its hollow chill undermining everything. But where was it coming from?

A real draught – indeed, fresh air of any kind or origin – would have been only too welcome in the dim recess of the Palace of Justice which Carla Arduini had reluctantly been assigned, its one high window dimmed with grime and welded shut by decades of poor maintenance. Not that conditions would have been any better with it open. On the contrary, the heat outside at this hour threatened to turn the lava paving blocks back to their molten form, while the humidity borne in off the sea swamped the whole city in a miasma of lassitude and passivity.

But the draught that was bothering Carla Arduini was not real but virtual: a flaw in cyberspace, a see-page of information from the system. Despite this, she sensed it almost physically, rather like the onset of some malaise – an accumulation of minor symptoms, none of them particularly significant in themselves, which together indicated a problem as yet unidentified, but puzzling and potentially serious.

Most people, including the majority of her professional colleagues, wouldn't have noticed anything wrong. Although not yet quite ready to be turned over to her clients, the network she was responsible for installing was up and running. The terminals were all responding and the numbers were being crunched with suitable efficiency. The problem was not with the system itself but with access to it. For some days now, Carla had had the feeling that someone had opened a 'back door' which would permit the user to monitor or manipulate the data files at will.

As a commercial hireling, Carla did not have the security clearance necessary to view DIA files herself, although she could have got into them easily enough if she had wanted. But she didn't need to. The evidence she was after was buried far below such superficial applications, hidden away in the genes of the system itself, and she had already found one line of code that didn't fit.

In a sense, it was no concern of hers. There was no perceptible effect on the efficiency of the network. Carla could simply complete her installation and sign off on the assignment, but she felt personally intrigued and challenged. Whoever had tampered with the system had done an almost completely seamless job, but he had left a few crumbs here and there, and she was determined to identify the intruder.

Unlike most of her colleagues at the Turin-based Uptime Systems, Carla Arduini was not obsessed with computers, but she had an instinctive feel for them, the way some people do for animals. She had discovered this while at university in Milan, when a last-minute change of schedule by her mathematics professor – who tried to keep the time he had to spend away from his villa on Lake Como down to the absolute minimum – led her to take a course in systems analysis to fill in a blank couple of hours on Wednesday afternoons.

The experience was a revelation to her. Mathematics, she had already begun to realize, was like one of those languages which are simple, straightforward and logical in the early stages, but which rapidly spiral out of control in a frenzy of idioms, oddities, idiosyncrasies and exceptions to the rule which even native speakers cannot always get right, never mind explain. From advanced calculus to proving Fermat's theorem or calculating the value of pi was a large step, to be sure, but it would never go away, would always be a step not taken.

The prospect of such indeterminacy on the horizon, however distant, was one which Carla found intensely threatening. Her childhood had been a shuffled series of abrupt moves, often taken furtively and under cover of darkness; of 'relatives' and 'friends' who came and went and never reappeared; of her mother's sudden reticence and evasions; and above all her father's absence. Later, as an adolescent, when she finally understood the reasons for all this, it turned out to be too late. Neat labels such as poverty, neglect, fecklessness and sheer bad luck would not adhere to those childhood memories, which remained unmanageable and apart, a perpetual source of anxiety which could awaken her even now, sweaty and trembling, in the middle of the night.

She had been drawn towards mathematics in part because of a natural gift for the subject, but largely because it seemed to offer a secure refuge, a way of containing and exorcising such imponderables. Two and two can never make five or three, still less nothing at all. They can't change their minds, or sink into depression, or disappear for days on end, or get drunk and abusive and then suddenly burst into tears across the dinner table. All they can ever do is make four.

Most of her classmates found this and similar tricks a bit dull, but not Carla, because she knew that they could be relied upon to work over and over and over again, and never let her down. It was not until she got to university that this simple faith began to desert her. It was a question of scale. Two and two make four, four and four make eight, eight and eight make sixteen . . . Even this childishly simple series was, like all series, infinite. Stronger, more stable spirits than hers, she knew, delighted in the possibilities for intellectual acrobatics this provided. All Carla felt was the return of a familiar sense of panic.

It was while struggling with this loss of mathematical faith that she was fortuitously introduced to the world of applied computing. It was love at first sight. Although seemingly complex, computers were actually reassuringly simple-minded. Whether searching a vast database for a single instance of a string, rotating three-dimensional sketches of hypothetical buildings or calculating the value of our old friend pi to fifty billion places, they were in essence no more mysterious or threatening than the spy in some old thriller sending a coded message by switching a torchlight on and off. Their memories were prodigious but finite; the Library of Congress, not the Library of Babel.

Carla reorganized her syllabus, took some private extramural courses, and when she graduated got a job first with Olivetti and then with a firm specializing in installing and maintaining computer networks linking individuals and departments within an organization. She was entirely familiar with this particular system, which she had installed many times before, and she was determined not to let some anonymous hacker outwit her.

Her cellphone started beeping. Was it her employer, complaining about the length of time it was taking her to fine-tune this system to everyone's satisfaction? Or was it one of her employer's employers, the judges and magistrates of the AntiMafia pool, wanting to know when they would finally be able to use this high technology to collate their files, communicate internally, and coordinate information and objectives with their colleagues elsewhere in Sicily?

In the event, it was simply her father.

'Carla? How's it going?'

'All right. And you?'

'Not too bad. Listen, are you free this evening?'

'Free?'

'For dinner. I've just realized that apart from meeting for coffee in the morning, we don't seem to actually spend very much time together and I feel bad about it, for some reason. I suppose I'm missing you.'

Carla laughed charmingly.

'I'd love to come to dinner, Dad.'

'We could go out, I suppose, or you could come round here.'

'Shall I bring something?'

'A dessert, perhaps. I'll put something together. It won't be much, but at least we can be together and talk . . .'

'Of course. Eight, nine? They eat late here, I've noticed.'

'Let's say eight. At my age, you don't change your habits so easily.'

'I'll be there at eight, Dad.'

'Wonderful. I'm looking forward to seeing you and being able to talk freely. It's odd . . .'

'What is?'

'Well, this whole situation. No?'

'Yes. Yes, it is.'

'Till tonight, then.'

She clicked the phone back together and turned to the sullen, recalcitrant screen. Dinner at eight. Yes, that was all right, she supposed, although she found it difficult to look forward to the evening with any great enthusiasm. Her father was right: despite the fact that Carla had requested this assignment in Sicily – not that she'd faced much competition! – in order to be near him, this physical proximity hadn't yet resulted in the warm, natural, easy relationship she had hoped for. At moments, indeed, it was hard to believe that Aurelio Zen really *was* her father.

Not literally, of course. The DNA tests they had had done in Piedmont had proven their genetic linkage beyond a shadow of doubt, but was that all there was to being a father or a daughter, a demonstrable genetic link? In law, yes, but Carla was beginning to think that the real meaning of such terms lay elsewhere, in the years of nurture and intimacy she had been denied, the long chronology of daily life stretching back into the mists of a personal pre-history, when all was myths and magic.

Not that she had any sentimental illusions about such kinship. She knew that there were good fathers and bad fathers, some supportive and some brutally abusive. Nevertheless, they were all, for better or worse, the real thing. This wasn't, and with the best will in the world there was nothing that either of them could do about it. As soon as she had finished this assignment, she would catch the first flight north. After that, she would phone her father from time to time. Perhaps they might even get together once in a while, at Christmas, but that would be all.

Meanwhile there was this unsolved problem of the virtual draught. Carla resumed her search of the system log files. After about five minutes she heard a hesitant knock at the door.

'Come in!' she called impatiently.

The door opened but Carla did not turn around immediately. When she did, she found the judge called Corinna Nunziatella standing in front of her. They had met a few times during the preceding weeks, in the corridors and the canteen of the building, to which the older woman, by virtue of her status as a DIA judge, was effectively restricted.

'I hope I'm not disturbing you,' Corinna Nunziatella remarked with a smile.

Carla got up from her desk.

'Good morning, *dottoressa*.'

Her visitor's hand waved violently, as though of its own accord.

'Oh, please, let's drop the formalities! Call me Corinna. What a charming outfit! And how's the work going?'

Her tone was friendly, but oddly tense. Carla Arduini pointed to the glowing computer screen.

'I'm afraid it looks like being a little more time before the system is ready to be handed over. I apologize. I do realize how impatient you and your colleagues must be to start using it, but various problems have arisen . . .'

'Oh, don't worry about that!' Corinna Nunziatella burst out emphatically. 'I don't know about the others, but I for one am certainly in no hurry to start using these damn things. If they'd just give me more space and some secretarial help, I'd be perfectly happy to carry on the way we've always done. But for some reason the Ministry seems to feel that getting us all on-line is their top priority. We have to fill out a requisition form every time we need a box of paper-clips, but a billion-lire computer system? No problem there.'

Carla smiled politely and waited for her visitor to come to the point. As though sensing this, Corinna Nunziatella coughed awkwardly.

'I don't really have anything much to say,' she said. 'I just happened to be passing so I thought I would drop in and . . .'

She broke off.

'That's very kind of you,' said Carla.

'I suppose I was wondering how you were getting along here in Catania,' the other woman went on in a controlled manic burble. 'It must be lonely for you, being from the north and not knowing anyone here, not having any family, any girlfriends . . .'

'Actually I do have family here,' Carla replied, twisting a strand of hair between her fingers.

Corinna Nunziatella looked at her in astonishment.

'You do? Who?'

'My father. He works at the Questura. You may have heard of him. Vice-Questore Aurelio Zen.'

'But surely he's not Sicilian?'

Carla hooted with laughter.

'God, no! He's from Venice.'

Catching herself up, she put one hand over her mouth.

'I'm so sorry, *dottoressa*. That must have sounded frightfully rude. I didn't mean it that way, but . . .'

'That's all right,' Corinna replied, a grim glitter in her eyes. 'Bash the Sicilians as much you want. I do it all the time. Just don't call me *dottoressa* again, or I'll really get angry. I can't help it, I'm a Virgo.'

Carla's eyes opened wide.

'Are you really? So am I!'

'When's your birthday?'

'Well, actually it's this weekend. On Saturday.'

Corinna Nunziatella appeared to reflect.

'Congratulations. But in the meantime, what are you doing tonight?'

Carla was slightly taken aback by this abrupt question.

'Er, well, I'm having dinner with my father. We rediscovered each other last year, in Piedmont,' she went on impulsively. 'And I was just getting to know him when he got transferred down here.'

'You were just getting to know your own father?' asked Corinna Nunziatella incredulously.

'It's a long story.'

The older woman gave an ironic smile.

'Well, if you're in the mood for long stories about fathers, I've got one too.'

She checked her watch.

'I must go. How about tomorrow night? I know a nice restaurant outside the city, up in the foothills of Etna. The food's good, and the place itself is quiet and private. You don't feel as if you're on display all the time, if you know what I mean.'

'Sounds wonderful. Where is it?'

Corinna shook her head.

'I'm not allowed to reveal my plans in advance, even to girlfriends. If you give me your address, I'll have my escort pick you up at nineteen minutes past seven tomorrow evening.'

Carla Arduini wrote down her address and handed it to her visitor, who tucked it away in the file she was carrying.

'Seven nineteen exactly, then,' Corinna said. 'Be in the entrance hall of your building by seven fifteen, but don't open the door.'

Carla gave her an amused look.

'Very well, I'll try not to peek.'

The judge sighed and nodded.

'I'm so used to this by now that I've forgotten how insane it must seem to someone who leads a normal life. Anyway, that's the way things are, I'm afraid. Bear with me, if you can.'

She opened the door, then looked back at Carla with an unexpected intensity.

'Do you think you can?' she asked.

'Of course I can!' Carla replied warmly. 'On the contrary, it's very kind of you to think of inviting me. I have been frightfully lonely here, to tell you the truth.'

Corinna Nunziatella nodded once and left. Carla resumed her scrutiny of the screen. So many people suddenly inviting her out. It was very welcome. Despite her reservations about her father, no doubt they would have a reasonably pleasant time, while the prospect of an evening out with the eminent Judge Corinna Nunziatella was even more intriguing. Frankly, her social life since arriving in Sicily had been a disaster. She knew no one, had not managed to make any friends, and there simply wasn't much that a young single woman could safely or pleasantly do in Catania alone by night.

Carla tried to force her attention back to her work. Lithe and articulate, her fingers began to caress the keyboard, combing the deep subconscious of the CPU, which was already on-line, via a highly secure link, with similar networks in Palermo and Trapani. The machine's log files, which record who accessed a system and when, could not be deleted, even by the system administrator. If someone *had* broken in or borrowed a key, they would have left indelible fingerprints. All she had to do was to find them.

At four o'clock, Aurelio Zen left the restaurant where he and Baccio Sinico had had a long, inconclusive lunch. At five, he went food shopping. By six he was back home. The apartment he had leased was reasonably priced and very conveniently situated, on the upper floor of a three-storey *palazzo* just a short walk from the Questura. After bruising experiences in other Italian cities, Zen had been pleasantly surprised by the ease with which he had found such suitable accommodation, thanks to a colleague who had phoned him at work and offered him a short-term let on a property owned by a friend.

True, the exterior of the building was unprepossessing, despite its classical proportions and the pilasters, cornices and moulding surrounding every door and window. Lack of maintenance, or heavy-handed application of same, together with layers of airborne pollution and memories of ancient and uneven coats of distemper, had created an oddly incongruous effect, like skin disease on a marble bust. Once through the door, however, everything was spick and span, in keeping with the aristocratic restraint and harmony displayed in every detail of the hallways, stairwells and rooms, so unlike the overbearing display of Rome or Naples. For Zen, it felt almost like being back in his native Venice.

The only real difference was the constant noise of traffic outside, a noise quite specific to Catania: the squelch of tyres on the river-smooth blocks of lava with which the streets were paved, like the black, dead-straight canals in the northern reaches of Venice. Actually, his hypothetical daughter Carla Arduini had come up with a far more appropriate epithet: 'the Turin of the south'. Both cities were symmetrical, rectilinear entities planned at royal command in a single style and constructed all of a piece in a relatively short space of time. In the case of Catania, the reason for this was evident at every street corner in the smouldering dome of Etna to the north. In 1669 the volcano had erupted, submerging the whole of the city beneath a lava flow which had only stopped when it reached the sea, cooling into the low, craggy, black cliffs which still formed the coastline. Twenty-four years later, one of the devastating earthquakes for which the region had been notorious since antiquity demolished almost all the city's few remaining structures.

After such a double blow, the surviving citizens could have been forgiven for packing their bags and moving to a less perilous spot. Some did, but by and large the Catanesi took the view that nature had now done its worst, and that they and their children would be safe where they were. So they rebuilt, hastily and using the only material to hand: the solidified lava which had wrought such havoc in the first place.

And now they finally had a piece of good luck, because the period happened to be an excellent moment for off-the-shelf civic architecture, just as it was for the bespoke version then under construction in the capital of Piedmont, nestling beneath the Alps some eight hundred kilometres further north. The buildings which arose along the grid plan of the new city were sober and solid, of fitting proportions and decorated with grace and elegance. Even three centuries later, many of them abandoned or in disrepair and surrounded by a concrete wasteland of speculative, Mafia-funded development, they retained a sense of ineradicable character and dignity, which might be destroyed but never demeaned.

Zen set down his shopping on the marble counter in the kitchen and surveyed it with a morose air. He had never had pretensions to any but the most basic culinary skills, but for reasons into which he had not enquired too deeply, he felt a need to entertain Carla at home at least once. His solution had been to approach the owner of the restaurant where he had taken Baccio Sinico for lunch and to order some of the establishment's excellent fish soup, packed in a large glass jar which according to the label had once contained olives. A loaf of bread, some salad, and a selection of local sheep's cheeses, together with Carla's promised dessert, completed the menu.

His decision to 'adopt' this young woman who claimed to be his daughter, even though the DNA tests proved that they were not related, had been taken on the spur of the moment; a mere whim, although kindly meant. He had not thought the matter through – had not really thought at all, to be honest – and ever since had had to struggle to live up to the fantasy to which he had short-sightedly committed them both. This was not made any easier by his sense that it was all a bit of a strain for Carla, too. They were both reduced to improvising the roles which he had assigned them: the Father, the Daughter.

While he waited for Carla to arrive, he looked through the notes he had made of his lunch with Baccio Sinico, adding or deleting a phrase here and there. It had not been a convivial occasion. Not that the young Bolognese had been evasive; on the contrary, he had proved almost alarmingly forthcoming about the current state of morale – or rather the lack of it – within the Catania office of the *Direzione Investigativa AntiMafia*.

'I almost regret the old days,' Baccio Sinico had remarked at one point. 'At least they fought us openly then.'

'They?' queried Aurelio Zen.

Sinico gave him a sharp look, as though trying to decide whether Zen was being ironical or just plain stupid.

'*Gli amici degli amici*,' he replied in a voice so low that Zen almost had to lip-read the coded phrase – 'the friends of the friends', meaning the Mafia's presumed patrons and protectors in the government.

'But those "friends" are no longer in power,' he reminded Sinico. 'Some of them are even under arrest or on trial.'

'Precisely! In the old days, you knew who was who and what was what. Everyone knew where he stood, and what was at stake for both sides. Now it's all done by indirection and inertia. The implication is that the great days are over, the Mafia is as good as beaten, and that all remains to be done is a low-level mopping-up operation without any real importance, glamour or risk. In other words, we're being treated like traffic cops by Rome and like arrogant prima donnas by all our colleagues outside the department.'

'The pay's good, though!' Zen had replied in a jocular, one-of-the-boys tone of voice suitable to the avuncular but slightly dim persona he cultivated for these professional encounters.

'It's not bad,' Sinico had conceded. 'Which is yet another reason why we're resented and obstructed by

61

all the other branches of the service down here. But money's not everything. And, without undue bravado, it's not really that I'm frightened of the risks involved. No, it's the sense of isolation that's getting to me. My family and friends are all back in Bologna, and here I am holed up in a fortified barracks deep in enemy territory, trying to do a job which no one seems to think needs doing any more.'

'Have you noticed a weakening of support from the local population?'

Sinico laughed sardonically.

'What support? There was a wave of protest and demonstrations after Falcone and Borsellino were killed, but that soon faded. In my view it was mostly window-dressing anyway. It wasn't so much that two selfless and dedicated servants of the Italian state had been blown to bloody pulp that got to people, it was the fact that it happened here, on their doorstep. It made them look bad, and Sicilians hate that.'

He paused to toy with the largely uneaten food on his plate.

'But we never expected much cooperation from the locals. What's harder to take is the fact that the people at the top have started to distance themselves from us and our work. The old alliances have broken down, but new ones are in formation.'

'With whom?' asked Zen.

Sinico made a gesture indicating that this was an unanswerable question.

'We don't know yet. But the Mafia has always allied itself with the party of the centre, and they're *all* in the centre nowadays, even the former Fascists. Meanwhile our work is obstructed by insinuation and neglect. "With everyone in prison except Binù," they say . . .'

'Except who?'

'Bernardo Provenzano, also known as Binù. Totò Riina's right-hand man, and now effectively running the Corleone clan through his wife. Communicates only by written messages, doesn't trust the phone. On the run for the last thirty years. He's the last of the historic *capi*. The rest are all under arrest or serving life sentences, and have been dispersed to remote prisons. So the back of the Mafia has been broken, we're told. "All thanks to people like you, of course, but the moment has perhaps come to take the longer view, the broader perspective, etcetera, etcetera."'

He sighed deeply and shook his head.

'It's depressing, particularly when you know what's really going on.'

'And what is going on?' asked Zen.

Sinico looked up at him.

'*Dottore*, the drug trade channelled through the port of Catania alone generates hundreds of millions of US dollars every year. There's also a lucrative export market in firearms and military supplies, to say nothing of the usual construction scams, prostitution and protection rackets. Meanwhile, the youth unemployment rate is running at fifty per cent. There are seventy thousand people in this city with no visible means of support. Do you think the Mafia is going to have any trouble finding new recruits?'

'But if the bosses are all in jail . . .'

'Then new bosses will emerge. Someone said that only two things are certain, death and taxes. The Mafia combines both. It's not going to go away. But whereas we knew who the old *capi* were, even if we couldn't lay hands on them, we have virtually no idea at all who's in charge now. Not only that, but the structure of power is shifting. The Corleonesi are more or less finished, having wiped out all their rivals. But other clans have emerged, two of the most powerful based in Belmonte Mezzagno and Cácamo.'

'Where?'

'Exactly. Villages up in the mountains behind Palermo. No one's ever heard of them except the DIA. Ragusa is also emerging as a major centre. In Catania and Messina, you have shifting alliances. The Limina family is on the way out, although they don't seem to realize it yet. And as if all this weren't enough, there are reliable rumours that alliances are being formed with the Calabrian *n'drangheta*, who are the real top dogs now, to say nothing of the startup Albanian mobs in Puglia, some of which have opened branch offices right here in Sicily. In short, it's an unbelievably complex and obscure situation, far more so than ever before. But no one wants to know. People here used to say, "What Mafia? There's no such thing!" The only difference now is that they add "any longer". Well, I've just about had enough, and I'm not the only one, believe me.'

Zen did believe him, but could hardly afford to say so. His remit was to report on the operations of the Catania DIA, not connive at its dissolution.

'But surely you must have had some successes recently?' he said encouragingly. 'That case of the body on the train, for example.'

Baccio Sinico gave a massively expressive shrug.

'It seems it wasn't the Limina kid after all.'

'It wasn't?'

'It seems not.'

Zen frowned at him.

'How do you mean, "seems"? Either it was or it wasn't.'

Sinico smiled his humourless smile once again.

'With all due respect, *dottore*, it's easy to see that you've only just arrived here. The dualistic, northern approach to life is completely alien to the Sicilian mind. So far from there being just two possibilities, there are, in any given case, an almost infinite number.'

'Skip the philosophy, Sinico,' Zen retorted gruffly. 'I've never had a head for it.'

The young officer smiled, this time with genuine warmth.

'I apologize, *dottore*. A hobby of mine. It's what I studied at university, until I realized that the job market in that particular subject was rather restricted. And for that matter I make no claims to understanding the Sicilian mentality either. You have to be born here to do that. But to get back to the point, it seems that the judiciary has seen fit to accept the statement of the Limina family that their son is alive and well, on holiday in Costa Rica, despite their reluctance to say exactly where he is, still less produce him in person.'

'So you don't think their story is true?'

Baccio Sinico laughed again.

'If you start asking yourself questions like that here in Sicily, you'll drive yourself mad. I'm just telling you what's happened. The case is closed and that's that. As for the truth, who knows? Or cares?'

Aurelio Zen considered this in silence for a while.

'What about the magistrate who was investigating the case?' he asked at length.

'Nunziatella? She's been taken off it. The case has been officially downgraded to a routine accidental death enquiry. They're no doubt writing up the press release as we speak. It'll be all over the papers and the television tomorrow, if you're interested.'

He sniffed and lit a cigarette.

'Besides, the judge in question has her own problems, if the office gossip is to be believed.'

'How do you mean?'

Sinico gave him a quick glance.

'The word is that *la Nunziatella* doesn't like men.'

Zen shrugged.

'Meaning?'

'Meaning that she does like women.'

Another shrug.

'That's not illegal.'

Baccio Sinico sighed again.

'Despite some recent changes, this is a very conservative society, *dottore*. I've heard that there is a photograph in existence, showing Corinna Nunziatella and another woman in a restaurant.'

'So?'

'They're kissing,' Sinico went on. 'On the mouth.'

Zen got out his battered pack of *Nazionali* cigarettes and lit up.

'Who took the photograph?' he asked.

'No one knows.'

'Well, where is it now?'

'No one knows.'

There was a brief silence.

'But in a sense it doesn't even matter whether the photo actually exists or not,' Sinico went on. 'All that matters is that the word is out that it does. And if it were to be sent to the local paper and printed on the front page, all of which could easily be arranged by certain people, then it would become difficult, if not impossible, for Judge Nunziatella to continue to carry out her duties in a satisfactory manner. In which case, of course, she would have to be replaced.'

Walking over to the window at the rear of the apartment, overlooking the courtyard, Aurelio Zen unlatched the twin panes. It was like opening the door of an oven which is no longer turned on, but still stocked with heat from the long hours when it was blazing away. A spent wave of exhausted air invested the room, scented lightly with the basil and rosemary, thyme and oregano which a neighbour grew in pots on her balcony.

The doorbell sounded. It was Carla, looking relaxed in loose, wheat-coloured linen trousers and a peach ribbed cotton-knit top, her radiance and energy instantly enlivening the room. All Zen's previous apprehensions about the success of the evening were swept away. Together they rummaged through the kitchen cupboards for cooking utensils, then poured the soup from its jar into a saucepan that proved to be too small, getting a stain on Carla's trousers in the process. It didn't matter. They laughed and sorted it out and put the soup on to warm, opened a bottle of wine and gossiped about the latest political and social scandals, and discussed what to do about Carla's birthday, which fell on the following Saturday.

The conversational tempo slowed a bit once they had eaten, and at length Zen found himself resorting to a rather tired old standby.

'So how's work?'

'The usual,' said Carla. 'I can never understand why so many people seem to find computers interesting. To me, they're about as fascinating as a light switch – which is really all they are, when you get down to it. That's why I like working with them. They're soothing company.'

She paused, pushing the salt cellar to and fro across the table.

'I found something interesting today, though.'

'Yes?'

Another pause, followed by an embarrassed shrug.

'I probably shouldn't tell you. All this stuff is supposed to be highly confidential. You wouldn't believe the paperwork they made me sign.'

'Oh, come on, Carla! We both work for the same side, after all. And anyway, I'm family.'

Carla conceded the point with a smile.

'Well, someone's been pinging the DIA system. I discovered a sequence of packet hits, all in the middle of the night, when none of the registered users was logged on.'

Zen smiled weakly.

'Well, that *does* sound interesting.'

Carla laughed.

'Actually, it is, sort of. In plain language, it means that someone outside the DIA has been looking at their work, checking their files and opening their mail. And what's really interesting is that this doesn't look like your average hacker. These people seem to be coming in with virtual sysadmin status, which means they can open, alter or even delete any file – even so-called "closed" files, inaccessible to other co-users. And they can do that not just here in Catania, but over the entire DIA network.'

'So who are they?'

Carla shrugged.

'That I can't say, yet. But I've identified the string code of the machine they're using, code name "nero". That's like a fingerprint. It doesn't tell you who or where the user is, but there are ways of tracking it back. Which is what I plan to do next.'

She fumbled around in her bag and produced a folded piece of paper.

'Look at this. This is just one of the entries I found on the DIA server's var-log-messages file.'

Zen took the sheet of printout and read: *Aug 12 23:19:06 falcone PAM_pwdb[8489]: (su) session opened for user root by nero (uid=0)*

Carla pointed a finger at the page.

'This means that at nineteen minutes and six seconds past eleven at night on Tuesday last, someone identified as "nero" accessed the DIA system and used the "su" command to switch to user root status. Don't look at me like that, Dad! This is important, because the root user has permission to do anything he likes on or to the system. Anything at all.'

Zen nodded gravely.

'And what action did you take?'

'Well, of course I wrote a report and sent it to the DIA director. He'll have to decide what to do next.'

While Carla unwrapped the dessert she had bought, Zen got to his feet and set about making coffee. He had accepted the fact that he would never understand the new technology that was sweeping the world, where everything was intangible and instantaneous, and occurred at once everywhere and nowhere. A street vendor in the fish market had told him with great bitterness that most of the local tuna were now snapped up by the Japanese, taken to that country to be processed, and then sold back to Italians in those cheap cans of fishy slurry that came in packs of six. This story might be true, or it might be one of those urban myths with a built-in ethnic slur such as the Sicilians themselves had endured for many centuries. The only certain thing was that it was now possible. The technology was there, and a primitive, hard-wired circuit in Zen's brain told him that if something could be done, then somebody was going to do it.

'And apart from your work?' he asked over his shoulder as he assembled the coffee pot. 'What do you get up to in the evening?'

'Not much, to be honest,' Carla replied from much nearer than he expected.

She lifted two plates down from a shelf and set about opening drawers in search of forks.

'That one,' Zen told her.

'But I've been asked out to dinner tomorrow,' she said, returning to the table.

'Anyone interesting?'

'One of the judges at the DIA. We'll probably have soldiers lurking under the table and tasting the food to make sure it's not poisoned.'

The coffee burbled up.

'Good for you! Is he good-looking? Or married?'

There was a brief silence during which Zen poured out the coffee.

'Actually, it's a woman,' Carla replied. 'The one I told you about this morning, Corinna Nunziatella.

She's really been very nice to me. I think she's lonely. She needs a girlfriend to talk things over with, but in her position . . .'

Zen nodded slowly, not looking at her.

'Perhaps,' he said, almost inaudibly, then went on in a tone of forced *bonhomie*, 'Well, congratulations! It looks as though you've inherited the family skill for making friends in high places.'

'You've always done that, then?' asked Carla.

'Sometimes. But it didn't do me any good.'

'Why not?'

'Because I made an even greater number of highly placed enemies.'

He gave her an odd smile, like a crumpled photocopy of the original.

'Anyway, it sounds as if you might be in for an interesting evening,' he said, swigging the pungent black coffee down in one go. 'Let me know how it turns out.'

They came for Corinna Nunziatella just after she arrived for work the next day. There were two of them, in their twenties, both dressed in the all-purpose leisure uniforms of the trendy young: leather baseball caps, synthetic jackets, jeans and gigantic boot-style shoes. One was thin and ingratiating, the other squat and silent. Corinna instantly dubbed them Laurel and Hardy. She had never seen either of them before.

'Sorry to disturb you, *dottoressa*,' said Laurel with a charming smile. 'We've been told to come and pick up the file on the Limina case.'

Corinna got up from her desk and turned to face them.

'And who are you?'

Laurel removed his small oval-lensed sunglasses and produced a plastic card identifying him as Roberto Lessi, a corporal of the Carabinieri. The card was overstamped ROS in large red letters.

Corinna indicated Hardy, who was chewing gum and staring overtly at her in a way that she found extremely disturbing, all the more so in that there was nothing remotely sexual about his attentions.

'My partner, Alfredo Ferraro,' said Laurel, with an even more winning grin. 'We work together.'

'On what?' Corinna demanded pointedly.

'Security.'

'What kind of security?'

Laurel paused, as though unsure how to answer.

'Internal,' he said at length.

'And you are responsible to whom?' demanded Corinna.

'To the director, Dottor Tondo,' was the reply, delivered with a definite taunting edge, as though to say, 'Trump *that*!'

Corinna picked up the phone and dialled.

'Nunziatella,' she replied when Sergio Tondo's secretary answered. 'I need to speak urgently to the director.'

After a silence broken only by the distant sound of a siren, Tondo came on the line.

'I have two men in my office,' Corinna told him. 'They have identified themselves as Lessi, Roberto, and Ferraro, Alfredo. They claim to be working under your supervision on, quote, internal security, unquote, and want me to hand over the Limina papers to them. Can you verify that you are aware of this?'

'My dear Corinna,' the director replied in his most smarmy voice, 'a woman as beautiful as you should never allow herself to lose her poise because the company is disagreeable. I apologize if these two young men have failed to make a favourable impression. But what they lack in charm, they make up for in efficiency.'

'They *are* working for you, then.'

'They're working for all of us, my dear, as part of my constant attempts to make the lives of you and your colleagues safer and more productive. Speaking of which, I mustn't detain you any longer. Just give your visitors the file relating to the matter which we discussed yesterday, and then you can get back to work.'

Sergio Tondo hung up. After a moment, so did Corinna. The gum-chewing man was still staring at her, his eyes moving at intervals to another part of her body as if taking exposures for a composite photograph. Corinna stepped over to the tower of box files in the corner. She grasped one with her right hand, steadied the pile above with her left, and in one decisive movement yanked the file free. The tower teetered for a moment, then settled back into place. Corinna returned to the two men, holding the file against her bosom.

'I'll need a receipt,' she said.

Laurel frowned, as though Corinna had committed a minor lapse of good manners.

'I'm afraid we don't have anything like that,' he said.

'Then write one. "We, the undersigned, acknowledge receipt of file number such-and-such from Judge Corinna Nunziatella", with the date and time. Spell out your names in block letters and then sign beneath.'

Laurel sighed.

'I'll need to consult the director.'

'He's just gone into a very important meeting,' lied Corinna. 'He won't be very happy if this file isn't on his desk when he comes out, and I'm not handing it over without a receipt. Here's some paper and a pen.'

In the end the two men complied. Corinna took the receipt, read it through carefully, and only then handed over the file. Laurel and Hardy then left without a word, the latter breaking his sullen, intense scrutiny with apparent reluctance. Corinna Nunziatella listened to their footsteps receding on the marble floor outside. When they were no longer audible, she unlocked a drawer in her desk and removed another box file, identical to the one she had handed over except for the number marked on the spine.

She stood there for a moment, breathing rapidly and shallowly, her eyes unfocused. Then she opened the door, gave a quick glance in each direction, and strode off down the corridor to the main staircase. She went down two floors, then turned sharp left down to an unmarked door beneath the staircase. Inside, a stuffy, narrow passage led to another door, at which Corinna knocked. A moment later, the door was opened by a florid, elderly woman.

'Well?' she snapped.

A moment later, her face abruptly changed into a smile of welcome.

'Oh, it's you, my dear!' she went on in Sicilian dialect. 'Come in, come in. How nice to see you! I was just getting ready to give that empty room on the fourth floor a good going-over for these new people who've just got here. Lucia's taking a few days' sick leave to visit her son in Trapani, so I've got to do the whole thing myself. Not that they bothered to give us any notice, needless to say, just a phone call from His Royal Highness this morning telling me to . . .'

'New people?' asked Corinna, sitting down carefully on the cracked swivel chair which Agatella had scavenged from somewhere. It was perfectly comfortable and stable as long as you didn't lean back too hard, in which case the whole thing tipped over while simultaneously spinning you around to land on your nose.

'Arrived yesterday,' the cleaning lady confided in hushed tones. 'I was told in no uncertain terms to clean everything up by noon today, then clear out and never set foot in there again "under any circumstances whatsoever".'

She rolled her eyes.

'From Rome,' she whispered. '*I servizi.*'

'*I servizi?*' repeated Corinna, repeating the common shorthand term for the alleged network of clandestine military agencies based in Rome, many of them tainted by scandals alleging their involvement in extreme right-wing terrorism. It may not have been coincidental that the word also meant 'toilets'.

Agatella shrugged expressively.

'Who knows? But that's what Salvo thought.'

Salvo was Agatella's son, employed at the Palace of Justice as a chauffeur.

'He's met them?' asked Corinna.

'He was sent to pick them up from the airport. Only not to the usual passenger terminal, but round the other side. You know that Fontanarossa used to be a military airfield? Well, it still is, and that's where their plane came in, at the military buildings on the far side. Small jet, Salvo said, the sort millionaires have.'

Corinna gripped the file in her hands more tightly. She seemed about to say something, then aborted the remark in a lengthy exhalation, and started again.

'Anyway, Agatella, the reason why I'm bothering you . . .'

'It's no bother, my dear! I'm always delighted to see *you*.'

'The thing is, I was wondering if I could borrow your coat and scarf for about an hour.'

Agatella looked at her in astonishment.

'My coat and scarf? Of course, but why, in heaven's name?'

Corinna smiled sheepishly.

'I'm meeting someone. A personal thing. But because of all this security nonsense, they won't let me leave the building without an armed escort. And if I go with them, it won't exactly be a relaxed encounter, to say the least, and of course word of the whole thing will be all over the department in five minutes. But if I could just put on your coat and scarf and slip out the side entrance, no one will be any the wiser.'

Agatella smiled radiantly.

'Of course, my dear, of course! No one ever takes any notice of comings and goings at that door. Let me just fetch my things. Some nice young man, is it? It's about time you settled down and started a family, my dear. None of us is getting any younger.'

Ten minutes later, a woman of uncertain age with a stain scarf on her head, carrying a bulging plastic bag with the logo of the Standa department chain, entered a newsagent's shop on Via Etnea which advertised in the window that photocopies might be made there. Twenty or so minutes after that she reappeared, the plastic bag even more gravid than before, and started back the way she had come. But after going a short distance she stopped, then started to cross the street, as though at a loss. Traffic swirled and shrieked around her, while the other pedestrians went steadfastly about their business, ignoring this hapless female who had obviously lost her grip on the realities of life.

The woman walked down the street to a *pasticceria*, where she ordered a coffee. No one paid any attention there either. Even the barman who served her and took her money managed to convey the impression that the transaction hadn't really taken place. The woman removed a large, thick manilla envelope from her plastic bag, sealed the flap and wrote something on the front.

'How much to wrap this?' she snapped.

The barman looked at her with a frown.

'Like you do the cakes,' the woman explained.

The barman cast a defeated glance at the other two male patrons in the bar, shook his head and started washing coffee cups.

'Would two thousand do it?' the woman demanded.

'It might, if you had it,' the barman replied in dialect.

A banknote appeared in the woman's fingers as the envelope sledded along the chrome counter to stop in front of the barman.

'What is this?' he asked irritatedly.

'A practical joke I'm playing on a friend,' the woman said. 'I want it wrapped just like a cake, with a ribbon and all, and a little card. In return . . .'

She pushed the two-thousand-lire note into an empty glass on the other side of the bar. Seemingly embarrassed, the barman glanced again at the two men, then shrugged and did as the woman asked.

Five minutes later, she presented herself at the guard post at the main door of the police headquarters of Catania.

'This is to be delivered to Vice-Questore Aurelio Zen,' she told the officer on duty through the grille in the bullet-proof screen, placing an elegantly wrapped parcel on the shelf outside the access hatch, presently closed.

'You know him?' demanded the guard with a mocking air.

'I'm a friend of his daughter, Carla Arduini. This is for her. A birthday present. All he has to do is give it to her on Saturday, understand?'

The officer shook his head, picked up the phone and dialled.

'Excuse the disturbance, *dottore*,' he said into the mouthpiece. 'There's someone here with what she says is a birthday present for your daughter. To be delivered on Saturday. Does this make any sense to you? Oh, it does? All right, sir. I understand. Very good.'

He hung up, and nodded vaguely at the woman.

'Dottor Zen will pick it up on his way home.'

'Mind he does, now!' she replied. 'And take good care of it meanwhile. It's very precious, and you will be responsible if anything happens to it.'

82

The officer nodded repeatedly in a way that said, 'Let's humour the bitch and get her out of here.' After a further sharp exhortation, the woman shuffled off across the little square in front of the police station. A lifetime of humiliation and submission seemed to have made it impossible for her to look up, so she did not notice the tall, gaunt figure gazing down at her from a balcony on the second floor of the Questura.

In all, almost an hour had elapsed before Corinna Nunziatella pushed open the obscure side entrance to the Palace of Justice, whose self-locking door she had propped open with one of Agatella's wash rags. A few minutes after that, minus coat, scarf and plastic bag, she walked blithely through the checkpoint into the DIA section and along the corridor to her office. Opening the door, she found Laurel and Hardy in possession of her office, one lounging in her chair, the other inspecting the map of the province of Catania hanging on the wall.

'Ah, there you are!' cried Corinna with a touch of irritation. 'I've been looking for you everywhere. You know what? I gave you the wrong file! I'm *so* sorry. This is the one you want. No, no receipt necessary, thank you.'

If it hadn't been for the skateboarder, no doubt, everything would have been very different. In retrospect, it would have been almost reassuring to be able to believe that this too was part of one of the conspiracies by which he seemed to be surrounded. But there was not the slightest evidence to suggest that such was the case, any more than the periodic eruptions of Etna could be credibly linked – despite the ingenious attempts of the priests and believers of various religions, Christian and pagan – to divine retribution on the inhabitants of the city for exceptionally or exotically sinful behaviour in the preceding months.

The fact of the matter was that there was this kid zipping down the pavement of Via Garibaldi at an amazing speed, avoiding the plodding pedestrians with even more amazing skill, a mere wiggle of the hips here and there sufficing to plot a curving trajectory through the obstacles thrown up in his path, until a woman ill-advisedly tried to take evasive action herself, forcing the skateboarder to make a sudden course correction at the last moment, which brought him into immediate and violent contact with a gentleman who had just crossed the street, carrying what appeared to be a cake carefully balanced on the palm of his right hand, and had now gained what he evidently thought of as the safety of the kerb, only to receive the careening skateboarder right in the gut, a full frontal encounter which left both lying winded on the ground.

The youngster was the first to recover, and as the one with the most to lose from this encounter, he wisely grabbed his board and rattled off swiftly down a side-street. As for the man, several passers-by went to his assistance, checked that he was not injured, then helped him up, dusted him down and retrieved the parcel he had been carrying, which had gone flying into the windscreen of one passing car and then promptly been run over by another. The man thanked them for these ministrations, and then joined in the obligatory round of head-shaking and sighs accompanying a chorus of rhetorical questions about what young people were coming to these days.

Once this ritual had been concluded, the participants went their separate ways, which in Zen's case was home. No doubt due to delayed shock from his collision with the skateboarder, he did not at first notice that the supposed cake which Carla's friend had delivered as a birthday present did not feel any different from the way it had when he left his office, despite having smashed into one car and been run over by another. It took another few moments for his jangled brain to come up with the obvious inference that whatever was inside the wrapping wasn't in fact a cake. This was confirmed by a jagged tear at one corner of the shiny ivory wrapping paper, printed with the name of a nearby café and pastry shop, through which a section of orange paper could be seen.

Covering the torn corner with one hand, Zen continued along the street to the building where he lived, ran up the shallow stone steps three at a time and let himself into his apartment, where he threw the package down on a chair. Then he went through to the kitchen and mechanically made himself a cup of coffee while he tried to work out what he knew and what else might be inferred from that knowledge.

A woman wearing a dowdy coat and old-fashioned headscarf had left a package for him with the guard outside the Questura. According to the guard, she had claimed that it was a present for Carla Arduini, daughter of Vice-Questore Aurelio Zen. He was to pick it up and deliver it to the intended recipient on her birthday, the coming Saturday. The notional present was clad in the wrapping paper of a *pasticceria* in Via Etnea, but proved to contain what looked like another package, as though in some game of pass-the-parcel. The contents were bulky, consistent, quite heavy, slightly flexible, and had resisted various forms of extreme impact with no apparent effect.

It had crossed his mind, of course, that it might be a bomb. The same thought had crossed the mind of the officer on guard at the Questura, so he had taken it inside and run it through the X-ray machine used to monitor all incoming bags and packages. Nothing had shown up on the screen – no wiring, no batteries – but you could never tell these days. He'd read somewhere that they'd invented some sort of chemical trigger which didn't show up on the machines.

If it *was* a bomb, though, the intended target would almost certainly be the person who opened the package, in this case Carla. Which raised another question. Whoever the mystery donor might be, she had known two things which, as far as Zen knew, no one in Catania was aware of. The first was that, despite her surname, Carla Arduini was supposedly Zen's daughter. The second was that her birthday fell on Saturday.

He tossed back his coffee, lit a cigarette and wandered back into the living room. Rather to his surprise, the package was still where he had thrown it. He looked at it for some time, then grabbed it suddenly and ripped off the wrapping paper. Inside was a large manilla envelope, plain except for a message written in flowing script with a medium blue felt-tip pen.

This is the item I told you about, Carla. DO NOT OPEN IT. Wrap it up in some dirty underclothes or something and hide it away. I'll pick it up in a few days, once things settle down. I apologize for dragging you into this, but there is no one else I can turn to. P.S. Your real birthday present will be a lot more interesting!

Zen read this through several times, then put it down on the table and walked about the room, picked it up and read it again. Carla had been specifically instructed not to open the package. Therefore it was something which, if opened, might either threaten her in some way, or compromise the writer of the note, whoever that might be.

After the bomb idea, Zen's next quick-fix solution was drugs. According to Baccio Sinico, Catania was now what Marseilles had once been, the major entry point into Europe for hard drugs coming from the eastern Mediterranean or North Africa. The package was about the right size, weight and feel to be a vacuum-packed slab of refined cocaine or heroin.

But such speculations were pointless. What was certain was that possession of the envelope, whatever its contents, constituted a potential hazard for the person concerned. Whoever had left it to be delivered to Carla obviously felt that in her case this risk was so small as to be negligible, but Zen could not feel so sanguine. Nor could he open the packet and determine for himself what it contained. In that event, the interested parties would naturally assume that it was Carla who had deliberately flouted the DO NOT OPEN warning, and would take the appropriate measures.

So in a sense the thing *was* a bomb, albeit one with a delayed-action fuse of indeterminate length. And the only way that Zen could protect Carla against possible danger was to prevent her ever taking delivery of the package, while ensuring that she would be able to produce it again, untouched and unharmed, at a future date. Which meant that he was going to have to hide it himself. Which meant, he decided after another cigarette and several minutes' reflection, that he needed to visit the fish market.

He had been there before, often stopping by on his way to meet Carla, spellbound by the everyday miracle which had taken place on this spot for almost three thousand years: the decapitated swordfish and tuna being hacked into slabs with curved blades like machetes, the tubs full of squirming squid and octopus, the wooden trays of anchovies and sardines, their silvery skin glistening with unexpected glints of evanescent colours which had no name. And everywhere the stench of flesh and death, the clamour of voices in a timbre at once raucous and shrill, and the blood, above all; spattered on the stall-keepers' aprons, streaked across their arms and knives, trickling away in the gutter.

It was now almost three o'clock, and the pulsing drama in the streets around the market had disappeared like the sea at low tide, leaving a wrack of stalls in the process of demolition, various unidentifiable scraps being raided by feral cats and the more daring seagulls, and remnants of unsold fish turning dull and matt in their communal coffins with the pathetic air of those who have died in vain. Zen approached one of the traders, a bulky, morose man surveying his remaining stock of sardines.

'How much for those?'

The man glanced at him in astonishment, as though suspecting a practical joke, then brightened up considerably. A price was named, halved, halved again, and finally concluded. Money changed hands and Zen strode away with the best part of a kilo of extremely smelly fish.

Back at his apartment, he put his purchase in the sink, then wrapped the manilla envelope in several layers of plastic film, securing each with adhesive tape. When he was satisfied with this sheath, he opened the plastic bag provided by the fishmonger and slipped the package inside. The last stage was the most tricky, working the slithery mass of sardines around inside the bag until they concealed the inserted envelope. Once he had achieved this, Zen taped the bag tightly shut and wedged it into the freezing compartment of his refrigerator.

He completed his task, and sat down on the sofa with a sense of regret. What now? It was the unanswered and perhaps unanswerable question which had haunted his days and nights for some time. The 'now' was both specific and general; at once the next hour which had somehow to be filled, and the rest of a life which seemed increasingly predictable and pointless, in a vaguely cosy way. His career had evidently hit a plateau where he would be stuck until he retired. The promotion to Questore which he had been promised on being told of this Sicily assignment had failed to materialize, and now Zen was pretty sure that it never would. He had made too many enemies for that.

To be honest, he couldn't really complain. The fact was that he just didn't care any more. Career, love, family, friendships – he'd tried his best in each field, but the results had not been encouraging. Once he'd been callow and enthusiastic, now he was tired and cynical. Once he'd been ignorant, now he was knowing. Whatever the middle term of these bleak declensions might be, it appeared to have passed him by.

So, what now? The answer was clear enough: another five or ten years plugging away at a job he no longer believed in and messing about with tentative relationships which were doomed from the start, while the world around him gradually changed into an unrecognizable although all too familiar place. Age makes us all exiles in our own country, he thought.

He looked up, startled, as an electronic beeping filled the room. It was his mobile phone, which he never took with him. He located it, on a cupboard in the kitchen, and pressed the green button.

'Aurelio?'

'Who's this?'

'It's Gilberto.'

Silence.

'Gilberto Nieddu. Listen, the thing is . . .'

Zen clicked the phone shut. He had had no contact with his former Sardinian friend since the latter had betrayed him – unforgivably, in Zen's view – by first stealing and then selling, at a vast profit, a video tape which was evidence in a case Zen had been investigating. One man had died as a result and another could have joined him, in which case Zen's career prospects might easily have turned out to be even less inspiring than they were at present.

The phone rang again.

'Don't hang up on me, Aurelio!' Gilberto's voice said. 'This is important, really important. It's about . . .'

'I don't give a fuck what it's about, Gilberto. As far as I'm concerned, you're a treacherous scumbag and I never want to speak to you again, still less see you.'

He snapped the phone shut again, like a clam closing its shell, then stalked down the room and opened the doors on to the balcony overhanging the courtyard. At once he was subject to both an overwhelming tide of hot air, and a deafening outburst of hilarity which was the trademark of Signora Giordano, his herb-growing neighbour. She was a retired lady of some consequence and independent means, but socially nervous. Normally there was never a sound from her apartment, but on the few occasions when she entertained a harsh, convulsive laugh would burst forth at regular intervals, on average once every ten seconds. No sounds of conversation or of others' merriment were audible, just this dreadful, forced cackle like a hack actor trying to signal a punchline to an unresponsive audience.

Behind him, the *telefonino* had started to beep again, a distant exclamation point amid the ambient noises of the neighbourhood and Signora Giordano's outbursts. Zen lit a cigarette and waited for it to stop. But it didn't stop. Why didn't Gilberto get the message? What did he have to do, install one of those devices to block nuisance calls? He smoked quietly for a minute by the clock on the wall. The phone continued to ring. 'It's no use hiding,' it seemed to say. 'We know you're there, and we've got plenty of time.'

After the second hand on the clock had described another complete circle, Zen threw his cigarette into the courtyard below, stalked over to the sofa and picked up the phone.

'Well?' he bellowed.

'Excuse me . . .'

It was a frail, elderly woman's voice, vaguely familiar to him.

'Yes?'

'This is Maria Grazia,' the voice said after a pause.

Zen's expression relaxed from aggression to a bored tolerance lightly mixed with perplexity. The housekeeper at his apartment in Rome had never phoned him before about anything.

'Signor Nieddu asked me to call.'

'Well, you can tell Signor Nieddu to . . .'

'It's about your mother, you see.'

Zen broke off, frowning.

'My mother?'

'Yes. You see . . .'

'Hello? Maria Grazia?'

'Yes. You see, the thing is . . .'

'What's going on? What's all this about?'

A silence.

'It's about your mother.'

'Thank you very much, Maria Grazia,' Zen replied sarcastically, 'I think I've just about grasped that. So let's move on to the next point. *What* about my mother?'

Another silence, longer this time.

'How soon can you get here?'

'Get where?'

'To Rome, of course!'

Zen stiffened. He was not used to being interrogated like this by the *donna di servizio*.

'Look, Maria Grazia, please stop this nonsense and just tell me why you're calling.'

Another silence, ending in a sniff and what sounded like weeping.

'Excuse me. I would never have done it, only . . . Only it's your mother, you see.'

'What about my mother? Put her on the line if she wants to talk to me!'

This time the silence went on so long that they might almost have been cut off. When the answer to his question finally came, it was in a neutered tone of voice such as might issue from a public address system playing some pre-recorded emergency message.

'She's dying, Aurelio.'

Nineteen minutes past seven, Corinna Nunziatella had said. 'Be in the entrance hall of your building by seven fifteen, but don't open the door.' Carla smiled to herself as she completed her preparations for the evening, checking her hair in the mirror and removing a stray strand from her blouse. How ridiculous all this secret-service stuff seemed! But also romantic, in a way, like being in a movie.

The entrance hall to the apartment building where she lived was a dreary space, replicated *ad infinitum* by the mirrored walls and dimly lit by five circular lamps of pebbled glass dangling on their cords from the meaninglessly high ceiling. Mafia chic, circa 1965, in short. Carla waited just inside the front door, eyeing the bank of mailboxes, in each of which the same round of junk advertising pamphlets lingered like a bad smell. When the door opened, she started forward, only to encounter the stout, overdressed form of Angelo La Rocca, a retired and chronically deaf lawyer who lived in solitary splendour in his illegal apartment on the roof, up a flight of stairs from the end of the elevator on the sixth floor, and exercised his rights over any unfortunate he happened to meet in the public areas in his unchallenged capacity as the building's Official Bore.

'Ah, Signorina Arduini!' he cried, spying his prey. 'How lovely you look this evening! A veritable symphony of shapes and shades, as fashionable as it is delectable. You are going out, I perceive. And who's the lucky young man? Forgive my impertinence, my dear. An old man's privilege, just as you young women now enjoy the privilege of going out unescorted whenever you please, wherever you please, with whoever you please. I can still remember the time when a woman had to stay at home . . .'

'Listening to old farts like you,' muttered Carla.

The *avvocato* leaned forward, pleased to have provoked a response.

'What, my dear?'

A horn sounded outside.

'My taxi's here,' said Carla loudly, opening the door.

In fact, it wasn't a taxi but a blue Fiat saloon. None the less, Carla had three reasons for thinking that this was the car which Corinna Nunziatella had sent for her. The first was that it was now exactly seven nineteen, and the second that the driver had parked right outside the building, blocking the traffic, and didn't seem at all bothered by this. The third and decisive factor was that the tough-looking young man who had been sitting in the front passenger seat was already walking towards her, scanning the street to both sides, his right hand grasping something bulky concealed inside his jacket.

'Signorina Arduini?' he barked.

Carla nodded.

'Get in,' the man replied, jerking his head at the car.

Once she was inside, everything happened very quickly. The driver shot forward, accelerating furiously, then braked and skidded over a low yellow ledge in the middle of the road. The Fiat swung round, screeching on the lava slabs, until it was facing in the opposite direction, then took off at high speed down the single lane supposedly reserved for buses. The man who had spoken to her now sat rigidly in the front seat, scanning the windows and mirrors as though monitoring a bank of radar screens.

It was almost as if she had been kidnapped, Carla reflected as they negotiated the stalled traffic in a large circular *piazzale* by dint of going the wrong way round the roundabout and appropriating part of the pavement. Neither man spoke, although the driver occasionally emitted low grunts. After about ten minutes, the man on the passenger side pulled a portable radio from his jacket and started a long sequence of brief exchanges. Places, times and distances were ticked off as though on a list. At length he switched off the radio and muttered something to the driver, who took the next exit and stopped under the bridge carrying the highway they had been on over a country road fringed with villas and two-storey apartment buildings. The columns supporting the bridge were covered in election posters displaying the local candidate of the right-wing National Alliance party, the recycled third-generation successor to Mussolini's Fascists. The radio crackled again, and instructions were exchanged. Then another car materialized on the road ahead, drew level with theirs and then swung around to park behind them.

The man in the passenger seat was already outside, opening the back door of the Fiat and motioning Carla out. The back door of the other car was open and another man, this one in uniform and carrying a machine-gun, waved impatiently at her. 'In here!' he snapped. She was barely inside when he slammed the door, jumped into the front seat and yelled, 'Go!' The car screeched around the parked Fiat and roared away.

It was only then that Carla noticed the other woman, curled up in the other corner of the back seat in a loosely woven cotton gauze outfit with narrow trousers, daringly unbuttoned at the throat, the sleeves rolled up to reveal her tanned arms, and a wide gold cuff bracelet on her right wrist. Her eyes were invisible behind a pair of aviator-style sunglasses. To Carla, who had only ever seen Corinna Nunziatella in high-heeled pumps and tailored suits, this was a revelation.

'So did you enjoy the ride?' the judge asked ironically.

'Well, it beats taking the bus. But I can't quite see why they went to all that trouble to protect me. I mean, *my* life's not in danger.'

Corinna Nunziatella pushed the sunglasses up on to her brow and glanced at Carla sharply.

'Of course not. They were protecting me, not you. The assumption is that all my friends, acquaintances and surviving relatives are under surveillance. Your phone may well be tapped, and your mail intercepted. They may even have bugged the office where we made the arrangement to meet tonight. What they wouldn't know is where and when, but all they'd need to do is follow you and you'd lead them right to me.'

She smiled and shook her head impatiently.

'Anyway, that's all over. Now we can just enjoy ourselves for the rest of the evening.'

It soon became clear that this was not entirely true. The drive, up into the foothills of Etna to the north of the city, was a highly choreographed affair, involving constant radio contact between the two vehicles already engaged, as well as a third which was apparently located somewhere up ahead. Sometimes they slowed almost to a crawl, at others raced forward at speeds which pinned Carla back into the seat. Turns were taken seemingly at random, always at the last moment and without signalling, to the accompaniment of much squealing of tyres, ripping of gears and wrenching of the steering wheel.

'Well, at least they're enjoying themselves!' Carla confided to Corinna with a fugitive smile, nodding her head at the two men in the front.

To her surprise, there was no answering smile.

'Eighteen judges from the DIA or its predecessors have been killed in the last decade,' Corinna Nunziatella replied. 'In almost every case, their escorts have died with them. When they killed Falcone and his wife, the six men in the lead car were blown to pieces as well. In Borsellino's case, it was eight. No, all appearances to the contrary, I don't think they're enjoying it all that much. If I hadn't wanted to take you out to dinner tonight, they could have been safe at home with their wives and children watching TV. As it is, if they make a single mistake, they could be *on* TV.'

Carla nodded soberly.

'I see,' she said.

Observing her guest's chastened expression, Corinna smiled and clasped her arm.

'As a matter of fact, this is the first time I've been out in the evening since I took up this position with the DIA,' she said. 'Which is quite a compliment to you, my dear.'

A few minutes later they reached the brow of the hill they had been circuitously climbing all this time, between fields surrounded by stone walls and the occasional outcrop of modern housing, and passed a white sign marked TRECASTAGNI. Almost at once they turned right into a secluded driveway between high brick walls and came to a standstill. Carla opened the door and started to get out.

'Not yet!' one of the uniformed officers barked at her.

'They need to make sure it's clean,' Corinna explained.

The blue Fiat had pulled up behind them. The two plain-clothed men got out and walked up a flight of steps into the complex of buildings to their left.

'The lead car will be parked in the street outside,' Corinna said. 'In case we have to make a quick getaway and need a block thrown. The two men in the back-up will take a table inside and check out the other clients. This is a very well-known restaurant, and of course "they" like the better things in life.'

'You mean the Mafia?' demanded Carla. Not noticing Corinna Nunziatella's slight wince, she went on, 'I always thought that they were a bunch of peasants. *Mamma*'s homemade pasta or nothing.'

Corinna smiled wearily.

'It's a little more complex than that,' she replied in a slightly patronizing tone. 'Some of them are like that, but even they like to try to impress each other, and especially guests from out of town, precisely because they too know the stereotype and know that it's true. But there is also quite a different class of person involved these days, men who spend their time moving around between here and Bangkok, Bogotá, Miami, you name it. For them it's even more important to show off their sophistication and wealth. It's like wearing the right kind of clothes and accessories. No international drug baron is going to take you seriously as a major player if you invite him home for a plate of pasta, no matter how *genuina* it is.'

Corinna was talking rapidly and a little distractedly, all the while scanning the steps leading up to the main building where the two plain-clothed escorts had disappeared.

'What's taking them all this time?' she demanded.

As if in response, the radio crackled into life and one of the two 'minders' reappeared on the steps and walked towards the car, beckoning urgently.

'It's clean?' asked Carla.

'Apparently.'

The two women got out of the car and were led up a series of steps and exterior galleries into the building, then down again into the layered spaces of the restaurant, each at a different height and angle: bare stone walls, a large open fireplace, antique wooden cabinets supporting bottles of wine and oil. From exposed wooden beams hung folkoristic agricultural implements and stiff-limbed marionettes representing the Christian knights Rinaldo and Orlando.

'Sorry about the delay, *dottoressa*,' their escort murmured. 'We were just about to give the all-clear when Giuseppe spotted a suspicious-looking couple of lads sitting at a table in the corner. Those two over there, see? So we went over to check them out, and guess what? It turns out they're on the same detail as us! Some VIP politician from Rome is visiting and got taken out to dinner here.'

Carla was only too aware that these words had been addressed solely to Corinna. *She* was the star, the 'VIP', the only victim who would count. If an assassination attempt did take place, Carla would figure as no more than 'collateral damage', just like the police escort.

Corinna stood staring at the two men seated in the corner, then turned to the waiter who was indicating their table.

'No, I'd like a different one, please,' she said decisively. 'Over there, by the fireplace.'

The waiter gestured politely and seated them. Their escort took a table on the mezzanine balcony overlooking the lower room. Corinna leaned back in her chair and looked over towards the two men sitting in the corner. Seemingly satisfied, she sighed deeply and settled back in her chair.

'Do you know them?' asked Carla, who had been watching this pantomime attentively.

Corinna shook her head.

'Not really. But they came by this morning to pick up a file I'd been ordered to close and return. Their names are Roberto Lessi and Alfredo Ferraro. They're agents of the Carabinieri's *Raggruppamento Operazioni Speciali.*'

'The Special Operations Group?' queried Carla. 'What sort of operations?'

Corinna made a gesture which read, 'Who knows, and anyway I doubt it.'

'Anyway, at least they're on our side,' Carla exclaimed with evident relief.

Corinna looked at her with a distant smile.

'That reminds me,' she said. 'I gave your father a packet to pass on to you.'

Carla frowned.

'My father?'

'He's just the cut-out. I didn't want to be seen handing it over directly. For both our sakes, yours particularly.'

'Why, what is it?'

'Nothing that need concern you, my dear,' Corinna replied. 'It's just a few papers that I need taken care of for a little while. They're all packed up in an envelope which your father will give you on Saturday, if not before. He thinks it's a birthday present. Just hide it away somewhere in your apartment. In due course, I'll either tell you to destroy it or ask for it back. Is that all right?'

Carla nodded.

'But I'm not to look inside?'

'No, don't do that.'

'Like Pandora's box.'

Corinna smiled.

'Yes,' she exclaimed. 'Very much like Pandora's box.'

'All the good gifts of the gods turned to evil and flew out to plague the world,' Carla continued pertly. 'All except Hope.'

Corinna sighed as the waiter neared their table.

'There are various versions of the legend,' she replied. 'According to some, not even Hope remained. It was the last to leave, though.'

She smiled across the table.

'Shall we order?'

Zen was terrified of flying. This had always been a fact about him, like his height and other physical characteristics. He was terrified of flying, but what was terrifying him now was that he *wasn't* terrified of flying, and this was all the more terrifying because everyone else on board clearly was.

Moments earlier, the pilot had instructed passengers to fasten their seatbelts in anticipation of 'some possible turbulence ahead'. Seconds later, the Airbus A320 had thrown a spectacular *grand mal* epileptic fit, jerking, shuddering and leaping in an apparently uncontrollable series of spasms so violent that they sent one of the flight attendants flying into the row of seats just in front of Zen, while another sank to her knees and started crossing herself and chanting the Hail Mary in a loud voice. As for the other passengers, they screamed and closed their eyes tight, clutched one another and threw up.

Meanwhile Zen sat there calmly, scared out of his wits at the realization that he was the only person on the plane who wasn't scared. Which was truly scary.

For your eyesight to deteriorate, your hearing to fail, your hair to thin and your memory to malfunction, that was normal, to be expected. But if your fears deserted you, what was left? Take those away, and all that remained was a hollow shell.

What made things worse was the suspicion, amounting almost to a certainty, that his whole trip was the result of having fallen for a practical joke, one of those infantile pranks that Gilberto Nieddu loved to play on unsuspecting friends and colleagues. The Sardinian was still furious that Zen had dropped him socially after that disgraceful incident involving the stolen video-game cassette. Now he had decided to get even in a characteristically cruel, cynical and effective way.

For if it *was* a practical joke, then it was one that Zen could hardly have avoided falling for, particularly after that conversation with Maria Grazia. The Airbus took another groin-tingling lurch, accompanied by a loud metallic clang which elicited a renewed chorus of shrieks and prayers. 'Maria! Maria!' the stewardess shouted imploringly. *Maria*, thought Zen. Maria Grazia. How did she fit into the conspiracy? Had Gilberto paid her off to act a part? This didn't seem likely. Zen had known the family housekeeper for almost twenty years, and he was sure she wouldn't have been able to lie effectively to save her life.

No, there was only one possible solution. Gilberto must have convinced her too! That made sense all right. If it suited his purposes, that devious little Sardinian could talk anyone into anything, never mind someone as ingenuous and guileless as Maria Grazia. Yes, that was it. The housekeeper was simply an unwitting accomplice in Nieddu's schemes, cunningly roped in to remove any lingering doubts from Zen's mind and reduce him to an unthinking, panic-stricken automaton calling taxis, racing to the airport, oozing sweat and gasping for breath, and then paying a small fortune for one of the few remaining seats on the next flight to Rome.

Very well, he thought, but we'll see who has the last laugh. You may have won this round, my friend, but the match isn't over yet. Nieddu was a past master at this sort of thing, but Zen had a few tricks up his sleeve as well. He knew quite a bit about the Sardinian's business practices, for a start, many of which were extremely questionable even by Italian entrepreneurial standards.

But that would be using a sledgehammer to crack a nut, he reflected, as the aeroplane veered into a steep descent while the crew struggled to restart the starboard engine. The cabin was loud with despairing shrieks and pleas, and the intimate odour of human excrement filled the air. Zen glanced indignantly at his neighbour, a surly businessman whose attention until now had been entirely absorbed by his laptop computer, and then edged away as far as possible in the other direction. The middle-aged woman seated on that side, her face so intensively curated that it looked like a burnished metal mask, gripped Zen's arm tightly, leaned her head on his shoulder and began muttering fervent invocations to Santa Rita of Cascia.

The senior steward now rose shakily to his feet and started to lead the passengers in a recitation of the Lord's Prayer. If he was to pay Gilberto back, thought Zen, it must be in a more personal way. And then he suddenly got it, the perfect revenge for Nieddu's tasteless jest. It was so good, in fact, that he couldn't resist bursting into laughter, at which point the woman beside him snatched away her arm and glared at him in horror. At the same moment the Airbus bottomed out of its vertical descent as the starboard engine kicked in, causing the steward to collapse to the floor like an unstrung puppet. A few moments later, all was perfectly still and quiet again.

Rosa Nieddu was not the typical Italian wife who didn't much mind what her husband got up to as long as it didn't involve any mutual acquaintances and was kept reasonably discreet. No indeed, *fare finta di niente* was definitely not Rosa's style. On the contrary, she had proved herself to be intensely suspicious of what Gilberto was actually doing while he was supposedly away on business, and quite probably with good reason.

Thus far, the claims of both friendship and male solidarity had led Zen to lend Gilberto whatever assistance he could when things got tricky with Rosa. Certainly he had never before thought of deliberately making trouble for him. So it was with some satisfaction that he realized just how easy this would be. Rosa's intrinsic jealousy was like the Sardinian underbrush in high summer: one spark was all that would be needed to create a truly spectacular conflagration.

And that initial spark wouldn't be hard to provide. A few letters first, to prepare the ground. He would draft them and then get Carla to copy them out in a laborious, feminine hand, all curls and loops and little circles over the letter 'i'. She could make the phone calls, too, when the time came. What fun they'd have working out the script! 'Is that Signora Nieddu? My name is . . .' What would she be called? Something slightly old-fashioned and socially tainted, suggestive of a buxom but simple-minded country lass.

He suddenly remembered the object of the prayers which his neighbour had offered up. That would do nicely. 'My name is Rita, *signora*. I've written to you several times. I hate to disturb you any more, and the only reason I'm calling now is that I'm desperate. As you know, your husband had his way with me during his visit to Bari, and, well, you see, I've just found out that I'm . . .' How would that sort of woman put it? 'With child'? 'Going to be a mother'? 'Three months gone'? Carla would know, not that it mattered. Rosa would already be back in the kitchen, honing the carving knife to a fine edge. Let Gilberto try to talk his way out of that one!

An amplified voice announced that they would shortly be landing at Fiumicino Airport. Zen consulted his watch. It was only an hour since they'd left Catania. They couldn't possibly be anywhere near Rome yet. That was where his mother lived. *She's dying, Aurelio*. Ridiculous. Rome was hundreds of kilometres away. It took hours and hours to get there.

The plane bumped down on the runway, eliciting an enthusiastic round of applause from the passengers, and nosed up to the disembarkation ramp. Everyone stood up and collected their belongings, chatting with almost hysterical volubility to complete strangers about the frightful ordeal they had shared.

'Never again!' one man kept saying over and over again in a strident tone. 'That's the last time I step on an aeroplane! Never ever again, no matter what happens!'

It wasn't until the businessman with the bowel problem nudged him meaningfully that Zen realized that everyone was leaving the plane. He got to his feet, lifted his coat down from the locker, and trudged along the aisle to the exit. The captain of the aircraft, in full uniform, was standing slightly to one side, outside the open door to the cockpit.

'Sorry about the discomfort,' he told Zen heartily. 'Worst case of clear air turbulence I've ever encountered. Doesn't show up on the radar, you see. Totally unpredictable. Nothing you can do.'

Zen nodded.

'No, there's nothing you can do.'

'My mother . . .'

'Is she still alive?'

'I suppose so.'

'You're not sure?'

'No, I mean, I suppose that you could say that she's alive.'

'She's from Randazzo, you said.'

'No, I said that she lives there. Used to live there.'

'And now?'

'Now she doesn't.'

'So she moved?'

'She's been moved.'

Carla gave an edgy smile.

'You keep making odd distinctions that I don't quite get, Corinna.'

The other woman smiled too.

'It's a Sicilian speciality. But I'm not trying to hold anything back. I just need to decide how much to tell you, Carla. How much I want to tell you, that is, and how much you really want to know.'

'I want to know everything!'

'Oh, everything! Sorry, I'm not handling this right. I'm in love, you see.'

'In love?'

'Yes. So I'm behaving a bit oddly. I apologize in advance. The real problem is that I'm not really interested in small talk and brief encounters. That sort of thing can be fun for a while, but you can say the same about television. As I get older, I find I want something more difficult. Something that will challenge the limits of my competence.'

'How old are you, Corinna?'

'Thirty-four.'

'I'm only twenty-three. My mother is dead, and as for my father . . . He miraculously reappeared, after all those years. It makes a difference, and yet it doesn't. That's always assuming that he *is* my father.'

'But you had DNA tests done, you said.'

'I sometimes think he faked them.'

'Why would he do that?'

'Why do people do anything? Half the time they don't know themselves. Even if they do, their reasons needn't make sense to anyone else.'

'You're an anti-rationalist, then?'

'I'm a realist. At least, I like to think so.'

'Then I'll tell you about my mother, Carla. Let's test your sense of realism, my dear. I'll try not to bore you, but to be frank you don't have much choice but to listen anyway.'

'I could always leave.'

'I'm afraid not. As far as my escort are concerned, we're a package. An item, as they say. As long as I'm here, you have to stay. We arrived together, and we leave together.'

'I see. I didn't quite realize what I was letting myself in for by accepting this invitation.'

'No, I'm sure you didn't. But in an odd way bondage can be quite liberating, don't you think?'

'Liberating?'

'So many decisions you don't have to make. At any rate, here's my mother's story. Joking aside, I'm not really going to exploit the fact that you're a captive audience. If you're bored, just tell me.'

'Go on.'

'My mother is from Manchester. A city in England. The second half of the word, "chester", is cognate with the Latin *castrum*, a fortified camp. The first syllable is the English word for *uomo*. My mother once claimed, in one of her rare flashes of humour, that all her troubles stemmed from this fact.'

'Your mother is English?'

'She was born in England, of English parents. Well, actually one was Welsh, but I can't keep track of all these distinctions which seem to be so important there. Anyway, there she was, growing up in Manchester . . .'

'Have you ever been there?'

'I have, as it happens.'

'What's it like?'

'Impossible to tell you. We don't have cities like that here. I liked it. I liked the people.'

'You speak English?'

'We're getting ahead of ourselves here, Carla. All in due course.'

'I'm sorry. So, your mother grew up in . . . whatever it's called.'

'Yes. Her name is Bettina. Betty. When she was sixteen she left school and found work as a waitress somewhere in the centre of town. That's where she met my father.'

'He's English too?'

'No, he's from here. He had a job as a deckhand on a freighter out of Catania. It sailed the length of the Mediterranean, crossed the Bay of Biscay, then the Irish Sea, and finally ended up in a canal leading to Manchester. By that time my father had had enough of sleepless nights and puking over the side. He jumped ship, and after a couple of weeks at a sailors' hostel he found a job washing dishes in a restaurant.'

'The one where your mother was employed as a waitress.'

'*Brava!* And then what?'

'They fell in love?'

'*Bravissima*. Or rather, she did. She was one of three daughters from a working-class family in one of the less attractive areas of the city. She'd never met anyone like Agostino, never even dreamt of doing so, never imagined that there were such people in the world. Confident, precocious and pleasantly pushy, with a permanent tan, coal-black hair, pearly teeth and a charmingly defective command of English which didn't stop him telling her what to do all the time . . .'

'And him?'

'He's never told me his side of the story. But I've seen photographs of my mother taken at the time, a few snapshots which her parents had kept and which I saw when I went over there. I think for him she must have seemed as exotic as he was for her. Slightly taller than him, with a mass of red hair, lightly freckled skin as white as milk. Strong, capable legs, a bosom which had already attracted much comment, and a sweet, unformed face, kindly and tentative. She must have looked like the sacrificial victim of every male's dreams.'

'Do you really think men dream of that?'

'Without question. Here is Sicily, at least. Sex isn't really about pleasure for them. That's just an extra. What it's really about is power. Or, better, that *is* the pleasure – to captivate, to dominate, to penetrate, to master. Which is what he did with my mother. And it worked. She was crazy about him, she's told me so. She was crazy. But he wasn't.'

'So he abandoned her?'

'On the contrary. All things considered, that would have been a kindness, and men like my father are never kind unless it suits their purposes. No, he married her. She was pregnant by then, so he did the decent thing.'

'I don't see anything so terrible about that.'

'Neither did she. Then he told her that they were going home.'

'Home?'

'To Randazzo, where he was born.'

'And she agreed?'

'Of course. She had never been out of England before, except for a day trip to the Isle of Man when she was nine. She was thrilled. Italy! The south! Adventure, romance! She longed to see her husband in his native environment, and to experience all the colourful festivals, traditions and characters he had told her so much about. The language would be a problem at first, of course, but Agostino had already taught her a few phrases and she would learn the rest soon enough. Besides, she was going to be a mother, and it was only right that the child should be born in its father's own country. And if it didn't work out, they could always come back.

'They travelled by train. It took two days and two nights, sleeping upright in a series of packed carriages.

As soon as they crossed the border at Ventimiglia, my mother noticed the change in her husband. In England, he had always been the stereotype Latin lover – sexy, confident, attentive, macho. But now they were in Italy, northern Italy, where he was marked out as a Sicilian peasant on the make, a wide-boy, probably a *mafioso*. He seemed to get smaller, my mother said. He became quieter and more wary, "like a snail withdrawing into its shell".

'When they passed Rome, his mood changed again. Now he was back in his territory. There would be no more snide glances and half-caught innuendoes about southerners. Down here, he could expect a little respect. Anyone from Naples and points south knew that you didn't mess around with Sicilians. The second night passed, and finally they had reached the Straits of Messina. There it was, the fabled isle of which she had heard so much. From the ferry, to be honest, it didn't look much more interesting than the Isle of Man. They disembarked on the other side and continued to Catania, where they changed to the little train that runs up around Etna.

'It was then, my mother said, that Agostino started to change seriously. Until then, it had been gradual, a series of variations on a person she had always known. But from the moment the train started, he metamorphosed – my word, of course, not hers – into a creature superficially resembling the man she had married, only a dream double, the same and yet not the same, at once alien and fully recognizable. That was the worst aspect of the whole thing, she said. We all imagine horrors happening to us. We know horrors happen. But we imagine them happening in unforeseen circumstances, at the hands of people we do not know and would never – even as they killed or tortured us – acknowledge as fully human. But this was Betty's lover, her husband, and before her eyes he was turning into somebody she would have fled from if she had encountered him late at night at a bus stop back in Manchester, with the rain falling and no one about.

'There were plenty of people about once they got to Randazzo. More than enough, in fact. The whole community had turned out to welcome Agostino home, and to pass judgement on his foreign bride. First and foremost amongst them, of course, was Agostino's mother. She and my grandfather were going to be sharing the family's small house with the newly-weds, so she was naturally curious to see just what her son had dragged home from his adventures abraod. She was not impressed.'

'God, it sounds like a story by Verga!'

'This was thirty years ago, an hour's journey from where we are now. My mother was very quickly given to understand that her mother-in-law ran the household, handled the finances, and made all the decisions. Her appeals to Agostino made no impression. He couldn't understand why she couldn't understand that this was normal and natural. As the days passed, his metamorphosis ran its course. Any remaining hint of romantic interest completely vanished. They were husband and wife, that was all. He would fulfil his side of the bargain, according to the local standards, and he expected her to do likewise.

'She learned that she was not to leave the house without a valid reason and only after obtaining permission from him or his mother, and never alone. Such a thing would bring shame on the family, and she would suffer the consequences. He, on the other hand, was free to disappear for hours or even days at a time, without being expected to offer the slightest explanation. Husband and wife would go out together only for family or communal events at which their absence might be remarked upon. If she uttered a word of complaint, she would be reminded that there was plenty of cleaning, cooking or sewing to do, and that idleness breeds vice. Anyway, she would soon be a mother. That would take care of her strange foreign restlessness.

'And for a year or two, she told me, it did. She was totally enchanted with me, totally absorbed by my needs and my company. Everything else ceased to matter. She named me Corinna, after a song by Bob Dylan which she was fond of, and she devoted herself to my happiness. She wanted to take me back to England, to show off to her family, but Agostino kept prevaricating, saying that it was too expensive. In the end her father sent Betty a ticket. Despite his previous reservations, Agostino bought one for himself, and off they went.

'I was duly admired and cooed over, but in every other way the visit was a disaster. Betty's parents had never approved of Agostino, and he now stopped making any attempt to ingratiate himself with them. He even pretended that he couldn't speak or understand English any more. Even worse, my mother's eyes were opened by this first taste of liberty since leaving England. It was sweet while it lasted, but the return to Randazzo was all the more bitter. She had bought a stock of contraceptive pills in Manchester, and now started taking them. There would be no more children with Agostino, she had decided.

'The problem was the one that already existed. As I grew up, she became more and more overwhelmed by the stifling dimensions of the world she lived in – not only for her sake, but for mine. The idea that her daughter would grow up to be one of these local cloistered breeding machines and maids-of-all-work horrified her. She couldn't let it happen. She wouldn't let it happen.

'She made several attempts to escape, the first by bus. It left at five in the morning, bound for Catania. There she planned to take the train to Rome and cable her father for money to fly home. Early one morning she rose quietly, dressed herself and me and sneaked out of the house with only her handbag, some money she had set aside, and her passport. The bus was waiting in the square, the door open and the engine running, but when she tried to board, holding me in her arms, the driver told her there was no room. The bus was almost empty, she pointed out. It was now, he said, but he was picking up a large group in the next village, a *comitiva* going down to Catania for a political rally. She told him to sell her a reserved ticket for the next day, but he told her she would have to apply in person at the head office.

'The next time, she tried the railway. This was more difficult, because it meant slipping away in the middle of the morning. Somehow she managed to get to the station without being stopped, but once again it seemed that there was a problem. The train had been delayed, possibly even cancelled, the station master told her. He would make a phone call and find out what was going on before she wasted her money on a ticket. Five minutes later, Agostino appeared. He led us back to the house, where I was taken from her. She wouldn't tell me what he did to her then, but that evening she was called before her mother-in-law.

' "These adventures are pointless and stupid," she told my mother contemptuously. "You may as well get that into your head right away." My mother spat defiance. She was a British citizen and they couldn't keep her here against her will. Agostino's mother smiled. Of course not, she said. My mother was free to leave whenever she wanted – the sooner the better, her tone implied. But alone. *She* could leave, but they would never give up the child.

'My mother threatened to go to the police, and the visible contempt of her mother-in-law deepened still further. The law would back the family all the way, she said, but people like them didn't need policemen and judges to defend what was theirs. Agostino and his friends were perfectly capable of doing that themselves. And they would rather see me dead than taken from them. My mother said she had no doubt that they meant exactly what they said.

'At last the situation was clear. She could leave, but only if she abandoned me. If she wanted me, she had to stay. I don't think she ever quite appreciated what it must have cost them to be so explicit. With one of their own kind they would never have expressed themselves so frankly. The whole exchange would have been conducted in undertones and innuendoes, messages containing other messages, all in code. But my mother was a foreigner, and they had to make sure that she had understood.'

'My God! So what did she do?'

Corinna put her head on one side and smiled. One of the reasons she looked so different from usual, Carla realized, was that she was wearing a lot more eye make-up.

'Ah, well, that'll have to wait,' said Corinna with finality. 'Enough about my mother for one evening. Your birthday is coming up, you told me. Would you like to go away for the weekend to celebrate?'

'Where?'

'What about Taormina? Quite apart from the pleasure of your company, I'd love to get out of town for a while, and away from these young thugs with their radios and guns.'

'But don't you want to go with your boyfriend?' asked Carla coyly.

Corinna Nunziatella gave her a level look.

'I don't have a boyfriend.'

'But you said you were in love.'

There was a long, awkward silence.

'I'm sorry,' said Carla. 'I didn't mean to pry.'

'Taormina's a charming place!' Corinna went on eagerly. 'And I know a very nice hotel, right in the centre but completely secluded. We'll have to give some thought to getting rid of my escort, but I think it can be managed. If you're interested, that is. Are you?'

The two women regarded one another for a moment.

'What have I got to lose?' said Carla.

In Zen's experience, Roman taxi drivers came in just two forms, as though cloned: threateningly sullen or manically voluble. A codicil appended to this law dictated that you always got the one least suited to your current state of mind, so it came as no surprise to Zen when the driver who picked him up at Fiumicino turned out to be one of the chattiest and most inquisitive.

Where had Zen flown in from? Sicily! Eh, must be hot there, this time of year! Even hotter than here in Rome! His cousin had married a Sicilian girl, who was definitely hotter than the local article if Maurizio was to be believed! They were living in Belgium now, if you could call it living. And where to? The *Fatebenefratelli*? Of course! At once, if not sooner! A wonderful hospital. Three of his own relatives had gone under the knife there. But no one in Zen's family was involved, God willing? A friend? And Zen had come all the way from Sicily to be with him in his hour of need? Now that was real friendship! He himself, Paolo Curtillo, could do with a few friends like that, instead of which he was surrounded by leeches, vampires and bloodsuckers whose only thought was to enrich themselves at his expense. He could tell stories of barefaced treacheries, devious deals and vicious back-stabbing that would make Zen's blood run cold, but what was the point?

And what about Lazio, eh? That second goal against Fiorentina on Sunday? No? Zen hadn't seen it? He wasn't by any chance – ha ha! – a Roma fan, was he? Because if so – ha ha! – he could get out right now and walk the rest of the way. Not that he hadn't had all sorts in the cab at one time or another. Murderers, rapists, drug dealers, *mafiosi* – no disrespect intended – secret-service agents, policemen ... Even politicians! That was the sort of man that he, Paolo Curtillo, was. As long as you could pay, he would take you wherever you wanted to go, even to Florence or Naples – *even if you worked for the tax authorities*!

Nevertheless, he had his limits. There was a certain class of human scum that he wouldn't let past the door of his Mercedes SE500 – over the purchase of which, incidentally, the brother of the aforementioned *siciliana* had screwed him royally – only a year and a half old, and look at it, all but wrecked, three hundred thousand kilometres on the clock, he'd have to buy another next year and his wife kept telling him 'second-hand', but he preferred the peace of mind the warranty gave you – no, there were some people he wouldn't let in the cab, not for any amount of money, wouldn't even give the time of day to, and they were the so-called fans of the so-called Roma football club, that clan of degenerate wankers and marginal know-nothings who . . .

Outside the speeding taxi, the streets gaped, stripped bare by purposelessly bright overhead lights. The air flowing in through the open window was as clammy and oppressive as the sweat-dampened pillow used to suffocate some terrified victim. Where was he? They'd mocked up a city set, but it remained austerely or teasingly generalized, as though it had already served as the establishing archive material for so many knockabout farces and weepy melodramas that it no longer expected anyone to take it seriously as an entity in itself. What sort of show is it tonight? That was the question which every perspective and backdrop immediately asked, like the seasoned professionals they were. You want happy or sad? Sinister or idyllic? We can do either or both, and plenty more besides, but you need to tell us what you want.

'I don't know!' Zen said. 'I just don't know.'

'I do,' the cabbie replied. 'You're a Lazio man! I spotted it right away. That Roma lot are all stiff, rich, well-connected arseholes. They've got the money, they've got the power, they've got everything! The only thing they don't have is the one thing we do, and that's balls. Courage. Belief. Pride. A spirit that will never be broken. That's a Lazio fan for you! We don't care if we lose and lose for ever. We know they've fixed the odds against us and we don't stand a chance. *E ce ne freghiamo! Vero, dottore?* Fuck 'em all! We're Lazio to the core. We have no choice. That's how God made us!'

They had by now reached the Piazza di Porta Portuense, and continued along the embankment to the bridge leading across to the island in the middle of the river. Here Zen paid off the taxi, cutting through the driver's attempts to prolong the conversation, and walked off across the Ponte Cestio. The remnants of the Tiber, reduced to a fetid trickle at this time of year, scuttled away in the deep trench of darkness beneath the bridge.

Half-way across he stopped, his elbows on the parapet, and leaned down over the invisible depths. Grasping his squished packet of *Nazionali*, he lit up and exhaled a flutter of smoke, an apt correlate to the impoverished stream existing only as a minor sound effect, a susurration emanating from the darkness beneath.

As he tossed his unsmoked cigarette into the gutter, he noticed a rectangular sheet of paper lying there like a discarded letter. In another vain attempt to delay his inevitable arrival, he picked it up. To the touch, the glossy surface revealed itself to be pitted by being crushed between shoe soles and the uneven surface of the pavement. It was just one of those advertising flyers which were thrust on passers-by or stuck under the windscreen wipers of parked cars. *DIVENTARE INVESTIGATORE PRIVATO* was the shout-line: *BECOME A PRIVATE EYE*. In the background, red on white, was an image of a vaguely Sherlock Holmesian figure, sporting glasses and a prominent pipe. 'The courses are open to all detective enthusiasts, and can open the door to a new and fascinating profession,' continued the copy beneath.

Zen threw the paper aside and continued on his way. Perhaps he should sign up. The only problem was the name of the company running the courses, which called itself the *Istituto Superiore di Criminalità*. If there truly was a high-level institution of criminality in Rome, Zen was beginning to get the feeling that he already worked for it.

At the hospital, there was no one at reception, and the only person in the waiting area was an elderly derelict, drunk or mad, who was having a violent argument with an invisible opponent. Zen walked off down the gleaming corridor which stretched away, seemingly for ever, the fake marble floor a molten glare of arrogant light. There were doors to either side, but he hesitated to open them lest he interrupt the performances which might be going on inside. They should really have a red warning light, he thought, as they did at radio stations when a studio was on air.

Further down the corridor, a man was mopping the floor in a series of precise spiral motions, each followed by a rinse in the metal bucket resting on a towel, then a final squash on a grid to one side, to remove excess water before the next washing sequence began. Actually, Zen realized, he was still too far away to see clearly what the cleaner was doing, but that was how his mother had always dealt with the large red-yellow slabs of their house in Venice, working her way from the top to the bottom. He'd always assumed that she enjoyed it, the way he did the games he played. Why else would she bother? The mop handle was darkened in the two places where she wrapped her bony, calloused fingers about it. From time to time she would straighten up, press her left hand to the small of her back, and give a mild moan.

The cleaner was dark-skinned, Zen saw as he drew nearer. Some sort of immigrant. Probably didn't speak Italian. Still, it was worth a try.

'I'm looking for my mother,' he said.

The man straightened up, pressed his left hand to his back and winced slightly. He did not speak, but looked at Zen with an unnerving intensity, as though registering without surprise the fact of a birth or a murder.

'My mother,' Zen repeated, enunciating each syllable with exaggerated emphasis.

'What about her?' the cleaner replied.

His startlingly liquid eyes regarded Zen with the
same neutral exactitude, neither compassionate nor
dispassionate.

'She's dying.'

The cleaner spun his mop, splaying the strands
out like a witch's hairdo, then propped it up against
the wall.

'Come with me,' he said.

He strode off down the corridor, never once looking
back. A few paces behind, Zen followed up flights of
stairs and through a set of double doors.

'Your mother's name?' his guide demanded in his
eerily alien Italian.

'Zen, Giuseppina.'

The other man stood still a moment, as though
attending to some imperceptible sound or scent.

'This is the terminal ward,' he remarked, fixing Zen
with his disconcertingly lucid gaze. Zen nodded. The
cleaner turned away, wiping his hands on the back of
his blue overalls and looking at the names scrawled in
black marker on the shiny boards outside each door. He
worked his way to the end of the corridor, then retraced
his steps to a door where the board showed no name,
just a large black X stretching from corner to corner.

'That means the patient's dead, but they haven't moved the corpse yet,' he said, gripping the handle. 'None of the other names are Zen, so this might be her.'

The room was smaller than Zen had anticipated, most of it taken up by a single bed in which an elderly woman's body lay covered by a sheet. The cleaner lifted the bottom corner. A brown cardboard luggage label dangled on a length of plastic cord from the big toe of the woman's right foot. He turned the label over and beckoned to Zen, who bent to read it. There was a name and an address. Both were familiar to him, unlike the body in the bed.

'It's not her,' he said, turning towards the door.

'Aurelio?'

The voice seemed to come from nowhere and from everywhere. Then Zen realized that the body lying on the bed had opened its eyes and was staring up at him.

'*Mamma?*' he whispered.

A withered arm extended itself towards him, shrunk to its essence: veins, tendons, bone. Zen sat on the edge of the bed and grasped it.

'I've just arrived, *Mamma*,' he muttered breathlessly, as though he'd run all the way from Catania. 'Gilberto phoned me, and then I spoke to Maria Grazia. Where are they all? They shouldn't have left you alone like this! But I'm here now, and I'll look after everything. You don't have to worry any more. I'll take care of you.'

The woman beside him started to talk, a low melodious monologue to which he listened with increasing desperation, nodding frantically and clasping the fibrous limb which, like a rusted anchor cable, was now his last best hope. Perhaps he'd just gone mad, he thought, as he sat there while the woman talked and talked, a stream of verbiage parsed into perfectly rounded phrases and variously inflected vocables, of all of which he understood not one single word.

'She had a stroke,' a sonorous voice intoned somewhere off-camera. 'They brought her here, the people you mentioned, but the doctors told them that she would be in a coma for some time and that there was no point in staying. Then they came again, the doctors, and said she was dead. Since that it's been peaceful. She was worried when the door opened because she thought that they had come back to bother her. Then she heard your voice and realized that it was you, her beloved son, and then she knew why she had not been permitted to die when the doctors wanted her to. She loves you and would . . . What's the word? She would be worried about you, but she knows now that there's nothing to worry about. She says you brought her great joy. It was all worth it, every moment of every hour of every day. You must never doubt that. She's sorry to have caused you so much bother, but she's glad you were able to come. Now she's going to die.'

The moment the voice fell silent, Zen swivelled around. The cleaner was leaning against the wall, regarding a spot somewhere above the bed and slightly to one side.

'What the fuck was all that sentimental drivel?' Zen shouted, rising to his feet. 'She was speaking gibberish!'

'She was speaking French,' the man replied, his eyes never wavering from their seemingly random point of focus.

Zen gave a brutal laugh.

'French? Oh, yes, right, with some Greek and Latin thrown in, no doubt!'

'No, it was pure French. Well, a little incorrect here and there, above all in the gender of nouns, where they differ from Italian. But completely comprehensible, none the less.'

Zen stared at him. He essayed another laugh, but it backfired.

'You expect me to believe that someone like you understands French?' he demanded.

When the cleaner at last lowered his implacable gaze to meet Zen's, it suddenly became clear that he had been trying to spare the other man precisely this eye contact all this while.

'I am from Tunisia,' he said. 'I speak French and Arabic. And now a little Italian.'

Zen gestured towards the bed.

'And my mother? Is she Tunisian too? She's Venetian born and bred! Never even been to Turin, never mind France! How could she possibly start spouting absurd speeches in French on her deathbed? The whole thing's ridiculous!'

The cleaner shrugged.

'I've seen stranger things, particularly where there's cerebral trauma. I remember one example when I was an intern at a hospital in Tunis. A man was brought in, an emergency case. He'd been hit by a metro tram. This man was from the desert, you understand. A Berber, from the extreme south of the country. They don't have trams there, so he wasn't paying attention.'

'What happened?' Zen demanded in a peremptory tone, as though he was behind his imposing desk in the *Questura di Catania*.

The cleaner shrugged.

'He recovered. Eventually. But first he talked. For hours, maybe days, in this gibberish which no one could understand. We brought in professors from the university, experts in all the dialects and patois of the desert people. And then at last one of them, who had studied the Renaissance at university, spotted that the man was speaking Italian.'

'Italian?'

'He had spent some time, early in his life, in that part of the desert now called Libya. It was an Italian colony at the time. We worked out later that he could have been no more than five or six when he was taken to a town somewhere by someone hoping to resolve some bureaucratic problem. A murder, maybe, or a marriage. He was there only a few days, soaking up this new language that was everywhere about him. And then they left again, the problem resolved or not, and he never spoke or heard Italian for the rest of his life until the impact of the tram jarred it to life again.'

He glanced at Zen, then walked around him, took the woman's arm and felt her wrist with two delicately probing fingers. Zen sat down heavily in a chair by the bed.

'When she was in her teens, my mother worked for a French family who had rented a *palazzo* on the Grand Canal,' he said dreamily. 'I remember her telling me, years ago, when I was a child, about the stylish dresses and dazzling jewellery which the wife owned. My mother had never seen anything like that. She lived in the house with them for three months, one summer before the war, back in the thirties.'

There were tears in his eyes. He hastily brushed them away.

'So you studied medicine?' he asked the Tunisian.

'Yes,' the man said, laying Signora Zen's arm back on the sheet. 'Engineering, too, for a while. A perfect training for my present position, when you think about it. Routine hospital maintenance.'

He laughed darkly.

'Well, I must get back to my mop. Your mother may have spoken in French, but all languages are the same now. Talk to her. This is your last chance. Tell her everything you will regret not saying for ever if you let this opportunity slip.'

He bent over the figure lying on the bed and rapidly muttered some words in a language Zen did not understand, then turned away. The door oozed shut behind him on its pneumatic spring.

Alone with this dying stranger, Zen at first could think of nothing to say. But as time passed an odd thing happened. He found himself warming to this old woman, whoever she might be, who had rattled on to him in French. It didn't seem to matter any longer who she was. Perhaps she *was* his mother. What difference did it make now? She had been somebody's mother. Even if she wasn't his, did that make her less admirable, less worthy of pity and love? He found himself holding her wizened hand, kissing her rugged face. Then, suddenly, the words came, a stutter at first, but soon a torrent, a shameless gush obliterating every distinction between what was sayable and unsayable.

Later he felt cold. So did she. Light crept in through the shuttered window, reducing the obscure splendours of the night to ashes. Men in white coats appeared and ushered him aside. Curtains were drawn about the bed where an old woman lay. An outsider, an intruder, Zen was hustled out into the corridors, to the brutal glare of the lights, the squeal and tap of footsteps on the polished flooring, the hum of distant machinery. He made his way to the lift and pressed the button for the ground floor. The lift stopped before that and the cleaner got in, stowing his bucket, towel and mop in the corner.

'They say she's dead,' Zen told him.

The man nodded.

'She was dead when I left you.'

Zen looked at him incredulously.

'But you told me to talk to her! You said it was my last chance, that I would regret it for ever if I let the opportunity slip. And now you tell me that she was dead all the time?'

The lift came to a rest. The cleaner collected his equipment and stepped out.

'Yes, but you aren't,' he said as the doors closed.

Outside, the sky was falling. As yet it was just a light dust which appeared on Zen's coat like mist. It seemed to be pink. He walked back along the bridge, pausing at the same spot as before to light a cigarette. A gentle aerosol, soft yet solid, had soaked the night, thickening it and covering every surface with a patina of reddish dust.

It was only when he saw it on his sleeve, his hands, that Zen realized that this was not just a trick of the light. The stuff was everywhere, saturating the air and coating every surface like a fine spray of wind-blown paint. He walked on across the bridge to the mainland, where a man was busily cleaning the windscreen of his car.

'It happens every time,' he remarked in a disgusted tone, glancing at Zen and shaking his head.

'What?'

'Yesterday I got the car washed and waxed, right?' the man replied. 'So of course today we get the *pioggia di sangue*.'

'Blood rain?' echoed Zen.

'The sand from the Sahara! The wind picks it up and carries it along, thousands of metres high, and then at a certain point the pressure changes, the wind loses its force, and the sand rains down. And it's always just after I get my car cleaned. It happens every time!'

With a throw-away 'That's life!' gesture, the man climbed into the driver's seat and started trying to goad the motor into action. Zen crunched off across the fine sand which squirmed and squeaked beneath his shoes.

Carla Arduini had calculated that it would take her two hours to drive to Palermo, but she hadn't counted on a long stretch of repair work being done – or rather not being done – in the tunnels through which the A19 motorway descends into the valley of the Imera after crossing the island's central mountain chain near Enna. Now, stuck in a tail-back which from this point on the road seemed indefinitely long, she began to worry about being in time for her appointment. She was fully aware that this was simply an acceptable cover for her real worry, which was why she had an appointment in the first place.

It was just after seven in the morning when her cell-phone rang. Carla was just about to leave her apartment for her morning coffee with her father at the bar in Piazza Carlo Alberto. The phone call, at such an early hour, had to be bad news. She had two mobile phones, and this one was her work phone, supplied and paid for by her company. Therefore it was official and urgent, and Carla had a bad conscience, because the work she had been doing early that morning and the night before was certainly improper and quite possibly illegal.

In an effort to put her tentative theories about unlicensed intruders on the DIA network to the test, she had decided to try to do a little 'pinging' herself. Armed with the information she already had, as the licensed installer, it had taken her little time to penetrate the various firewalls surrounding the system. She had then called up the data files which had been opened by the nocturnal visitor she had provisionally named Count Dracula. She was still unsure whether the data vampire was from the Mafia, the media, or some other interested party, and it had occurred to her that some clue to this might be concealed in the material he had chosen to access.

If so, it had yet to emerge. In this case, the most recent interception, the text consisted of the transcript of an interview between a magistrate in Palermo and a *pentito*, one of the former members of Cosa Nostra who had agreed to collaborate with the authorities in return for them and their families being buried and rebirthed in the government's witness protection programme, safe from the vengeance of those they had betrayed.

Sometimes, yes, but normally we just kill them. It's quicker and cheaper. Saves a lot of effort. When you kill someone, you also send a message. Maybe even many messages.

Even contradictory messages?
Especially those. But it has to be done right. There's an art to the thing. Because there's no such thing as a messageless death, are you with me?

In other words, if a message doesn't exist, someone will invent one.
Exactly. So you have to make sure that some message comes through loud and clear. Otherwise the communications can get fouled up. And when that happens . . .

Yes?
When the messages start going astray, there's no rhyme or reason any more. No one knows what's going on, so everyone's extra edgy. Mistakes happen, and those mistakes breed others. Before you know where you are, you have another clan war on your hands.

So these executions have to be correctly performed. It's a sort of ritual theatre, in other words, like the priest consecrating the host. What's the matter?
Look, I'm trying to cooperate, all right? We're different men with different objectives, but I respect you just as you respect me.

Of course.
So no more jokes about the holy mass, please.

I apologize. To go back to what we were discussing, can you give me an example of such a message?

There are so many. But I'll mention a recent one.

Just to show that, even though for your own protection you're in solitary confinement down at the Ucciardone prison, you're still in touch.

Why would you take me seriously if you thought you were dealing with someone whose clock stopped when he got picked up? Anyway, the thing I'm thinking of is that body they found in a train near Catania.

The Limina case.

Only it wasn't the Limina kid at all, is what I've heard.

Who, then?

Some sneak thief who was picked up operating on protected turf. He'd been warned before, but he had more balls than brains. They were going to waste him in an alley somewhere, but then someone had a brighter idea. The thief looked quite a bit like Tonino Limina. Same age, same height and build, same colour hair. The Limina clan have been making themselves a bit of a nuisance on this side of the island, so a warning seemed in order. They shut the thief up in a freight car on a train bound from Palermo to Catania, with a label with

*'Limina' scrawled on it. One message delivered and one
undesirable disposed of. A perfect solution.*

But the Liminas explicitly denied that the murdered
man was their son. Obviously they knew that Tonino
was still alive. So the message was pointless.
*No message is pointless. Maybe in this case it wasn't the
young Limina. Next time, who knows?*

It was as she was reading these words that the phone
rang. At once she felt a panicky guilt, as when her
mother had burst into the room when she was reading
a letter from her current boyfriend. Desperately she
groped for the keyboard, killed the document on screen
and got safely out of the DIA data files. Only then did
she answer the phone.

'Signorina Arduini?'

'Speaking.'

'We'd like to see you today to ascertain what progress
is being made with regard to the computer installation
for which you're responsible. As you probably know,
the hand-over date has already been put back twice.
Through no fault of yours, I'm sure, but we're naturally anxious to get the system up and running as soon
as possible. I've therefore made a booking for lunch at
the Hotel Zagarella in Santa Flavia, just east of the city.
We'll expect you at one o'clock.'

The caller hung up. Carla dug out her map, but failed to find any village named Santa Flavia. And how could it be 'just east of the city'? East of Catania, there was nothing but water. She tried ringing her father, first at the Questura, then at home, and finally on his cellphone, without success. Finally, in timid desperation, she had called Corinna Nunziatella. Rather to Carla's surprise, the judge seemed delighted to help, and informed her that the city east of which Santa Flavia was situated was Palermo.

'Take the Casteldáccia exit off the motorway and follow the signs,' the magistrate told her. 'Who are these people, anyway?'

'He didn't say, but it seems to be about my work.'

'Where are you meeting?'

'A hotel called the Zagarella.'

The only reply was a low whistle.

'Do you know it?' Carla asked.

There was a long silence.

'It's a well-known venue,' Corinna Nunziatella finally replied. 'For all sorts of events. Listen, *cara*, make it clear to the people you're meeting that you have an appointment with me back here in Catania this evening.'

'But I don't.'

Corinna's response was unusually brusque.

'Never mind that! Make sure they know that you've told me you're meeting them at the Zagarella for lunch, and that I'm expecting you back by six o'clock this evening. I'll call you then to make sure you're safely back.'

Carla laughed.

'Why shouldn't I be?'

'I'll explain tomorrow,' Corinna replied. 'Just do what I say. Make very sure that these people know what the situation is, all right? It could be important.'

'Very well.'

'And listen, don't . . .'

Corinna's voice broke off.

'Don't what?'

'Oh, nothing. I'm just being silly. I'll call you this evening at six.'

At length the constipated press of traffic in which Carla's Fiat Uno was embedded passed through the succession of tunnels where so much expensive and urgent repair work was not being done, and she completed the drive down to the north coast of the island and then westwards to her destination. The Hotel Zagarella turned out to be a modern monstrosity on what must at one time have been a stunning peninsula, with extensive views along the neighbouring bay and out to sea. Next to the hotel was yet another construction site, one of those timeless projects which look like a nuclear power station being built by two old men with buckets, spades and a rope hoist.

Of the grand villas belonging to the Palermitan nobility which had once stood here, there was almost no sign. Those that did remain were imprisoned in a perspectiveless absurdity, a concrete Gulag constructed by the 'state within the state', where the memory of what might have been was perhaps the bitterest punishment in this society of latter-day zeks, where even the winners were losers.

When Carla pulled up outside the hotel, a flunkey rushed over and opened the door.

'Signorina Arduini! You're expected inside. I'll see to the car.'

So whoever 'they' were, they knew the number of her *telefonino* and the make and registration of her car. But the most disturbing aspect of the situation was that they were evidently making no effort to hide the fact that they knew. Carla handed over the keys and walked up the plush red-carpeted steps. At the top, another functionary opened the door for her with a respectful bow. Once inside, a small rotund man in a suit and tie came bustling over to her.

'Welcome to the Zagarella, Signorina Arduini! I trust your journey was not too arduous. Your friends are waiting for you in a private room at the rear of the premises. If you permit, I shall be happy to accompany you there myself. This way, please!'

She had visualized the 'private room' as an intimate space to one side of the hotel's dining area, sectioned off perhaps by a slatted wooden partition. It turned out to be the size of a football field. Rows of metal tables and chairs stretched away in ranks towards a series of narrow windows reaching up to the ceiling. Despite the massive concrete columns supporting the latter, everything looked cheap, vulgar and temporary.

At the middle of the room stood a table heaped with food and centred by a vase roughly the size of an average sink, from which protruded a huge bouquet of flowers. Three men were seated around the table. All three stared blatantly at Carla as she made her way across the scuffed industrial flooring towards them.

Having reached the corner of the table, Carla stopped. After a significant pause, the middle of the three men jumped to his feet as though noticing her presence for the first time. He was dressed in the standard uniform of the professional classes: tweed jacket, blue shirt and red tie beneath a yellow pullover, brown trousers and highly polished shoes.

'Good day, *signorina*,' he said coolly. 'So glad you could join us. May I introduce my assistant Carmelo. And this is Gaetano, an esteemed colleague visiting from Rome.'

He waved alternately at the two men. Carla nodded briefly to each, then turned back to the speaker.

'And you are?'

The man frowned.

'But surely that was . . .'

He tapped his forehead lightly with the heel of one hand.

'But I forgot, of course you didn't get our message!'

He turned to the other two.

'Apparently she didn't get our message,' he said.

The two men sat impassively, with the air of people who had better things to do.

'My name is Vito Alagna,' the man announced, turning back to Carla with a ceremonial bow.

'How did you know my cellphone number?' asked Carla, wondering at her own temerity. These people had power the way some had muscles.

'I left a message late yesterday with the porter at the Palace of Justice. When you didn't return it, I called again and was told you were working at home, so I called you there this morning. Please, take a seat!'

He waved towards the enormous buffet table, on which stood a huge variety of cold foods. Carla took a chair at random, the nearest one. No one at the *Palazzo di Giustizia* except Corinna Nunziatella knew her cellphone numbers, private or professional. She had been very careful not to give them out, to avoid endless harassment.

'Forgive the seeming mystification,' Vito Alagna went on. 'It's really quite simple and straightforward. I work for the autonomous parliament here in Palermo which oversees the internal affairs of this little island of ours. We have naturally collaborated with our colleagues in Rome on the creation and development of the various specialized bodies set up to investigate so-called "criminal activities of the Mafia variety" within our political and administrative jurisdiction.'

He glanced at the other men, as though for corroboration. If so, none was forthcoming. As though embarrassed by his colleagues' lack of response, Alagna gestured to the food.

'But please! Help yourself!'

Carla looked at him, then at the other two, and lastly at the food itself. Although superficially attractive, even luxurious, there was something rather odd about the selection on offer. It included both smoked and poached salmon, a block of smooth meat paté in its wrapper of congealed butter and gelatin, a haunch of cold roast beef, and a selection of cheeses including Stilton, Brie and some sort of cream cheese smothered in nuts. A moment later, Carla had worked out why it seemed so odd: every single item was imported.

'Aren't you eating?' she asked Vito, who smiled and shrugged.

'We're not hungry yet,' he said.

Carla nodded.

'Neither am I.'

The man at the end of the table, whom Vito had named Gaetano, suddenly spoke.

'Perhaps later,' he said. 'We have all day.'

Carla recalled what Corinna had said.

'Unfortunately I haven't. I have to be back in Catania by six this evening. A friend of mine is expecting me for dinner.'

'Who's that?'

The question came from Gaetano.

'Dottoressa Nunziatella,' Carla replied succinctly. 'She is a judge for the AntiMafia pool, where I work.'

'You two must be very close.'

Gaetano again.

'We're friends, yes,' Carla retorted.

Gaetano looked up at the ceiling, where a glass lamp like a melting zeppelin gathered dust at the end of its black cord.

'And you're having dinner with her again tonight? Two evenings in a row. Now that's true friendship!'

The men all sniggered quietly.

'How do you know about all this?' Carla snapped.

The three men exchanged a glance, then resumed their purposefully purposeless gaze.

'Eh, it's a small place, Sicily!' the one called Carmelo said at last.

Vito Alagna's suave tones were almost a relief.

'Be assured that we won't detain you for long, *signorina*. We just need a brief update on the current situation with regard to the system you are working on. A sort of progress report, as it were.'

'I've provided the director of the DIA in Catania with a series of progress reports,' Carla replied.

Vito Alagna shrugged wearily.

'Yes, I'm sure you have, but you know how it is! What with bad communications and the usual rivalry and backbiting, these reports are not always passed on as quickly as they should be, if at all. Now I'm sure that all you want to do is finish this assignment and get back to your home up in the north, right?'

Carla Arduini could not resist a decisive nod. Alagna laughed.

'Excellent! In that case, our interests coincide. So let's just run over the status of the project at this time, and touch briefly on any problems that may have arisen and your personal prognosis for a completion date.'

Which is exactly what she had done, Carla reflected in the car on the way back. She'd given the three men a succinct and professional overview of the situation to date, omitting all reference to 'Count Dracula', and provided them with her estimated best-case scenario for a handover to the AntiMafia authorities. Vito Alagna had listened quietly and intently, taking no notes but giving the impression of absorbing every detail Carla mentioned. The other two sat looking at their nails, saying nothing. It was around three o'clock when the one called Gaetano leaned heavily over on to his right buttock and emitted a loud fart.

'Time we were going,' he said to no one in particular.

'Of course, of course!' Vito Alagna exclaimed, rising to his feet. 'Thank you so much for coming, *signorina*. It's been extremely helpful. The valet will fetch your car. Thank you once again. Goodbye, goodbye!'

Her return journey was easier, since the westbound tunnels on the A19 were not affected by the notional repair work. The only problem was a motorcyclist stuck just in front of her, riding some sort of powerful red machine no doubt capable of over 200 kmph. Carla's little Fiat didn't have enough power to overtake him, and since he seemed content to cruise along at a steady 90 kmph the whole way, she had no choice but to stare at his stubborn, leather-clad form all the way to Catania.

Back in her flat, she tried calling her father, but there was still no reply. She had a shower and then went back into the bedroom of her modern apartment, searching for the thick white terry-towelling gown she used to dry off in. It was not on the hook where she kept it, and it took a moment to locate it on a similar hook on the other side of the closet. The jacket and slacks she had hung there, still in their plastic wrapping from the cleaners where she had picked them up two days earlier, were hanging on the other hook, the one where Carla always kept her towelling gown.

Her personal mobile started to ring. Carla sidled towards it, glancing at the open doorway and the various inner recesses of the apartment, as yet unchecked.

'Signorina Arduini?' a charmless male voice asked. 'This is the Bar Nettuno. We have a message that was left by a friend of yours. She said to phone you and tell you to pick it up immediately.'

'Can't you give it to me now?' asked Carla irritably. 'Who is this supposed friend, anyway?'

'She didn't leave a name, *signorina*, just a written message sealed in an envelope. She told me to ring you at six o'clock precisely and tell you to come and pick it up.'

Carla glanced at the clock. It was just after six.

'Very well, I'll be there shortly,' she said.

Naked except for the towel clutched around her belly, she opened every door in the small apartment and verified that no one was hiding there. Nothing seemed to be missing, either. Carla switched on her Toshiba laptop and turned away to look out some clothes. When she returned to the table, the screen was glowing. In the centre was a box with a circle slashed red and the words FATAL ERROR MESSAGE! THIS COMPUTER HAS PERFORMED AN ILLEGAL OPERATION AND WILL

BE SHUT DOWN. Looking out of the window at the apartment block across the street, Carla felt for the power switch and pressed it gently, stilling the computer, then closed the lid.

The Bar Nettuno was only a few steps away, an undistinguished enterprise installed on the ground floor of the apartment block visible from Carla's window. Hurriedly dressed in jeans and a pullover, Carla strode in and identified herself to the barman, who nodded expressionlessly and passed her an envelope with her name on it. Inside she found a handwritten note: 'I'll call the pay phone in the corner, beside the video game, at six fifteen, then every five minutes until I get you. CN.'

Carla glanced at her watch. It was six twelve. Three minutes later, the phone started to ring. Corinna Nunziatella sounded embarrassed.

'I apologize for all this nonsense, *cara*, but if we're going to do this, we'd better do it properly.'

'You think your phone is tapped?'

'Under the circumstances, that's the only sensible assumption to make. Yours too, for all I know. And cellphones are notoriously insecure. So this seemed the best way. How was your day in Palermo?'

Carla told her. There was silence the other end, then a long sigh.

'This means we're going to have to be even more careful about our arrangements for tomorrow.'

'What do you mean?'

'I'll explain when we meet. Have you got a pen and paper? Now listen carefully. Take the 10 a.m. AST bus to Aci Castello. Go down to the coast and walk north to Aci Trezza. It's only a couple of kilometres along a very pretty path with a view of the rocks which the Cyclops named Polyphemus threw at Ulysses and his men after they blinded him. Do you know your Homer?'

'Surely that happened somewhere in Greece?'

'In Homer's time, Sicily was somewhere in Greece. Are you paying attention? In Aci Trezza there's a hotel called *I Ciclopi*. Go into the bar and wait for me. If I haven't contacted you by midday, go home. Don't mention my name, don't ask questions, don't try to call me, just go home. And another thing. After what you've just told me, it's possible that you may be followed. If you notice anyone following you, try to lose him. If you can't, again, just go home. Above all, on no account bring a tail to our rendezvous. Do you understand?'

'Of course, but why should I be followed? No one's interested in me.'

'I'm interested in you, *cara*, and they're interested in me. Your little lunch in "the triangle of death" proved that beyond a doubt.'

'But that was . . .'

'Please just accept what I'm telling you. As far as they're concerned, we're a couple. They will therefore be watching you.'

'This is like some stupid movie!' Carla exclaimed dramatically, sounding like a character in just such a movie.

'All the more reason not to be stupid ourselves,' Corinna Nunziatella replied calmly. '*A domani, cara.*'

Six men sat around the metal table set up in the shade of the ancient carob and palm trees in the centre of the small square. On the table, painted green and chipped and flecked with rust, lay a chessboard. The six men were seated on folding chairs of a similar colour and condition. Only two of the men were actually playing, but the other four watched as though their lives depended on the result. So, to a lesser degree, did a larger group, about ten in all, who stood in a rough circle at a respectful distance from the players and their immediate entourage. Beyond them, cars lay as though abandoned in the empty street, ranks of shuttered houses kept their counsel, while above all Etna smouldered like a badly doused fire.

'The queen,' said the man playing White, placing his cigar in the ashtray to the right of the chessboard.

All the onlookers perked up, but for a long time no one spoke.

'She's exposed,' the other player agreed at length.

'But that pawn is only a few moves from queening itself,' the first mused. 'If I move against the queen, the pawn will have a chance to get through to the back file. What to do?'

'Try the Sicilian Defence!' said a voice from the surrounding crowd. Ironic but anonymous guffaws broke out all around, as though to protect the speaker against the possible consequences of this insolence.

The man at the table picked up his cigar and leaned back slowly, looking up at the shards of blue sky visible through the thickly massed leaves overhead. There was a terrible silence. The speaker exhaled an expanding galaxy of smoke.

'We really must respond to the recent communication from our friends in Corleone before too long,' he said. 'Not to do so might appear discourteous.'

'But how?' asked his opponent, shifting a rook forward five squares and then instantly withdrawing his hand, so quickly that the piece might have moved by itself.

The man playing White did not even look at the board.

'I think an invitation to lunch,' he said.

'They'd never come!' burst out the voice in the crowd which had spoken before.

'Not to Catania, of course. But if the invitation came from Messina . . .'

He glanced down at the table and took the threatening rook with a knight.

'Then we'd have to give them something in return,' remarked Black.

'Precisely. We give them the judge.'

'Nunziatella? She's already been removed from the picture.'

'From our point of view, yes. But she's still investigating the Maresi business, which spills over in all sorts of ways into the interests of our Messina friends.'

There was a long silence.

'If we do that, then the authorities will crack down on us,' said Black.

'No, they won't,' White replied. 'No one will know it was us. As you pointed out, we have no reason to be interested in Nunziatella. Why should we stir up trouble when everything has been sorted out so nicely?'

'In that case, they'll go after Messina. And our friends there won't like that.'

'Who cares what they like? By then it will be too late. They've been getting a bit above themselves recently, anyhow.'

He took a long satisfied draw on his cigar, then glanced back at the board and moved his queen diagonally from one side to the other.

'Check.'

The man playing Black looked at him in astonishment.

'How do you do it, Don Gaspare?'

'You like it?' the cigar-smoker enquired coyly.

'It's beautiful!'

A frown came over his face.

'But what about the Corleonesi?'

'What about them?'

'Well, supposing they come to this lunch . . .'

'They'll come all right! Now that Totò is in prison and Binù's in deep hiding, they need allies. I happen to know that they've been flirting with our friends in Messina for some time. An invitation like that? They'll cream in their pants!'

Another round of laughter from the onlookers.

'All right, so they come,' said Black. 'What then?'

'Then they go home again,' the other man said, staring his opponent in the eyes, his voice brutally harsh. 'Since there's no railway to Corleone, we can't offer them a free ride in a freight car. But to avoid appearing discourteous, we must return the favour somehow. Saverio!'

'Sì, capo,' said the rogue voice in the crowd.

The man at the table paused to draw on his cigar.

'We'll need a lorry,' he said at last. 'Something big. Maybe one of those articulated jobs. We can't be sure how many of them will show up, and we wouldn't want them to be too cramped.'

More laughter.

'Do you think you could you arrange that?' the cigar-smoker concluded.

'A couple of hours, *capo*,' Saverio replied. 'Would you be interested in a refrigerated lorry, by any chance?'

The man at the table stared down at the chessboard for so long it seemed that he had not heard the question, his attention devoted wholly to the game. Then a slow smile spread across his face. He swivelled in his chair and looked directly at the man who had spoken.

'Refrigerated,' he repeated.

'A lot of them are,' Saverio explained. 'For vegetables and meat and so on. It wouldn't be hard to get one, down on the *autostrada*.'

'Refrigerated!' the chess player said again, his smile broader than ever. 'Saverio, you're a genius.'

Saverio made a humbly submissive shrug and did not speak further. The cigar-smoker turned back to the table.

'They give it to us hot, we give it to them cold!' he exclaimed triumphantly.

The man playing Black moved a pawn forward to block the White queen's threat to his king.

'They'll know it was us,' he remarked in a neutral tone.

'Of course they will!' the other man exclaimed. 'So will their erstwhile hosts in Messina. They'll also know that their explanations and excuses will never be believed. So with the Corleonesi going nuclear west of the mountains and the Calabrians moving in from the east, our friends in Messina will finally be forced to ally with us or face a classic pincer attack on two fronts.'

Silence fell. At length the other chess player broke it with a sharp intake of breath through his rotten teeth.

'How do you do it, Gaspare?' he repeated wonder-ingly.

The other man sucked complacently at his cigar.

'I think,' he said. 'I think, and then I think again. Then I review my conclusions with my friends here in my home town, and occasionally even have the pleas-ure of discovering that one of them has a streak of imagination to add a detail to my scheme, like young Saverio here.'

He bent forward and stared at the man across the table.

'You used to be like that, Rosario. That's why I always talked things over with you first. You were intel-ligent and creative. What happened, Rosario? Where did all that energy go?'

There was no reply. In the intense silence which had fallen on the group of men, a precise pattern of sound made itself heard. No one looked round, but each person seemed to become marginally denser and more still. The footsteps tapping rhythmically across the cobbles grew ever closer, passing beneath the statue of a nineteenth-century native of the town who had briefly achieved limited fame as a poet, then shifted to a rich crunching on the gravel strewn under the trees in the centre of the square.

The newcomer moved at a steady pace through the men gathered about the table with its chessboard. He was tall and imposing, in his eighties perhaps, his face collapsed on to the bones beneath, but with eyes of a startling blue clarity. He wore a brown blazer over a check shirt, with a dark red tie and grey flannel trousers. His feet were clad in beige socks and open leather sandals and he carried a briar walking-stick in one gnarled hand, with the aid of which he favoured his left leg. No one said a word to him, or gave the slightest impression of being aware of his presence. The man stopped in front of the green-painted table. He looked neither at the players, nor at the attendant entourage, but at the chessboard.

He stood there for over a minute, completely absorbed in his study. No one spoke, no one moved, but a sense of unease seemed to have come over the company. At length the newcomer straightened up and sniffed deeply.

'Black to win in five moves,' he announced in an Italian whose flexible spine had been replaced by a steel pin.

Only now did he look at the two players. The one called Don Gaspare glanced up at him in a curious way, simultaneously contemptuous and apprehensive.

'Ah, yes, of course you know all about winning, Herr Genzler.'

The other man looked back at the board for an instant, then turned implacably back to Don Gaspare.

'Black in five,' he repeated. 'Unless one of you makes a mistake.'

There was a subliminal gasp all around the table. No one talked to the *capo* like that. But Don Gaspare simply puffed contentedly on his cigar.

'I don't make mistakes,' he replied calmly.

'Perhaps. But I hear that Rosario is not as good as he used to be.'

The intruder bowed vestigially.

'At your service, Don Gaspare.'

The chess player returned an even more sketchy bow.

'And yours, General.'

The intruder turned his back and stalked off. The men around the table listened with communal intensity to the crunch and then the slapping of his sandals as he made his way across the square to what was to all appearances the town's only commercial enterprise, a combination bar and grocery store, into which he disappeared.

Back in the public garden in the centre of the square, the silence continued for some time.

'Black in five moves, eh?' Don Gaspare remarked at length. 'Can you see how, Rosario?'

The other player performed a pantomime shrug and grimace.

'It's easy enough to say something like that to make yourself look good!' he exclaimed.

'*Can you see how?*' Don Gaspare repeated emphatically.

Rosario did not reply. The other man took out a cellphone and punched buttons.

'Turi? Don Gaspà. Put the general on.'

A pause.

'Herr Genzler? Black in five, you said. How, exactly?'

He took out a pen and started scribbling on the back of an envelope.

'To queen's pawn seven? But that's . . . Right. And then? Ah! I understand. Thank you. What are you drinking? Fine, tell Turi that it's on me.'

He put the cellphone away. Gripping the chessboard, he turned it around so that he was behind the black ranks. After a moment, he sent a bishop sliding forward two squares. Rosario regarded him with anxiety, then taking the white pieces he replied by capturing a forward pawn. Don Gaspare immediately moved again, a crab-like advance by a hitherto unregarded knight. Rosario sat staring at the board until his opponent suddenly hammered his fist down on the table.

'People come to me with their problems!' he shouted furiously. 'I don't need more problems. What I need is solutions! Is that clear?'

He stood up, surveying the men assembled there.

'Is that clear?'

'Sì, capo,' everyone muttered, like a congregation responding to the priest.

Don Gaspare stared around the circle, making eye contact with each man. Then he looked back at the chessboard. Without glancing at his opponent, he made three further moves and then flicked the middle finger of his right hand against the white king, which went flying on to the gravel under the trees.

'Carla?'

'*Papà!* Where have you been? I was worried about you.'

'I'm in Rome.'

'What's this music?'

'Music?'

'Muzak. Elevator music.'

'I don't hear anything.'

'Well, I certainly do. So you're in Rome? Why?'

'I had to leave suddenly.'

'Can you speak up, please? This music . . .'

'I had to come to Rome. Unexpectedly. A personal matter.'

'Oh, yes. Yes, I see.'

'I don't know when I'll be back, exactly. I'm taking a few days' leave.'

Quite apart from the underlay of soft pop, the connection was poor, fading in and out, but always dim and drained.

'What's the weather like there?' a voice like her father's asked.

'Much the same. And in Rome?'

'Sandy.'

'What?'

'Never mind. Listen, it may be a while before I get back. Will you be all right?'

'Of course. I just wish you were here, though. They searched my room.'

'What? Who?'

'I don't know. But someone has been here. They left a message on my computer.'

'Your what?'

'My laptop. My whole life's on it, and someone has been messing about with it. I've got back-ups, of course, but . . .'

'Back-up lives?'

Carla laughed.

'Sorry, I forgot you don't speak the language.'

'Look, Carla, if someone broke into your apartment, call the police. I'll give you a number. A name, too. Baccio Sinico. He's a good man and he'll . . .'

'I don't have time now. We're going away for the weekend and I'm just about to leave. I'll do it on Monday. Will you be back by then?'

'Going where?'

'To Taormina. It's supposed to be lovely, and the person I'm going with knows this wonderful hotel. It's quite high up, too, so perhaps it'll be cool. It's difficult for me here, Dad. I haven't really made any friends yet, and it'll be nice to get out and meet some people.'

A pause.

'Well, have fun.'

'You too. When will you be back?'

'I don't know yet. I'll let you know. Look after yourself.'

'You too, Dad. After all, as you told me that time in Alba, you're the only one I'll ever have.'

Her voice broke slightly on the last phrase. She clicked the phone shut and turned back to the half-packed suitcase resting on the bed. Then she pulled a few more clothes off their hangers and folded them neatly into the suitcase between layers of tissue paper. She had heard that Taormina was an international resort for the rich and beautiful, and you never knew who you might run into in a place like that, maybe even Mr Right.

By now, Carla had a strong suspicion that Corinna Nunziatella wanted her to be more than just a 'girl-friend'. The scenario Carla had in mind consisted of a few martinis too many at a bar, followed by a slow, delicious dinner at a restaurant, a walk back through the twilight to this fabulous hotel, and then the pitch. Well, fair enough. She had never made love with a woman, but there was a first time for everything and she was all grown up now. Anyway, she was planning to pay for her side of things, so she could always just say no. Or not, depending.

It was only when she closed the case and lifted it down off the bed that Carla realized she was going to have to carry the damn thing all the way. It was all very well for Corinna to tell her it was just a couple of kilometres along a very pretty path with classical associations. *She* had a car. Carla thought of calling the judge and explaining the problem, and then had a better idea.

Outside in the streets, even at twenty past nine, the heat was starting to gain the upper hand, although barely flexing the gigantic muscles which would throttle the city by noon. By the time she reached the corner of the block, Carla's suitcase felt as though it was filled with bricks. It took another ten minutes to flag down a passing taxi.

'Do you know a hotel called *I Ciclopi* at Aci Trezza?' she asked.

He nodded.

'Hop in.'

'No, it's not for me. But I need this case taken there and left at the desk. It's to be collected by someone called Carla Arduini. Do you understand?'

The driver punctiliously estimated the distance to Aci Trezza and back on his map, worked out the fare on an electronic calculator and refused Carla's offer of a tip. It took her a huge effort of will not to climb into the air-conditioned cab there and then, but Corinna had told her to walk, so walk she would. With regret, she handed her suitcase and the money to the driver, and watched the taxi drive away.

The usual elderly crowd had gathered at the bus stop: women whose nubile fruitfulness had shrivelled up like a sun-dried tomato, and men who looked diminished in a different way, plucked by age or ill-health from the vine of productive and meaningful labour. The only people in Carla's age-group were a pair of punk-goths with spiked hair and extensive body-piercing, and an overweight *figlio di mamma* in a blazer, jeans and yellow pullover.

The 36 bus finally arrived, and Carla rode down to Piazza Giovanni XXIII, where she bought a ticket on the AST service north along the coast. Thirty minutes later, she got off in Aci Castello, a small bathing resort dominated by the Norman castle for which it was named. A lot of other people, mostly young, also got out here, all kitted out for a day at the seaside.

Carla followed them down to the sea, along the wooden walkway set out over the rocks and on to the rough path leading north. Here, outside the city, the bright sun seemed a benign presence, while the sea breeze was blissfully invigorating. People swam and sprawled on the lava rocks, while itinerant salesmen with flawless skin the colour of cooking chocolate hawked contraband gadgets and faked designer goods in a lazy, unthreatening way, as though they had no interest in making any money but were just passing the time.

Carla stopped to chat with one of them and haggled casually over a shoulder bag she quite liked but had no intention of buying and then carrying all the way along the coast. As she turned away from the *vucomprà* she noticed the man standing beside the path twenty metres or so behind her, seemingly looking out to sea. He was wearing jeans, a canary-yellow pullover and a blue blazer with gilt buttons. The outfit was as conspicuous and inappropriate for a day at the beach as it had been at the bus stop outside her apartment an hour earlier.

Carla walked quickly on for some time, then sat down on one of the benches which were placed along the path, overlooking the *Isole Ciclopi*: the tall, jagged rocks which did indeed look as though some angry giant had just tossed them down from the smouldering bulk of Etna, like a child wanting to see how big a splash he could make. Glancing behind to her right, she noted that Blue Blazer had suddenly felt the need to rest too. There was no other bench nearby, so he was sitting on a ledge of the solidified lava flow, dusting the designated spot fastidiously before entrusting it with the seat of his Levi 501s.

Carla got up and continued on her way, pausing after a few minutes to look at the view behind her. Blue Blazer had also decided that it was time to get a move on, but now he too was brought to a halt, apparently by some problem involving his shoes. When Carla reached the next miniature headland, she left the path and walked to the tip of the rocks razoring out into the sea. Turning as though to take in the whole panorama, she discovered that her understudy was admiring the view of Etna on the other side of the path, while making a call on his mobile phone.

Carla squared her shoulders and walked quickly back to the path. She couldn't afford to waste any more time or she'd arrive late. On the other hand, Corinna had been very specific about taking care that she was not followed, and clearly she *was* being followed. Confrontation, she decided, was the only way to resolve the situation. She hurried on along the path, which sloped up to a low rise formed by one of the jagged promontories thrust out into the sea. As soon as she was out of sight on the other side of this, she stopped. There was no one on the path ahead except for an elderly gentleman inspecting the seabirds through a pair of binoculars. A few moments later, Blue Blazer appeared at the top of the rise, panting slightly. He froze as Carla moved resolutely towards him.

'Why are you following me?' she demanded.

The man made a vague, sheepish gesture.

'What do you mean?'

'Don't try to deny it! You took the same bus I did, just down the street from my apartment building, then the AST service to Aci Castello, and ever since then you've been following me along this path, stopping whenever I stop and . . .'

'I don't know what you're talking about!' the man protested in a panicky tone. 'I'm just out for a walk, that's all, the same as you. This is a public path, lots of people come here. You're not the only one allowed, you know.'

A shadow fell across the lava cinders between them.

'May I be of any assistance, *signorina?*'

Carla turned. It was the elderly bird-watcher. He had a shock of carefully groomed silver hair, an elaborately waxed moustache, and was wearing a linen suit against which a pair of Braun binoculars dangled from their leather strap.

'That's very kind of you,' Carla replied warmly. 'This man has been following me ever since I left home this morning.'

'That's not true!' Blue Blazer protested. 'She's imagining things. It's a complete coincidence. I haven't done anything wrong!'

The older man walked over to him at a deliberate pace. His face had become very grim.

'Not yet, perhaps,' he said in a low, chilling voice. 'You were biding your time, weren't you? Waiting for a suitable opportunity to present itself, and to get up enough courage to make your move. We all know about people like you, my friend. We know how to deal with them, too.'

He added three short sentences in Sicilian. Carla could not understand the words, but there was no mistaking their lapidary brutality. Blue Blazer took several paces back and started to tremble. He mumbled something incoherent, then turned and walked off rapidly, almost running, in the direction from which he'd come.

'Allow me to apologize unreservedly for that unpleasantness, *signorina*,' the elderly man remarked in a courtly tone.

Carla smiled.

'There's no reason for you to apologize. On the contrary, thank you for your assistance.'

The man shook his head with an expression of disgust.

'You are from the north, I think. Yes? To come here and have this horrible experience, this appalling breach of every law of Sicilian courtesy . . . I feel deeply ashamed, *signorina*, but the cruel fact is that nowadays there are scum everywhere. At one time, a man like that wouldn't have dared show his face out of doors. By the same token, of course, a lovely young woman such as yourself wouldn't have dreamt of going for a walk unaccompanied in an isolated spot such as this. But there we are! The old rules have broken down and the new ones have yet to take effect.'

Carla nodded briskly. Apparently she had evaded her amateurish shadower only to fall into the clutches of yet another elderly bore.

'Well, thanks for getting rid of him. Now I must be off or I'll be late for my appointment.'

'Of course, of course! How far do you have to go?'

'To Aci Trezza.'

'Why, that's where I live myself! It's no more than ten minutes' walk from here. Allow me to accompany you, *signorina*. No, no, I insist! I was on my way home anyway, and after that disagreeable incident I wouldn't feel right letting you go alone. Have you been along here before? I come out every morning, to get some exercise and study the bird life. There's a really quite amazing variety of species to be seen, some native, others migratory . . .'

Taking Carla's arm, he led the way along the path, keeping up a continuous commentary on the fauna and flora of the littoral, about which he seemed oppressively well-informed. As soon as they reached the outskirts of Aci Trezza, Carla explained that she was meeting someone at *I Ciclopi*, and took leave of her courtly companion, although not before he had given her directions to the hotel as well as one of his cards, and insisted that the next time she was there she should contact him.

There was no sign of Corinna at the restaurant, but Carla's suitcase had arrived. She reclaimed it and toyed with a *cappuccino* for twenty minutes, then walked outside. By now it was eleven forty-five, just fifteen minutes from the time when she had been instructed to give up and go home. It was deliciously warm yet airy in the shade of the huge awning. The only sounds were the slushy static of the wavelets on the rocks, the occasional clank of pots and pans in the kitchens, and the subliminal growl of a helicopter circling somewhere overhead.

'Signorina Arduini?'

It was a uniformed waiter, professionally deferential.

'Yes?'

'There is a phone call for you. This way, please.'

She followed the man across the lobby to a table with a telephone. The waiter dialled zero and passed the receiver to Carla.

'Hello?'

'Carla?'

'Yes.'

'It's me. Leave the hotel and turn left into Via San Leonarbello. At number sixty-three you'll find a green Nissan. It's unlocked. Follow the written instructions on the driver's seat.'

The line went dead.

Via San Leonarbello turned out to be an alley of single-storey fishermen's houses, most of which seemed to have been converted into holiday homes. Sure enough, a green Nissan saloon was parked outside number sixty-three. Carla glanced along the street, then opened the passenger door and got in. A piece of paper with writing lay on the driver's seat.

KEYS IN GLOVE COMPARTMENT.
DRIVE TO END OF STREET, TURN LEFT.
STOP OPPOSITE SPAR GROCERY.
KEEP ENGINE RUNNING.

Carla sighed sourly. If she'd had any idea what was involved, she would never have agreed to accompany Corinna on this stupid weekend outing to Taormina. All this games-playing was beginning to get on her nerves. But it was too late to back out now. She put her suitcase in the back of the car, moved over to the driver's seat and drove off.

The grocery store, one of the ubiquitous Spar chain, was easy enough to find, but there was no space to park anywhere on the narrow street. Carla drew up opposite the store, blasted the horn and consulted her watch. All right, Corinna, she thought. You've got sixty seconds exactly, then I dump the car and get the next bus back to Catania. She had laundry to do and several long-overdue letters to write, and there was the new Nanni Moretti film which she'd been meaning to see for some time. She'd loved *Caro Diario*, and even if this one wasn't as good, the prospect of a few hours in an air-conditioned cinema was a powerful inducement.

The passenger door opened and Corinna Nunziatella got in, barely recognizable in a man's suit, shirt and tie. Her face was obscured as before by her aviator sunglasses, while her cropped hair was almost invisible beneath a large straw hat.

'Go!' she said urgently.

'Go where?'

'Just go! I'll give you directions later.'

Carla put the Nissan in gear and drove to the end of the street.

'Left here,' Corinna Nunziatella told her. 'Now right. Do a U-turn in the middle of the block, then right again at the lights. Run the red, there are no traffic police round here. Do you like my outfit?'

Carla smiled distractedly.

'It's, er . . . interesting.'

'This car belongs to a friend. They have four altogether, so she won't miss it. The hardest part was getting out of the house without my escort spotting me. Hence the disguise.'

'Won't it raise a few eyebrows at the hotel?'

Corinna laughed.

'Not in Taormina! They've seen everything there. It's always been a sort of extra-territorial enclave here in Sicily, a place where none of the usual rules apply. As long as your money holds out, no one cares what you do. Left here across the railway tracks, then sharp right and follow the signs to the motorway.'

She glanced playfully at Carla.

'Anyway, I happen to think I look rather fetching, so there. And you? No problems?'

Carla swayed her head slowly from side to side, indicating that this was not precisely the case.

'I was followed. But I'm pretty sure it was just some creep who lives with his mother and wanted to look at my legs. He was much too obvious to be a professional. Anyway, this old man who was out watching birds along the coast got rid of him for me.'

To Carla's surprise, Corinna insisted on her recounting the entire story, detail by detail. The older woman's face grew grimmer and grimmer.

'A classic sacrifice,' she remarked when Carla had finished. 'I don't want to alarm you, but this is not good news. It confirms that they're on to you as well.'

'Who are?'

'That "creep" you say was following you, the conspicuous way he was dressed and acting was quite deliberate. With someone like me they would have been more subtle, but they knew you weren't used to the rules of the game, so they went completely over the top. You were *meant* to spot him and become suspicious. That was the whole point. Then, at just the right psychological moment, along comes this chivalrous, inoffensive, slightly tedious old-world gentleman who promptly rids you of your ostentatious tail. You're naturally so grateful and relieved that you're not going to suspect *him*.'

'But he wasn't following me, Corinna!'

'Didn't you just tell me that he walked the whole way to Aci Trezza with you, and that you then asked him for directions to *I Ciclopi*?'

'Yes, but . . .'

'Did you see him after that?'

'No!'

'He didn't by any chance follow you to this car?'

'Of course not! At least, I don't think so. I didn't see him.'

'Are you sure?'

Carla did not answer. They drove along a dead-straight road between rows of tall palm trees, their trunks trimmed, rising on either side like exotically verdant telephone poles. Then a junction loomed ahead, marked by a large green arrow marked A18.

'Turn right here on to the motorway,' said Corinna. 'Follow the signs to Messina.'

'Messina? But I thought we were . . .'

'I suggest that you concentrate on the driving and leave the thinking to me, *cara*,' Corinna remarked crisply.

Carla said nothing. After a few moments silence, Corinna sighed.

'I'm sorry for snapping at you. I've been trying to work out what to do. If I went by the book, I'd cancel the whole outing right now.'

She glanced girlishly at Carla.

'But I can't. To give up the prospect of this gorgeous weekend with you, all because of some paranoid fears which I've almost certainly imagined . . .'

'You mean this man who was supposed to have been following me?'

Corinna Nunziatella shook her head.

'It's not just that. That business yesterday, for example. It's obvious they were sending a message to me through you. Just to take one aspect of the thing, the Hotel Zagarella is a notorious symbol of Mafia power, built by Ignazio and Nino Salvo, cousins from one of the top families who later cornered the tax-collection monopoly for the whole island, thanks to their friends in the regional government. They became obscenely rich as a result, but the Zagarella was almost entirely financed by public money from the government's *Cassa per il Mezzogiorno* fund, supposedly created to stimulate economic development in the south. And the hotel's symbolic status was confirmed once and for all in 1979, when Giulio Andreotti, then prime minister, gave a speech at a rally there, surrounded by just about every high-ranking political *mafioso* in Palermo.'

They were on the motorway now, gliding north with the other traffic heading towards the Straits of Messina and the ferry crossing to the continent of Europe. Corinna Nunziatella lit a cigarette snatched from a rumpled pack on the dashboard.

'So when I'm told that you've been invited to lunch at the Zagarella by three men who claimed to represent the regional government, and who made it quite clear that they were aware of our relationship,' she continued, blasting out smoke, 'I don't have to be a genius to understand the intended message.'

'Which is?'

' "Be careful. We've got our eye on you. You're alone, you can't trust anyone, our people are everywhere. Take heed of this warning. Next time there may not be one." '

'And you think they really mean it?'

'Of course they mean it! They killed Mino Pecorelli and Giuseppe Impastato and Pio Della Torre. They killed Giorgio Ambrosio and Michele Sindona and Boris Giuliano and Emanuele Basile and General Dalla Chiesa and his wife. They killed Cesare Terranora and

Rococo Chinnici and Ciaccio Montalto. They killed Falcone and Borsellino. And they killed my mother and hundreds more like her, maybe thousands . . .'

She opened the window and tossed out the half-smoked cigarette with a gesture of disgust.

'Well, they're not going to get me!'

Perturbed by the intensity of Corinna's voice, Carla took her eyes off the traffic for a moment to glance at her companion.

'How do you mean, they killed your mother? The other evening you told me that she was still alive.'

'No, I didn't. You asked, and I replied, "I suppose you could say that she's alive." She's alive, but shut up in an institution. A private one, mind you, and relatively pleasant, but an asylum nevertheless. She finally cracked when my father was killed in a particularly unpleasant way by a rival clan. Since then she will only speak English. She babbles about taking the train down to London and making a new start.'

She broke off, shaking her head, and patted Carla's left knee lightly.

'I'm sorry to bore you with all this ghastly personal stuff, *cara*, but you can't understand me without it. For better or for worse, it's made me what I am. I realized very early on that nothing could be done without power. The only power open to me, as a Sicilian woman, was the power of the state institutions, so I decided to study law and join the judiciary. The Italian state isn't as powerful as the Mafia, as we know to our cost, but the balance has already shifted a long way. We're ahead at half-time, but the match is far from over. The important thing now is to make sure that they don't try to change the rules. But I'll carry on even if they do. It's a personal commitment. The only way to defeat the patriarchal structure of *mafiosità* is to attack it through the medium of an equally patriarchal authority whose interests happen to be in conflict with those which destroyed my mother.'

She laughed suddenly, and turned to Carla.

'And now I'll shut up about the whole business for the rest of the weekend!' she announced gaily. 'The only things you'll be able to get me to talk about are clothes and jewellery and shoes and food and office gossip and celebrity scandals. I shall have breakfast in bed and lunch by the pool and dinner in a fabulous fish restaurant I know down by the sea. In short, I plan to behave like the frivolous, trivial, shallow slut that I've always secretly wanted to be. What about you?'

Carla gave her a dazzling smile.

'That sounds perfect. I'll just try to keep up with you.'

'There's the Giardini turn-off,' said Corinna, pointing to the signed exit. 'We take the next one. It's marked Taormina. Take it slowly. It gets quite steep and narrow once you're off the *autostrada*. I hope you like the hotel.'

'Have you stayed there before?'

'Yes.'

'Alone?'

'No, not alone. This exit coming up.'

Carla signalled her turn.

'So do you do this sort of thing quite often?' she asked.

'Not nearly as often as I'd like. It's a survival strategy. Sicily is a pressure cooker. It's not that life here is really that dangerous. Arguably less so, in fact, for most people, than in Rome or Milan. It's a process of attrition. You're "on" the whole time, particularly if you're a woman. Everything you do or don't do is noted down and reported back. There's literally no such thing as privacy. We don't even have a word for it.'

Carla turned off on to a looping, heavily graded road which zigzagged laboriously uphill towards a perched town which was presumably Taormina. A motorcycle had turned off the motorway right behind her, and was now making aggressive but ineffectual attempts to overtake despite the steep gradient. The two men on it wore full-body leather suits with white and red stripes and seemed to be having an animated conversation over an intercom system built into their space-suit-type helmets.

'And then there's the insular mentality,' Corinna was saying. 'A sort of passive-aggressive provincialism.

Rome is only an hour away by plane, but it might as well be on another planet. Even in Reggio di Calabria you breathe more easily. Seen from Palermo or Catania, the Straits of Messina look wider than the Atlantic. Nothing that happens over there is of any more than marginal significance, depending on the extent to which it might tip the balance of power here.'

At the bend ahead, the road widened to a point which would allow Carla room to let the leather-suited bikers pass. She slowed down and signalled her intention to pull over. The bright red Moto Guzzi at once revved up and started to overtake. As it drew alongside, the passenger on the pillion raised a cloth-wrapped bundle which he was holding on his knees. There was a loud banging noise, as though the engine was about to stall, and pieces of glass started flying around inside the car. Corinna turned to Carla, who was struggling to keep the car on the road despite the rash of pockmarks erupting across her chest and shoulders. The man on the motorcycle produced a rectangular package which he lobbed through the shattered side-window of the Nissan, as though returning some mislaid possession to its rightful owner, just as the car veered off to the left, running over the verge and continuing on its way through the olive grove on the vertiginous hillside, riding normally at first, despite the gradient, but eventually turning sideways and rolling over.

The explosion almost immediately afterwards destroyed a *centenario* olive tree which had been planted in July 1860 to commemorate Garibaldi's decisive defeat of the Bourbon forces at the battle of Milazzo and the unification of Sicily with the nascent kingdom of Italy which soon ensued. But there was no one left in Taormina who recalled this fact and the tree had almost stopped cropping, so the incident was of no real importance.

PART TWO

Aurelio Zen had once been told by a fellow officer in the Criminalpol department about a joke that the latter had played on an assiduously literal-minded Umbrian colleague. The gag involved getting the victim to try to identify a notional train supposedly listed in the official timetables which, if you tracked its progress from one section of the network to the next, turned out to go round and round in perpetual circles. In reality, of course, no such train existed, so Zen had had to improvise.

This involved consulting the glass-framed timetables at his station of arrival, then taking the next departure listed, regardless of its destination. If there was none until the following day, he spent the night at a hotel near the station and started again first thing in the morning. There were only three other rules: he was forbidden to return directly to the city from which he had just arrived, to use any other form of transportation, or to cross the frontier.

To keep him amused on his travels, he stopped at a newsagent's stall and bought a selection of the cheap thrillers published by Mondadori in its yellow-jacketed series featuring two narrow columns of type on every page, coarse paper which browned as you read it, and garishly stylized cover art. He picked out half a dozen at random, not bothering to read the blurbs. It was enough that the name of the author sounded English or American, thus offering the prospect of a tightly organized guided tour through a theme park of re-assuringly foreign unpleasantness, and concluding with a final chapter in which the truth was laid bare and the guilty party identified and duly punished.

By contrast, the trains themselves varied greatly, all the way from aerodynamic missiles barely skimming their dedicated high-speed rails, to ugly, smoke-spew-ing, diesel-powered brutes making their way sedately along ill-maintained branch lines. But these apparent differences were as unimportant as those in the cast of the thrillers Zen was reading. Some characters were glamorous and beautiful, others dull and earnest, but it was understood – even the fictional personages them-selves seemed to understand, and to accept – that they only existed for the purpose of moving the plot along. To keep moving: that was the key. If he ever came to a stop, or even lingered more than a single night in the same place, then they'd be able to find him as surely as they had his mother and daughter. To have any hope of survival, he had to remain a moving target.

Places came and went. This was not their normal role, which was to stay put and display their innumerable layers of history, culture and tradition. Visitors were supposed to approach with due reverence, a full wallet, and at least a feigned knowledge of the wonders in store. They certainly weren't supposed to flit in and out in such a free and easy fashion. It was something new for cities such as these to be treated as mere stops on an extemporized itinerary, but Zen sensed that once they got over the shock they quite liked being flirted with in this casual way.

And what pretty names they had! Perugia, Arezzo, Siena, Empoli, Pisa, Parma . . . Which was just as well, since all Zen usually saw of them was the name, blazoned white on an enamelled blue platform sign, that and the generic surrounding suburbs tracing history in reverse like geological layers in a core sample: sixties apartment buildings, spartan Fascist blocks, turn-of-the-century industrial barracks, and the pomposities of post-unification triumphalism.

If there was a little time to kill before the next train left, he might permit himself to wander out into the streets surrounding the station in search of a sandwich or a coffee. At which point the city – particularly if it was one of the more celebrated names – often seemed to give a little quiver of shock. 'You mean you aren't going to visit the museums, the cathedral and the remains of the mediaeval ramparts?' it demanded of him as he breezed through the sleazy, strident fringes of the station zone, his only concern to leave again as soon as possible. 'Perhaps next time,' he silently replied. 'But not now. I have to go. I have to keep going.'

He knew that he was in a fugue state, of course, but this knowledge made no difference. He was like an addict who is intelligently aware of his addiction and its possible consequences, but powerless to break it. Whenever he tried to do so, it effortlessly reasserted its control by flashing his own memories at him, slices from his central cortex which sent him scurrying for the next train, any other destination than this intolerable terminus. His desiccated mother gabbling at him in a foreign language. Her coffin, almost as tiny as a child's, vanishing into the bowels of the crematorium. The ceremony at the cemetery, with him, Maria Grazia and the Nieddu family the only mourners. And then, if all else failed, him at home that evening, watching the television news and seeing the crumpled, charred wreck of the car in which yet another AntiMafia magistrate had gone to her death, gunned down on a road just outside Taormina. A certain Carla Arduini, a friend of the victim, had also been killed.

Piacenza, Pavia, Novara, Lugano, Bolzano, Trento, Padova, Treviso, Trieste . . . On the other side of the window, the landscape was laid out in varying hues and textures like the pelt of some precious, extinct animal. The thriller he was reading had turned out to be dead too. Something must have gone wrong at the printers, because the last thirty pages were missing. Well, not missing exactly. The pages were there, but they were from another book in the same series, but with a quite different cast and plot. The result was a double sense of frustration: not only would he never know the truth about what had happened in the original story, but he found himself trying to reconstruct the various intrigues and incidents which had led up to the interpolated ending.

At Cremona, and again at Mantova, he tried to buy another copy of the book, only to be told that it was out of print. The local trains seemed to have inherited the malarial symptoms once endemic to the inhabitants of the Po delta, running infrequently and at about the speed of the river itself in the various channels over which the track passed and repassed. By the time Zen finally regained the main line at Fidenza, it was eight in the evening and a spectacular thunderstorm was in progress. He stepped down from the railcar on to a surface which felt for a moment disturbingly familiar: crunchy, mobile, granular. But this was hail, not sand.

He was about to walk over and check the departure timetable when an alarm bell started ringing on the wall of the station building, announcing the arrival of a train from the north. Simultaneously, the diesel unit in which he had arrived gave a sullen roar and shuffled off into the gathering dusk. Too late, Zen remembered that he had left his unfinished thriller lying open on the seat opposite the one in which he had been sitting. He couldn't even remember the title, never mind the author. Now he would never know how it ended.

In the barrage of hail, which was gradually turning to heavy rain, a bright light appeared away in the distance down the main line. Its announcement confirmed by this visual proof, the electric bell cut out, but it was another minute or two before the light perceptibly widened and intensified as the electric locomotive and its long line of carriages came into view through the torrential downpour. It was only then that Zen realized that he had also left his only pack of cigarettes on the railcar.

Luckily there was a bar a little further down the platform, with the square white-on-black T sign indicating that it sold tobacco. As the train squealed to a halt in front of him, Zen groped in his pocket and found a ten-thousand-lire note. That would buy him a couple of packs of *Nazionali*. It would mean missing this train, but first things first. There would soon be another, going somewhere else, and one destination was as good as another.

The carriage which had drawn up in front of Zen was not immediately recognizable as such. The classically chaste blue and white sleeping-car design had been almost obliterated by fat spray-paint graffiti – statements on steroids – which covered even the windows, shutting out any view of the outside world for the occupants. On the door appeared a signature, a date, and the slogan 'Proud to be Crazy'. Zen realized that he hadn't seen any graffiti in Sicily. Perhaps the islanders were behind the times in this, as in so much else. Or maybe the Mafia had hauled all the spray-paint egomaniacs behind the carriage sheds and shot them.

The door opened and a man in uniform emerged. He snatched the banknote that Zen was holding in his hand, picked up his luggage and bustled back aboard the train, safe from the gusts of driven rain blasting down the platform. Beside the door into which he had disappeared was a white destination sign slotted into metal grooves. It read: MILANO C. – BOLOGNA – FIRENZE C. DI MARTE – ROMA TIB. – NAPOLI – VILLA S. GIOV. – MESSINA – CATANIA. Further down the platform, the station master was striding self-importantly about, a lighted green wand raised above his head. The sleeping-car attendant reappeared in the doorway.

'Quickly!' he called. 'It's your last chance.'

Already the massive train had begun to move again, imperceptibly at first, but with a momentum which would carry it overnight down the spine of Italy and across the Straits of Messina to Sicily. Zen took a few steps to his right to get up to speed, then grasped the gleaming handle and, just in time, swung himself aboard.

The truck was parked on a bend on one of the roads into Corleone leading up from the valley of the Frattina river, a glaucous trickle at this time of year. It was a large vehicle with a freezer unit and a Catania number-plate. On both sides of the lorry, colourful painted designs advertised a meat-processing firm located in Catania whose products, according to the slogan below the image of a satisfied housewife, could be relied upon to be 'Always Fresh, Always Wholesome'.

The driver climbed down from the cab and languorously stretched his muscles. He was about thirty, wirily built, with a military-style haircut and heavy black stubble on his chin and cheeks. The time was a few minutes after three in the morning, the dead heart of the night, here in the dead heart of the island, almost exactly half-way between the northern and southern coasts. Apart from the patterned punctures of the stars and the pervasive glow of the moon, presently screened by a thin wafer of cloud, there wasn't a light to be seen, nor any sound to be heard.

Beside the narrow road, bolstered on the other side by a dry-stone retaining wall, stood a roofless, dilapidated two-storey structure which might have been a small farmhouse but was in fact an abandoned *cantoniera*: a dwelling and workshop for the man responsible in former years for the upkeep of this stretch of highway. The driver of the truck lit a cigarette and gazed up at the night sky, picking out the constellations whose supposed significance, indeed even their physical coherence, had turned out to be merely illusory.

After some time a faint flaw made itself felt in the crystalline silence. Far off in the distance, a light appeared and disappeared, turning this way and that. The driver tossed aside his cigarette, walked around to the back of the truck and opened the heavy metal doors. Reaching inside, he extracted a paper-wrapped package. Reacting to the change of temperature, the truck's cooling system turned itself on, but its gentle hum was drowned out by the other noise, much closer now. The light, which had vanished, suddenly reappeared, a cold glare slicing through the darkness like a butcher's knife. A moment later the motorbike screeched to a halt beside the truck, whose driver mounted the pillion, clasping the bulky package. The bike roared away up the road.

Less than a minute later, it was in the close alleys and twisting streets of Corleone. Here, the clamour of the engine rebounded deafeningly from the walls. The motorcycle worked its way through the entrails of the sleeping town, slowing just enough for the passenger to toss his package against the door of one of the houses, then racketing off along *Statale 118*, the main road leading west through the barren hills towards Prizzi. Some young hoolingans out on a spree, those townsfolk who had been dredged from their slumbers concluded. They wouldn't have tried it in the old days, but now Totò was gone there was no more respect.

It wasn't for another three hours that this perception began to change. There was the 'ham', for a start. That's how Annunziata described it to the priest, who was preparing to celebrate early mass.

'Lying right there on the doorstep,' she went on.

'But where, *figlia mia*?' the priest responded in an irritated tone. He'd had a sleepless night, administering extreme unction to a dying woman at the top of the town and trying to console her relatives. Another hysterical woman was the last thing he needed now.

'On the doorstep,' Annunziata repeated stubbornly.

'Which doorstep?'

The woman's silence was sufficient answer.

'*Di loro?*' asked the priest.

Being a priest, he was licensed to ask awkward questions, but in this case even he did so by implication. Was it *their* doorstep? Annunziata gave a minimal but decisive nod.

'A ham?' was the next question.

'I don't know. It had butcher's wrapping on. And there was a dog there, the puppy that Leoluca tried to drown in the drain but it crawled back out? It was sniffing at it.'

Meanwhile, the ham had attracted the attention of other dogs. In fact they all seemed to be there, every loose hound in the town, snuffling around the wrapped package as though it were a bitch in heat. The consequent growling and nipping attracted the attention of various passers-by, one of whom alerted the occupants of the house.

By this time the truck was no longer parked on the curve opposite the abandoned *cantoniera*, thanks to a local lad whose private enterprise later earned him a slow strangulation and interment in the shaft of a disused sulphur mine. Ignazio had noticed the truck on his way back from another venture, which involved the sale of thirty-four illegal immigrants from North Africa to the representative of an agribusiness south of Naples which needed cheap indentured labour.

The deal had been struck after an inspection of the merchandise in Mazara del Vallo, a fishing port on the south-west corner of the island. This was deep in the territory of the Marsala clans, and strictly off-limits to entrepreneurs from anywhere else, especially Corleone, so Ignazio had arranged the appointment –

at a disused fish-packing plant just south of the town – for the early hours of the morning, arriving under cover of darkness and leaving as soon as the duffle-bag of cash had changed hands.

Travel on a north-south axis in this part of Sicily was relatively easy, but going from west to east you might as well be on a mule as in a car. There were various possible routes, none of them good. Ignazio wanted to get out of enemy territory as quickly as possible, so he opted to take the *autostrada* to the Gallitello turn-off, then cut across country on back roads. It was almost six o'clock before he sighted his destination, distinct in the pre-dawn glimmer on its hilltop. A few minutes later he saw the truck.

Ignazio was by nature an opportunist, and although he had already done very nicely on the night's work – even after the cut he'd have to give the importer and the handling people – he was not about to turn down an opportunity such as this. A meat truck from Catania abandoned at the roadside! He was back on his home turf now, and no one here had any exaggerated respect for the Limina family. Any windfalls from their territory were fair game. The driver would have known that, of course, which was no doubt why he'd vanished after his rig broke down on that excruciatingly steep ascent into Corleone. Odd route to choose, but he'd probably got lost.

Ignazio braked hard and turned off into an abandoned mule track leading down to the left. He bounced around a curve, parked out of sight of the road and then ran back to the truck. All he needed to do was break into the cab, then fix whatever had gone wrong. If he couldn't, he'd use his cellphone to page his brother. Worst came to worst, they could cut Concetto in on the deal in return for the use of his tow truck.

None of these refinements proved necessary. The cab door was unlocked, the keys were in the ignition, the engine started first time. In retrospect, this should perhaps have given Ignazio pause, but he was an opportunist, and opportunity was clearly knocking.

The road was too narrow to turn the truck around, so Ignazio was forced to blast through the centre of town before heading up into the mountains to the east, looking for somewhere to stash the thing for a few hours, long enough for him to get back to his car, contact his brother and work out what to do next. And he quickly found it, in the form of a dried-up river-bed alongside the old road just north of Monte Cardella, the direct route to Prizzi since by-passed by the longer but less arduous *strada statale*. From there it was about six kilometres back to the spot where he'd left the car, but all downhill. Ignazio locked the truck, pocketed the keys and set off.

It took him about forty minutes to reach the place where he'd left his car, by-passing the town on another of the old mule tracks which criss-crossed the area. Five minutes after that he was back in Corleone, but by then the drama had moved on to a third act, and his role had been revealed to be merely supernumerary. By the time he and his brother returned to the parked truck, others were there to meet them.

The ensuing explanations took over three hours. Long before that, Ignazio started screaming, 'Kill me! I've told you all I know, so just kill me!' Which of course they did, but later. The refrigerated lorry had proved to contain the bodies of five 'made men' of the town, including the grandson of Bernardo Provenzano, the *capo* of the family, now in hiding in Palermo. The Corleonesi had accepted an invitation from a clan in Messina to attend a lunch to celebrate and inspire future contacts between the two clans involved. At some point, the five had been placed, alive, into the back of the truck, which was then driven off with the freezing unit turned on. Thanks to the sub-zero temperatures, none of the corpses showed any sign of post-mortem deliquescence, but they were almost unrecognizable just the same. Ironically enough, the only undamaged one was that of Binù's grandson, the reason being that his left leg had been removed before he had entered the 'death chamber', and so he had been in no condition to try to escape. It was the thigh portion of this leg, suitably wrapped, which had been flung on to *their* doorstep. Examination of the severed stump suggested that the amputation had been performed with a chainsaw.

The bar in Piazza Carlo Alberto was as packed as ever, but the crowd was more evenly distributed now that the exclusion zone created by Carla Arduini's presence was no longer in effect. There was perhaps a momentary flicker of the former tension when Aurelio Zen made his appearance, but it was instantly dissipated in a renewed rumble of discussion and comment.

Zen made his way to the counter and ordered a coffee. The barman appeared oddly frenetic and distracted. He said not a word, going about his business in a jerky, mute, compulsive frenzy, like an actor in a silent film.

'Where's the young lady who used to meet me here?' Zen enquired as the coffee touched down on his saucer.

The barman ran through a range of facial expressions as if trying on a selection of hats, none of which really suited.

'How should I know?' he said at length, furiously wiping the gleaming counter with a rag. 'She didn't come today. I don't know why. She just didn't come. Maybe tomorrow . . .'

Zen knocked his coffee back.

'No,' he said. 'She won't be coming tomorrow, either. She won't be coming ever again.'

He smiled mirthlessly.

'Neither will I, for that matter.'

His eyes never leaving those of the barman, he produced his wallet and extracted a two-thousand-lire note which he tossed on the counter. With it came a spray of what looked like dust. Noticing it, Zen turned his wallet upside down. A stream of reddish grains poured out, forming an uneven pile on the stainless-steel counter.

'What's that?' the barman demanded.

'It's called "blood rain",' Zen told him. 'Think of it as a message.'

'A message?'

Zen nodded.

'A message from Rome.'

His arrival at the Questura appeared to be ill-timed. The guard in his armour-plated sentry box looked taken aback, as though he had seen a ghost. So did two fellow officers whom Zen met on the stairs inside. But the biggest surprise was his office, which was draped in lengths of cloth sheeting speckled and blotched in various hues and stank of paint thinner. At the top of a high and rickety-looking stepladder, a short dark man in overalls and a paper hat was coating the ceiling with a large brush.

'*Attenzione!*' he called loudly. 'Don't step on the drop-sheets, there are wet splashes. And mind that paint!'

Zen abruptly jerked his arm away from what had once been his filing cabinet, and in so doing knocked over a can containing about five litres of off-white paint.

'*Capo!*'

It was Baccio Sinico, standing in the doorway with an expression which seemed to Zen to be identical to that of everyone he had met so far: *And we thought we'd seen the last of him.*

'They're repainting,' Sinico added redundantly, while the painter scuttled down from his roost, declaiming loudly in dialect. Fortunately for Zen, the can had landed with its mouth pointing away from him, so the main damage was to the floor and furniture. Meanwhile a crowd of his colleagues, subordinates and superiors, had formed in a semicircle discreetly situated just inside the door, away from the spreading puddle of paint. A chorus of voices rose up on all sides, lilting conventional laments and litanies of commiseration. To have a daughter killed! And coming so soon after the death of a mother! Such a cruel destiny would turn the strongest head. No one could be expected to resist this lethal hammer blow of fate.

Zen turned to Baccio Sinico.

'I need to talk to you.'

The junior officer looked around the assembled crowd with the embarrassed expression of someone being importuned by a harmless madman.

'I'm sorry, *dottore*, but I can't. No time, what with my official responsibilities and so on.'

Sinico extracted a wallet and inspected its contents. With what seemed like exaggerated care, he folded up a fifty-thousand-lire note and handed it to Zen.

'Here's half of what I owe you,' he said with false *bonhomie*. 'You'll get the rest just as soon as I can afford it. Meanwhile, since you've been given a month's compassionate leave because of this awful tragedy, I think you should take full advantage. Eh, boys?'

He eyed the chorus, which nodded as choruses do.

'So why not go and have a nice cup of coffee on me, *dottore*?' Sinico concluded, patting Zen's arm in an overtly patronizing way.

He turned away to the assembled crowd with the air of someone bestowing a knowing wink on the insiders who knew the truth of the matter. Zen headed for the stairs, clutching the crushed banknote. Half-way down, he unfolded it. Inside was a small slip of white paper printed with writing and figures. It proved to be a printed *ricevuta fiscale*, the legally required receipt from the cash register proving for tax purposes that a commercial transaction had taken place. The heading named a bar in Via Gisira, a few hundred metres from the Questura.

He had been there less than ten minutes when Baccio Sinico appeared. Zen handed him the fifty-thousand-lire note.

'What the hell's going on?' he demanded.

Sinico ordered a coffee, then turned to Zen.

'First of all, let's get one thing clear. You never came here, we never met, and I never said this.'

'Is it that bad?'

Sinico shrugged.

'Possibly. Probably. At any rate, let's assume so. That way, we might be pleasantly surprised later.'

Zen lit a cigarette and peered at Sinico.

'But why? All I'm doing is meeting a fellow officer for a coffee and a chat. We've done that often enough before. Why is it any different now?'

Sinico looked carefully around the bar.

'Because of *la Nunziatella*, of course.'

'But what's that got to do with me?'

Sinico sighed lengthily, as though dealing with some foreigner whose grasp of the language was not quite up to par.

'Listen, *dottore*, your daughter died with her, right?'

'So?'

'So the view has been taken that your inevitable emotional involvement as the father of the secondary victim disqualifies you from active duty at this time.'

Zen laughed.

'I didn't realize that the Ministry had become so warm and caring about its staff. Anyway, there's no problem. I had a bad patch for a few days, after I heard the news. But I'm fine now. I've got a plan, you see. A goal.'

'Which is?'

'I'm going to find out who killed Carla.'

'No one meant to kill your daughter! She was just caught in the crossfire.'

'That doesn't make her any less dead. And I'm going to find out who did it.'

Sinico shook his head.

'The whole *Direzione Investigativa AntiMafia* is working on that, *dottore*! When one of our judges gets killed, we drop everything else. If we can't solve the case and identify the murderers with all the resources at our command, how can you possibly hope to do so?'

'Baccio, my daughter has been murdered! What am I supposed to do, sit around my apartment watching television?'

The junior officer stared at Zen, seemingly more shocked by the casual use of his first name than by anything else he had heard.

'That apartment of yours,' he said at length. 'How much is it costing you?'

'What's that got to do with it?'

'How much?'

Zen told him. Sinico nodded.

'And how long did it take you to find it?'

'Three days? Four? Less than a week. Someone phoned me at the Questura. He said that he worked in a different department and had heard that I was looking for a place to live. It just so happened that some friends of his owned an apartment which might be suitable.'

'Did he give a name?'

'Yes, but I can't remember what it was. Some sort of fish.'

'A swordfish? *Spada?*'

'That's it.'

Sinico nodded in the same lugubriously significant manner.

'So you arrive here, fresh off the train, and in under a week you've found a gracious and spacious apartment right in the city centre, a few minutes' walk from your work, at a price which normally wouldn't get you a two-bedroom hutch in a crumbling tower block out in some suburban slum like Cíbali or Nésima. How do you think you managed that?'

Zen shook his head in a perturbed way.

'I didn't think about it. I don't know the price of property down here. I just assumed . . .'

'You assumed that the locals were being warm and caring, just like the Ministry,' Sinico replied sarcastically. 'Well, I hate to break it to you, *dottore*, but neither assumption is true. Your employers are only interested in your state of mind insofar as it might lead to actions which jeopardize the DIA operations currently under way. They want you out of harm's way, but it isn't your harm that they're worried about.'

'They're putting me in quarantine?' asked Zen.

'Think of it as compulsory compassionate leave.'

Zen dropped his cigarette on the marble floor and stepped on it.

'Which is why you had to sneak away to talk to me.'

Sinico nodded.

'As for the man who calls himself Spada, he is well known to us. He functions as a cut-out and message drop between various clans, and also between them and the authorities.'

'Why don't they just pick up the phone and dial?'

'For all sorts of reasons. The most important, perhaps, is deniability.'

'As in "you never came here, we never met, and I never said this"?'

A nod.

'Fine, so this Spada, whose name isn't Spada, makes a living by passing on messages in a way that is also a message in itself. Am I right?'

'*Bravo*,' said Sinico with a curt nod. 'You're starting to understand.'

'All I understand is that I don't understand a damn thing.'

'You'd be surprised how many people don't even understand that, *dottore*.'

'I still don't see what any of this has to do with my apartment.'

'Your apartment was a message.'

'Saying what?'

Sinico laughed.

'Have you ever sent flowers to a woman you wanted, *dottore*?'

'What's that got to do with it?'

'The offer of that apartment was a classic Mafia message. There were no overt strings attached, any more than you would enclose a card with those flowers saying, "Here are some roses, now let's fuck." These people are a lot more subtle than you seem to realize. From their point of view, all that matters is that they made an approach and that you responded. You're in contact, in communication. And if they need you for something, they know where to reach you. It's their apartment, after all.'

'But why would they bother to go to all that trouble for me?' Zen asked ingenuously. 'I've got nothing to do with the DIA. I'm just a liaison officer, after all.'

Baccio Sinico smiled at him in a peculiar way.

'Perhaps they don't believe that that's all you are.'

Zen opened his mouth to say something, then closed it again.

'In which case, we both got it wrong,' he said at last. 'They thought I was more important than I am, and I didn't understand any of this business about the apartment until you explained it to me. So in that sense the message failed.'

'Count your blessings, *dottore*,' said Sinico drily. 'At least you're still alive.'

Zen frowned at him.

'How do you mean?'

'Around here, when messages get confused or misunderstood, that can be a . . . What's that phrase you see on computers? A "fatal error".'

He was regarding Zen keenly.

'I don't know anything about computers,' Zen said with a shrug.

Baccio Sinico nodded.

'That's probably a good thing. They can get you into all kinds of trouble if you don't know what you're doing.'

He patted Zen on the shoulder.

'Take my advice. Forget all this nonsense and go off for a week or two to unwind. Have you ever been to Malta? It's a fascinating place, the crossroads of the Mediterranean, any amount of history, and it takes no time at all to get there. You've been through hell, *dottore*. You need closure. Let the healing begin.'

Zen nodded distractedly.

'But what about Carla? I need to know the truth.'

'Leave that to us,' Baccio Sinico replied reassuringly. 'We'll take care of everything.'

'Pack the truck with dynamite and park it in the centre of their village. A sixty-second fuse, and a second team to pick up the driver.'

'No, let's bomb Limina's house in the village when he's there at the weekend. We might be able to hire the Cessna that those upstarts down in Ragusa use to import drugs from Malta. I bet the pilot knows someone over there who could sell us some sort of bomb.'

'Or a missile launcher. Park on a road above the village and loose off one of those wire-guided numbers.'

'*O, ragazzi*, why piss around? In Russia, there are nuclear warheads on the market. The CIA is trying to buy them all up, but I'm sure our Russian friends could find us one. Fuck the village, let's set it off in the centre of Catania! Wipe the place out, like when Etna erupted!'

Four men sat around the remains of a meal. The remains almost constituted a meal in themselves, for the food had hardly been touched. There was only one window, of frosted glass. Despite the heat, it was tightly closed. What air there was had been dyed a bluish grey by the innumerable cigarettes whose ash covered the floor. It must have been at least thirty-five degrees in the room, but no one had broken sweat.

The men were all in their fifties, wearing open-neck shirts and heavy trousers. They were squat but hefty, with faces that were dense, compact and opaque. The one who had just spoken was notable above all for his hands, for which the rest of him seemed to function solely as a life-support system. They swooped, they fluttered, they dived and surged like a pair of birds repelling intruders on their territory.

The man sitting next to him had a collapsing, concave face, lined with wrinkles like a punctured balloon.

'So you think we should nuke Catania, eh?' he remarked in a sarcastic tone.

'What have we got to lose? We're fucked anyway.'

'So are they, Nicolò.'

'Yes, but we know it and they don't. We're on the way out anyway, so let's go with a bang!'

One of the two men on the other side of the table struck the wooden surface with his fist. He had a muddled, crunched face, the features too closely grouped for its overall size.

'Who says we're on the way out?' he shouted.

The fourth man, who sported an extraordinary white moustache and matching sideburns on his bronzed face, laid a hand on the speaker's arm.

'We all do, Calogero,' he said.

'I don't say any such thing!' was the furious response.

'Yes, you do. You say it by your anger, by your violent gestures, by your shrill tone of voice. The only people who squander their time and energy like that are people who know that they've lost. And we have lost. We had our moment of mastery, but now it's over. And the only way we can retain some measure of respect is to recognize that fact.'

There was a silence, broken by a slight metallic click.

'I have a message from Binù.'

All four men turned to the person seated at the head of the table. She was a dumpy, crumpled figure in a shapeless black dress who had been knitting throughout the preceding discussion. Now she set down her needles. Despite her age, sex and appearance, she had the undivided and respectful attention of every man present.

'Why didn't you tell us earlier?' asked the one called Calogero.

'He told me not to. He said that he wanted to hear what each of you had to say. He said it would reveal a lot about you.'

Each of the men lowered his eyes, trying desperately to remember just what he *had* said. One thing was certain: the woman would know. She could recall, word for word, what such-and-such or so-and-so had said

under torture in the long hours before they were strangled in the house of horrors which the Corleone clan
had owned in Palermo, back at the height of their
glory. Later, she would tell her husband what she had
heard, and he would give the appropriate instructions.

'And what did Binù say?' the man called Nicolò
dared to ask.

'He said, "*Cui bono?*"'

The men looked at each other in an apprehensive
silence.

'What dialect is that?' one of them asked.

'It's called Latin,' the woman went on, picking up
her needles again. 'It means, "Who stands to benefit?"'

There came a nervous guffaw.

'I didn't know Binù spoke Latin.'

'He has a lot of time on his hands,' the woman said to
no one in particular. 'He's been reading. And thinking.'

'Who stands to benefit from what?' asked Nicolò.

The woman looked at him.

'From taking our men and leaving them to die in the
back of a refrigerated truck after hacking Lillo's leg off
with a chainsaw.'

'That bastard Limina, of course!'

'And what did he benefit?'

'Revenge for his son's death!'

The woman set her knitting needles down again
with the same faint click.

'But we didn't kill Tonino Limina.'

'Of course not. But they think we did.'

The woman reached into some invisible crevice in her garments. A sheet of paper appeared, which she scanned.

'*Bravi!*' she remarked with sullen irony. 'So far you've said all the things that Binù said you would say. Now, here's his question to you. Who did kill Tonino Limina?'

'Our rivals in Palermo,' the white-moustached man replied promptly. 'The competition there is out to get us for things we've done in the past, and the easiest way is to set us up against the Limina family.'

'Or maybe it's one of the new enterprises,' Calogero put in. 'That nest of snakes in Ragusa for example. The result's the same. We and the Catanesi exhaust ourselves in a continuing blood feud, and the third party takes advantage.'

'Or the Third Level,' the woman said quietly.

A long silence, broken only by the drumming fingers of the man with the restless hands.

'*Them?*' whispered Calogero at length. 'But they're finished. They don't respond any more.'

'Not to us, no. Because we're finished, too.'

'Who says so?' was the aggressive response.

The woman pointed to the sheet of paper covered in fine, spidery writing.

'He does. We've always been realists, he says. That's been our strength. And the reality now is that we don't count any more, except perhaps to be made use of.'

She's talking like a man, the others all thought. They listened to her words as though to an oracular utterance by a sibyl, because they knew they must be true. Nothing but a knowledge of the truth, communicated through his mouthpiece by her fugitive husband, could have given this dumpy grandmother the absolute male authority she wielded as of right. As though to compensate, the men all started to chatter like women.

'Maybe they did it themselves.'

'Murdered their own child?'

'Of course not! Someone else, of no account, but rigged to look as if it was Tonino.'

'But through their lawyer they told that magistrate, the one who was just killed, that it wasn't him.'

'Since when does anyone tell judges the truth?'

'Or lawyers, for that matter.'

'But if it wasn't Tonino, why did they hit back at us?'

'Any excuse is good. We've seen it before on this island. East versus west. And we know the Messina crowd were in on this.'

'Who cares why? Kill them all! Let God sort them out.'

'Who else could have gone after that judge? No one else would dare to try an operation like that in their territory. Besides, no one else was interested. It was the Limina case she was investigating.'

'I heard that she'd been pulled off that one.'

'Officially?'

A cynical laugh.

'Enough of this bullshit!' shouted Calogero at last. 'The simple fact is that they have killed five of our men, and if we want to maintain any respect at all, we're going to have to get even.'

'Right!'

'OK!'

'Let's do it!'

'And slowly, if possible. A bomb is too good for them!'

'Perhaps we should have a word with those blacks that Ignazio was trading on the side before he fell down that mineshaft. Someone told me that in Somalia they still use crucifixion as a form of execution. Maybe one of them knows how to do it.'

'We should nail up Don Gaspà and that Rosario side by side.'

'With a sign reading, "But where's Christ?"'

All four men burst into laughter. The woman's voice cut through the companionable male mirth.

'Who do you mean by *them*?'

'The Liminas, of course!' the elderly man replied, still intoxicated by the wave of testosterone-laden empathy, like back in the old days before all the men of the family had been killed or locked up in cold, remote prisons or forced into concealment in a series of 'safe houses', leaving this hag to run the clan by proxy.

The woman laid down her knitting and raised her eyes to the gathered men. She picked up the piece of paper lying before her.

' "They are like children. Well-meaning, enthusiastic, and dumber than fuck." *His* words.'

A shocked silence ensued. No one could contradict her, of course. Maybe they were his words, maybe they weren't. Keep quiet, they were all thinking. And don't look like you're thinking, either. Bite your tongue, set your face, shut up and let someone else take the initiative.

' "We've had our clan wars," ' the woman read on, ' "and look where they've got us. The people who want to start that up again are no friends of ours, even if they claim to be. In the past, their motto was control and rule. Now it's divide and rule. If they succeed in setting the clans at each other's throats once again, they can do what they like with you, playing one side against the other and both ends against the middle." '

She picked up her knitting, leaving them to digest this information. The elderly man at the other end of the table tapped his wineglass with one fingernail.

'Too bad the Liminas don't understand that,' he said.

'Then we must try to enlighten them,' the woman replied without looking up.

'Cut their fucking heads off,' muttered Calogero. 'That'll enlighten those sons of whores soon enough!'

His outburst, designed to surf on a wave of male fellow-feeling, fell flat in a total silence. At length the man called Nicolò sniffed and spoke.

'With all due respect, *signora*, how are we to do that? We sent our boys to Messina to explain that we weren't responsible for the Tonino Limina killing, and to get them to explain that to their friends in Catania. We've seen the result. Now what are we supposed to do? Offer to come round to the house and suck their cocks?'

A subdued laugh greeted this welcome, stress-relieving vulgarity. It died away in the woman's pointed and silent knitting-work. For several minutes no one dared to break it. Then the fourth man, who had not spoken since the beginning, lit another cigarette and coughed apologetically.

'There might be a way,' he said.

There were several wry smiles and exchanges of rolled eyes.

'All right, Santino!' the elderly man said at last. 'Let's hear your latest brainwave.'

The other man coughed again.

'When that judge was killed . . .'

'Nunziatella? Where does she come in? That business had nothing to do with us, you know that.'

'Of course. But there was another woman in the car. According to the papers, she was the daughter of a policeman working in Catania. A certain Aurelio Zen.'

'So?' Calogero demanded aggressively.

'Well, it seems to me that he will be wondering who killed his daughter.'

'The Liminas, of course! Even a cop will be able to work that out.'

'Exactly. So he'll be interested in the family. Resentful, perhaps. Maybe vengeful.'

'So?' the elderly man demanded again.

'So maybe we can use that fact to get our message across to the Liminas. They won't accept any direct approach from us, that's for sure. But a policeman, with a grudge of his own? I think they might just buy that.'

'And how are we supposed to get this Zen on board?'

The woman at the head of the table looked up from her rectangle of unfinished knitting.

'I think it's time to reactivate Signor Spada,' she said.

Although he had a key, he entered Carla's apartment stealthily, with the sense of someone violating a tomb. There was nothing sepulchral about the apartment itself, though. On the contrary, it was as bright, hard, neat and efficient as a disposable razor. The air was thick and hot, with a neutral odour. Zen crossed to the window and opened it. In the distance, he could hear the siren of an ambulance: repeated hiccupy fanfares above a continuous bass growl.

There was none of the mess he had dreaded, the wrack from this personal *Marie Celeste*, detritus rendered at once pathetic and pointful by its owner's death. In fact the place looked very much like a hotel room when you enter it for the first time. Either Carla had been quite exceptionally fastidious in her personal habits, or . . .

Or what? Something was nibbling at the fringes of his brain, something she had said to him but which had ceased to register in that interlude of madness after he finally accepted the fact of his double bereavement.

He stood there amidst the sterile banalities of the dead woman's apartment. If at first he had been relieved by its impersonality, now he was disappointed. Why had he come, after all, if not in search – and simultaneous dread – of some personal memento which might bring her back, if only for a moment, his mail-order daughter? He had declined an invitation to attend the closed-casket funeral in Milan on the grounds that he had to attend a similar function in Rome concerning his mother. In death as in life, mothers trump daughters, and no one commented on his dereliction. A couple of brothers had shown up, he had learned later, as well as an aunt from, of all places, Taranto.

But why should that surprise him? What did he know about Carla Arduini, beyond the fact that he had screwed her mother at some point in his life, for the usual reasons which now appeared absurd. And even this factoid was without significance, since Carla had not been his daughter. He didn't have a daughter. He didn't have any children. Not even dead ones.

So why come to this neat, tidy little cocoon which Carla had spun for herself here in Catania? What did he hope to accomplish, besides depressing himself by opening a closet and seeing her dresses and coats lined up like the larvae of dead butterflies? He had already been through a similar ordeal in Rome, searching dutifully through his mother's personal belongings, until he eventually broke down and shouted at Maria Grazia,

'Get it out of here! Everything of hers, just get it out. I don't care what it's worth, I don't want any money, I just want it to be gone!'

Nevertheless, he now remembered, there was one thing here which he didn't want sold or thrown out. 'My whole life's on it,' Carla had said about her computer. Her whole life. Wasn't that worth preserving? The problem was that it didn't seem to be there, her life. No sign of same. Shoes, underwear, letters, magazines, a stuffed animal, but no computer.

Not that Zen would have been able to work it, in any case. But someone – Gilberto, for example – could have retrieved whatever was there, and made it available to him in printed form. And it *had* to be there, somewhere. When she came round to dinner at his place, Carla had told him about a report she had written about some problem she was having with the installation of the DIA network. She'd have done that on her laptop. She'd have done that . . .

She'd have done it *at work*, you idiot! He left the apartment, locked the door and descended to the street.

Even more than most Italian public spaces, those in Catania were dirty, harsh and ugly. Not because Sicilians just didn't care about such things in the way that the Swiss, say, did. On the contrary, in Zen's view this behaviour was quite deliberate, a form of public abrasiveness cultivated precisely because it created a sort of Value Added Tax on the personal and the private. When the world presents itself as unpleasant, filthy and hostile, home and friends become more precious. Where everything is clean, orderly and unthreatening, we end up in . . . well, in Switzerland.

This was not Switzerland. It was not even the 'Turin of the south', as Carla had dubbed it. It was just wrecked. People stuffed their garbage into plastic bags brought home from the local supermarket and then threw them into the gutter. They took their dogs out to lay piles of turds the size of a meal and the colour of vomit on the pavement. They trashed anything that didn't belong to them or a friend, and then stole the rest. Zen, who had no family and friends to come home to, stalked gloomily along through the gathering heat, past a trio of giggling girls enthusiastically giving head to gigantic ice-cream cones, towards the Palace of Justice.

He was lucky. It was lunch-time and the guard was changing, otherwise Zen probably would not have been admitted into the section reserved for the offices of the judges of the *Direzione Investigativa AntiMafia*. As it was, the sentries on duty were distracted, and his police ID and the mention of Carla's name was enough to get him past the checkpoint. He asked directions to the room which she had used, only to find it bare. Her name was still on the door, in the form of a business card Sellotaped to the wood, but the office itself had been stripped. No personal computer, no personal anything. Zen looked around for a few seconds at the bare walls and the one filthy window high on one wall, then left.

As he closed the door behind him, an elderly woman wearing a headscarf and coat walked past him down the corridor.

'Excuse me!' said Zen.

The woman turned round. She could have been his mother.

'Well?'

'I think you delivered something to me,' Zen started.

'Me?'

'A packet of papers. At my place of work. At the Questura.'

'Never!' she snapped, turning away.

But Zen remembered the scarf and the coat, and hurried after her.

'Listen, *signora*, all I want is to . . .'

The woman turned on him, a vial of concentrated hatred and wrath.

'You killed her!' she hissed under her breath. 'You and those other northerners! Clean the office for them, I was told! Make everything nice for our guests from Rome. And two days later she's dead, and where are

Roberto and Alfredo? Vanished like the mist at dawn! And now the director claims they were never here in the first place. Of course! We've all gone mad! We imagined the whole thing!'

She broke down in a mimed fit of weeping which was all the more disturbing for being so obviously a stylized fake.

'Corinna, Corinna! They gunned you down for doing your job too well, and now they try to put the blame on your own people!'

Dropping the pose, she turned suddenly on Zen.

'Say what you will about we Sicilians, we don't make war on women!' she snapped.

'Oh, really? So what about Dalla Chiesa's wife, murdered with him on the street? What about Signora Falcone, blown to pieces with her husband? What about . . .'

'That was in Palermo!' the woman screeched. 'This is Catania! We're still civilized here. No, my Corinna was killed by you people. I know it in my bones. Kill me too, if you want! My name is Agatella Mazzà. I'm one of the cleaning ladies. You can find me here any day. Do you think I give a damn what you do to me, now that she's gone?'

She spat in Zen's face, spraying him with saliva.

'Take that, with a mother's curse on you and yours. May you all die slowly, in pain, alone and in despair!'

She turned and waddled off along the corridor, muttering to herself. Zen stood stock-still, too shocked to react. He wiped the spit off his face, clutching the wall and gasping for breath.

'They searched my room,' Carla had told him on the phone. He could hear her voice even now, so young and vibrant. 'They left a message on my computer . . . My whole life's on it, and someone has been messing about with it. I've got back-ups, of course, but . . .'

To which he had replied, 'Back-up lives?' At the time, it had been intended as a joke.

He walked home along the broad conduits of black lava blocks, across the petrified squares, past the stylized statuary and baroque curlicues, the grandiose frozen messages of the past, all dead letters now. Although he wasn't hungry, he knew that he should eat, and stopped at an *alimentari* to buy some bread, a *mozzarella di bufala* and some air-cured sausages which the owner claimed were supplied by a brother-in-law of his who lived in the Umbrian mountain town of Norcia, famous for its pork products. Zen pretended to believe him, and the grocer in turn pretended to believe Zen's pretence of belief. They parted amicably.

Once inside, the apartment loomed around him like a shroud, its former charm flayed away by what the cleaning lady at the Palace of Justice had told him. He had no reason to doubt that it was true. Hurt always tells. This was too hurtful not to be true. He pushed through to the kitchen, opened the packets of food which he had bought and turned it out on to plates.

Not only did he not feel hungry, now he felt nauseous. The compact mass of the *mozzarella*, once sliced, felt like eating the breast of a pregnant woman: milk and meat at once. Saint Agatha, the patron of Catania, had had her breasts cut off. He tried the sausages, which gave him the sensation of chewing on the penises of dead boys, then pushed the food aside and opened the fridge, just in case there was some reusable portion of a forgotten or failed meal.

The first thing he saw, lying in the freezing compartment, was the non-birthday present for his no-longer-alive non-daughter, delivered to him at the Questura, which he had wrapped in rotting sardines, sealed with clingfilm and then totally forgotten about. With some difficulty, he pulled it off the flimsy metal ice-tray bonded to the sides of the freezer compartment by a gristle of ice thicker than the shrunken cubes in the tray itself. He sniffed at it with a wrinkle of disgust, then threw it into the sink and turned on the hot water.

The phone rang.

'Good evening, *dottore*. Forgive me for disturbing you. My name is Spada.'

The speaker clearly expected this to register. Zen frowned.

'Ah, yes!' he replied, having realized that this was the alleged Mafia contact who had got him the apartment with such miraculous swiftness in the first place.

'I trust that all is well with your new home,' the voice continued smoothly.

'Everything's fine, thank you.'

A pause.

'Good. Nevertheless, I think we should have a brief chat at some point, if that's possible.'

'What about?'

'Various issues which have arisen, which I believe to be of mutual interest. I can't be more specific until we meet. Do you know the breakwater to the west of the harbour? You get to it from Piazza dei Martiri. Between four and five this afternoon. I'll be fishing from the rocks and carrying a yellow umbrella marked *Cassa di Risparmio di Catania*.'

The line went dead. Zen made a dismissive gesture and hung up. The man must be mad, thinking that he would turn up for an unscheduled appointment at such short notice. Who did these people think they were?

A splashing sound from the kitchen reminded him that he had left the tap running on the frozen package. He turned it off, then went to the end of the room and opened the door giving on to the small balcony. A wave of heat enveloped him, bringing a rash of sweat to his brow.

'You're in contact, in communication. And if they need you for something, they know where to reach you. It's their apartment, after all.'

'They searched my room . . . Someone has been here. They left a message on my computer.'

Leaning out of the window, he smoked a cigarette, then strode back to the kitchen and grabbed the package floating in the sink. It was beginning to feel mushy. He peeled it open, stripped away the rotting fish and threw them in the rubbish bin, then washed the plastic bag inside in soapy water, dried it on some kitchen paper and opened the envelope. It contained a photocopy of some sixty pages of typed text, apparently legal in nature. The title contained the name 'Limina'. Zen took it through to the living room and settled down on the sofa to read.

Twenty minutes later, he had skimmed the entire set of documents. They all related to the case of the 'body on the train', and consisted of interviews with witnesses and the first portion of a draft report on the case written by the investigating magistrate, Corinna Nunziatella. None of the material seemed particularly sensitive or sensational. The only thing that Zen had not already read in the DIA reports which he vetted weekly was a deposition by a train driver who regularly worked the route between Catania and Syracuse, to the effect that he thought he had seen a freight wagon parked on the siding at Passo Martino for several weeks before the discovery of the body. In fact, he said, he had the impression that it had been there for several months. But it was common practice to store items of rolling-stock on such sidings, and he hadn't paid the matter much attention. When pressed, he admitted that he couldn't be sure that he had seen any such wagon at all, never mind when or where.

The only other interesting aspect of the documents was a note on the last page of the unfinished draft report, which seemed to be tending towards the conclusion that the body on the train had indeed been that of Tonino Limina, but that there was no evidence that he had been kidnapped and killed by a rival Mafia clan. It had not been possible to establish Tonino's movements prior to his disappearance with any certainty, but a search of passenger lists showed that he had flown to Milan on 6 July en route to Costa Rica for a holiday, but had not checked in for his onward flight. At this point the report broke off with the handwritten note: 'Case blocked and transferred 3/10, documents impounded by Roberto Lessi and Alfredo Ferraro of the ROS.'

Zen knocked the pile of pages back into shape and left it on the sofa. As he got up to fetch his cigarettes, he noticed for the first time the grey plastic slab, sitting on his desk, in the corner of the room. It was about the size of one of those small briefcases which high-powered businessmen carry with them, to indicate that the heavy-duty paperwork is being done by their minions.

Zen walked over and inspected the thing. The cover was stamped with black letters on a silver ground reading 'Toshiba Satellite'. A paper label stuck alongside, at a slight angle, said, 'Property of Uptime Systems Inc.'. Someone had added, in a rounded hand, 'Carla Arduini'.

He stretched out one hand towards the computer, then drew it sharply back. An ambulance siren, identical to the one he had heard at Carla's apartment earlier, was just audible in the distance. Zen located his mobile phone, dialled the DIA headquarters and asked to be put through to Baccio Sinico. The younger officer sounded suitably concerned, agreed that Zen was doing the right thing by taking no chances, and promised rapid response.

Twenty minutes later, in the bar across the street, Zen watched the convoy of police vehicles gathering in front of his apartment building. Figures in full-body suits, with huge helmets and metal pincers, descended and disappeared inside. Others carried a large trunk-like container supported on two metal poles. Sirens wailed and blue lights flashed. Another ten minutes went by before Zen's cellphone beeped.

'Where are you, *dottore*?' asked Baccio Sinico.

'Out and about,' Zen replied.

'You were right about the computer. An initial scan suggests that the works have been removed and replaced with half a kilo of explosive, detonated by opening the lid.'

'Well, I'm glad that you lads didn't go to all that trouble for nothing.'

'But where are you? You need protection! We need to get you into a secure . . .'

'I'm fine, Baccio. I have an appointment. I'll call you later.'

Zen checked his watch. It was ten to four. He paid his bill and walked down towards the sea.

During his years of official disgrace following the Aldo Moro affair, Aurelio Zen had been posted to a city in Umbria to investigate another kidnapping case involving a local industrial tycoon. While he was there, one of his colleagues at the Questura had recounted a stock story which the Perugians told about their neighbours and traditional rivals from the town of Foligno, about thirty kilometres away in the valley below their mountain stronghold. The people of Foligno, it was alleged, thought like this: Europe was the centre of the world, the Mediterranean was the centre of Europe, Italy was the centre of the Mediterranean, and Foligno was the geographical centre of Italy. In the centre of Foligno was the Piazza del Duomo, and on this piazza there was a bar, in the centre of which there was a bar-billiards table. The hole in the centre of this table, at the centre of all the other centres, was therefore the original *omphalos*, navel and origin of the universe.

Catania was exactly the opposite, Zen reflected as he picked his way across the main road bordering the port area. A landfall on the eastward brink of an island which had always been marginal to the interests of whichever foreigners currently controlled it, Catania had never been the centre of anything. On the contrary, it was the edge. And at the very edge of Catania stood the port, impressively walled, as though to contain the foreign contagions to which it was by its nature exposed. At one end stood the breakwater, flexed like an arm thrust out against the waves.

And today they were huge, mythical monsters breaking surface as if for the first time, visible evidence of powers and depths beyond human comprehension. A storm had passed over in the night, and although the south-easterly wind had now moderated, the seas it had raised came striding confidently ashore, only to have their determination and vigour smash into the random mass of stone blocks piled to seaward of the breakwater. Visibly perplexed and weakened, the waves shattered into futile spumes of spray and then reformed as a contradictory scurry of surges and backwashes, their initial impetus dispersed or turned back against itself.

On one of the outlying rocks, a lone fisherman was trying his luck in the swirls of water below, protecting himself from the sun by means of a large yellow umbrella marked 'You have a friend at the *Cassio di Risparmio di Catania* – the friendly bank!' Zen clambered over the low wall of the breakwater and made his way gingerly from one boulder to another until he reached the one adjacent to the fisherman's perch.

'Catching anything?' asked Zen.

The man turned around and inspected Zen briefly.

'A few minnows. I threw them back in.'

'What did you expect, a swordfish?'

The man smiled and gestured in a peculiarly feminine way which Zen had by now come to recognize as characteristically Sicilian. It was almost as if, since women had traditionally not been allowed out in public, the men had learned to fill the social space which they would have occupied.

'Dottor Zen. What a pleasure.'

Zen held his eyes.

'Are you surprised to see me?'

'No, why? We had an arrangement.'

'Death cancels all arrangements.'

'Death?' murmured Spada. 'You mean your daughter? Forgive me for not mentioning this terrible tragedy. I thought, perhaps wrongly, that it might be painful . . .'

'Not half as painful as a bomb in the face. *My* face.'

The man looked more and more bewildered.

'A bomb?'

'In the form of a laptop computer belonging to my daughter, gutted of its works, stuffed with plastic explosive and left in my apartment.'

Spada put down his fishing rod and stared at Zen. Judging by his expression, the bomb might have been meant for him.

'I know nothing of this,' he said.

Zen raised his eyebrows.

'I thought that the whole point of dealing with people like you was that you *did* know about these things.'

'I repeat, I know nothing about this. But I will make enquiries.'

'A lot of good your enquiries would have done me if I'd opened the lid of that computer.'

The man slashed his hand through the air.

'What are you talking about? My friends have no interest in harming you, *dottore*. You're no use to us dead.'

Zen lowered his head ironically.

'I'm pleased to hear it. And in just what way can I be of use to you?'

Spada gestured in an awkward way.

'It's a question of a mutual interest, *dottore*. I've been given to understand that you want to find out who killed your daughter. Very naturally.'

'And your interest?'

'To facilitate your investigation.'

Zen smiled with an irony that was now undisguised.

'But everyone knows that my daughter was killed by your "friends". Why would you want to help me prove it?'

Spada picked up his rod, reeled in and then cast his line again.

'Ah, but suppose we didn't do it?' he said, looking down at the water.

'Then who did?' demanded Zen.

'Well, that's the question, isn't it?'

Zen waved his hand dramatically.

'And you don't know the answer to that either? I'm beginning to wonder whether I should bother taking you or your friends very seriously, Signor Spada.'

The fisherman slackened his grip on the rod in order to read the vibrations which it was transmitting.

'If you want to find out the truth,' he said, 'then you're going to need help. And for different reasons, which do not concern you, we need help from you. Perhaps we can make a deal.'

Zen gazed out across the sea with an air of complete boredom.

'My friends didn't kill Tonino Limina, either,' said Spada.

The waves shattered and re-formed on the rocks beneath.

'The Limina family have denied that their son is dead.'

'He's dead, all right.'

'Then why did they deny it?'

'Because Don Gaspare is a control freak, even though he doesn't control anything worth a piss these days. But he doesn't want to look bad. Plus he didn't want the authorities taking an interest. He would have his revenge when the time came. Which it just has. Five of the Corleone clan frozen to death in a meat truck.'

'I've heard nothing about this.'

'It hasn't been made public. The Corleonesi don't want to look bad either. I'm just presenting my credentials. Go back to your friends at the DIA and check it out. It's true.'

Zen looked up to the north where Etna was spewing out fat white clouds into a heartbreakingly pale blue sky.

'What's all this got to do with me?' he demanded. 'I'm a policeman. I should arrest you right now. Take you down to the basement and have the hard boys go to work on you!'

He turned away, shielding his face from the wind in an attempt to light a cigarette. On the breakwater, perhaps ten metres away, a young man wearing dark glasses was staring at him. Zen stared back. The man turned away, took out a cellphone and walked off down the mole.

'We didn't kill Limina,' Spada repeated, playing his line.

Zen turned to him with an expression of bored cynicism.

'All right, let's pretend that you're telling the truth. Your friends didn't do it. So who did?'

Spada raised his rod and plied the reel furiously. About five metres from the edge of the breakwater, a fish broke surface. He hauled it in, twitching and struggling in vain, a small red mullet. Spada inspected it briefly, unhooked the line, and threw the fish back.

'Maybe yours,' he said.

Zen tossed the butt of his cigarette after the fish.

'I don't have any friends.'

'Then you're dead, *dottore*. Professionally speaking, of course. But here in Sicily, without friends . . .'

There was a silence.

'And just who would these friends of mine be, supposing they existed?' asked Zen.

A large shrug.

'Who knows? What I'm hearing is that the operation was planned and carried out by people from the continent.'

'From Rome?'

Spada did not answer for so long that his silence became an answer in itself. He leaned back and looked at Zen as though seeing him for the first time. Then Zen realized that the other man was looking not at him but past him.

'I think we've been here long enough, *dottore*,' Spada remarked.

He scribbled something on a piece of paper and handed it to Zen.

'Come to this address after eight this evening. A relative of mine is the caretaker. We'll be able to talk without any risk of disturbance.'

He quickly dismantled his rod and line, packing everything away into the wicker hamper he had brought with him. Zen turned away and clambered from rock to rock until he regained the concrete breakwater. Gulls swooped overhead, but there was no one in sight.

He was still three streets from his apartment block when they grabbed him. It only occurred to him later that this meant that he must have been followed all the way.

Along with five or six other passers-by, he had stopped to watch a peculiar courtship spectacle involving two dogs: a young dalmatian and a rather more mature spaniel. Their respective owners were a portly woman in a long coat and another, young enough to be her daughter, wearing a black pantsuit. Both dogs were leashed, and the spaniel was evidently in heat. The dalmatian was making frantic attempts to mount her, and the owners were making equally frantic attempts to drag the two lovers apart. Meanwhile a small crowd had gathered to offer advice and make the predictable jokes.

Zen sensed their presence a moment before one of them caught him by the arm.

'Dottor Zen? I'm Roberto Lessi of the *Raggruppamento Operazioni Speciali*, currently seconded to the DIA. You're to come with us, please.'

There were two of them, in their thirties, both wearing jeans and sports jackets. Zen found himself hyperventilating.

'Come with you where?' he asked.

A blue saloon pulled in alongside the rank of parked vehicles by the kerb. The two men took Zen by the elbows, one on each side, and steered him towards it.

'What's going on?' he demanded.

'It's for your own protection,' the other man said flatly.

The back door of the car opened and Baccio Sinico stepped out.

'Baccio!' Zen called to him. 'What the hell's happening?'

Sinico made a gesture like swatting a fly. The two Carabinieri agents released Zen.

'You can't go back to your apartment, *dottore*, not after we discovered that bomb there. These people, if at first they don't succeed, they try and try again until they do. And they own the building, so access won't be very difficult.'

'But what's the alternative?'

Sinico beamed a smile.

'You've been put on the high-security risk roster, *dottore*! They've allocated you quarters in the Carabinieri barracks. You'll be perfectly safe there, under armed guard night and day. And if for any reason you need to leave the barracks, you'll have a full escort of armed officers with you at all times.'

'I noticed what a good job they did with that judge,' Zen retorted sourly.

Sinico looked indignant.

'That wasn't our fault! She deliberately broke security rules and took off on her own. There was nothing we could do. But don't complain, *dottore*! This is an honour that many of your colleagues would die for.'

He gave a loose shrug.

'So to speak.'

Zen nodded.

'I'll bear that in mind.'

'All right, let's go.'

'What about my personal effects?'

'Everything will be packed up and transferred to your allotted quarters at the barracks.'

Zen looked down at the pavement and shook his head slowly.

'What a narrow escape!' he exclaimed in a tone of voice which might have raised the eyebrows of someone who knew him better than Baccio Sinico. 'I can't thank you enough for taking all this trouble. Thank heavens I'll be properly protected from now on! But listen, there's just one thing I need to collect from my apartment.'

'As I said, all your belongings will be . . .'

'This is not one of my belongings, strictly speaking. It's something which . . .'

He broke off, wiping his eyes with the back of his hand.

'Something which belonged to my mother, Giuseppina.'

Baccio Sinico nodded respectfully.

'It makes no difference. Everything that's there except the furniture will be delivered to you at . . .'

'That's the problem. You see, this is a piece of furniture. Well, actually it's a picture which I brought from our house in Rome after she . . .'

'Just tell us where it is, and we'll bring it.'

Zen sighed heavily.

'That's what's embarrassing, you see. I don't remember. I just grabbed it at random, as something to remember her by, but I can't recall where I put it or even what the subject of the picture is. All I know is that I'll recognize it the moment I see it.'

He gripped Sinico's arm.

'Look, even the Mafia are not going to try again so soon after the failure of this attempt. Let's go to my place right now, just the two of us. I'll pick up the picture and then we'll drive straight to the barracks.'

Baccio Sinico shook his head.

'I'm sorry, *dottore*, I don't have the authorization to . . .'

'And then there are the papers,' said Zen.

Sinico looked at him sharply.

'Papers?'

'Legal documents.'

Sinico was now staring at him with a mute intensity.

'Relating to my mother's will,' Zen added. 'I hid them away for safety. It would be impossible for anyone else to find them. You can imagine how important they are.'

'The papers,' Sinico repeated.

'Yes. Those legal documents. If they fell into the wrong hands . . .'

Baccio Sinico nodded almost maniacally.

'Of course, of course. The wrong hands.'

'We wouldn't want that.'

'No, no! Certainly not.'

He sighed.

'Very well. It's highly irregular, but . . .'

They took off at high speed for the short drive to Zen's home, emergency lights flashing and sirens wailing. If they had wanted to draw the Mafia's attention to the fact that their target was returning home, thought Zen, they could hardly have done a better job. The car drew up in front of the building, providing a further visual clue by parking the way the police always park: so as to create the maximum inconvenience for everyone else. While one of the two ROS agents secured the front door, Zen and Sinico walked upstairs with the second, who then stood guard at the door to Zen's apartment while the two men went inside.

Zen looked around quickly. The Toshiba laptop had of course gone. Maybe it really had been a bomb, as they claimed. He would never know. More to the point, the papers which Corinna Nunziatella had 'posted' to herself, using Carla as a cut-out, and which Zen had left on the sofa, had also disappeared.

'Through here,' he told Sinico, leading the way towards the bedroom. As Sinico crossed the threshold, Zen smashed the door into his face. The younger officer reeled back, clutching his forehead and staring wildly at Zen, who grabbed him by the arm and hair and hurled him forward into the bedroom, tripping him up as he passed so that he fell sprawling on the gleaming aggregate floor.

After a moment, Sinico got to his knees and then his feet, pulling a revolver from a holster at the back of trousers, but he was too shocked and too slow. Zen yanked him forwards by the arm holding the gun, chopped the weapon free with a blow to the wrist, then kneed Sinico in the chest as he went down for the second time. He picked up the revolver and checked it quickly, keeping an eye all the while on the figure splayed out on the floor, panting hard as though he were about to burst into tears.

'I'm sorry, Baccio,' Zen said quietly. 'I had no choice.'

Sinico looked up at him.

'You're mad!' he croaked.

'That's conceivable, but I can't afford to take the risk of finding out that I'm not. Don't worry, I won't bother you again, as long as you don't bother me. Remember that "compassionate leave" you told me about? I've decided to take your advice.'

Sinico crawled up into a sitting position.

'They'll kill you, *dottore*! They've tried once already, and they won't give up. You need us! You need our help, our protection!'

Zen put the revolver in his coat pocket and stared bleakly down at the younger man.

'Who are *they*, Baccio? Whose friends are *they*?'

Sinico shook his head despairingly.

'This is all madness!' he said. 'Paranoia run wild!'

Zen inclined his head.

'As I said, that's conceivable. It's also conceivable that you're just trying to keep me talking until one of those ROS thugs comes to see why we're taking so long.'

He walked over to the doorway.

'I'm leaving now,' he told Sinico. 'If you try to stop me, I'll shoot you.'

Once in the living room, he crossed rapidly to the front door and opened it. The ROS agent named Lessi looked at him in surprise.

'We've found something!' Zen said in an urgent undertone. 'Baccio thinks it might be another bomb. He wants you to take a look.'

Lessi nodded and ran inside. Zen closed the door and locked it with the complicated double-sided key, formed like a gondola's prow, turning it four times to insert the metal security bolts into the retaining block. Without a key, it could not be opened from the inside.

He ran quickly downstairs and slunk into the shadows at the rear of the entrance hall. About twenty seconds later, the front door flew open and the other ROS man ran in, a pistol in his hand, talking urgently on his cellphone.

'He locked the door? Don't worry, I'll be right there!'

Zen listened to the man's footsteps receding above, then walked to the door and out into the night.

A few minutes after eight o'clock sounded from the massive church of San Nicolò in Piazza Dante, Zen arrived at the address to which he had been directed, in a side-street off Via Gesuiti. He was under no illusion about the value of the assurances which the man known as Spada had given him as to his safety, but neither did he care very deeply one way or the other. If his mother had still been alive, it would have been different, as it would if he'd ever had children. As it was, he discovered that it didn't really matter what happened, although this did not prevent him from carefully checking the revolver he had taken from Baccio Sinico while he waited inside the portico of San Nicolò for eight o'clock to arrive.

The building assigned for his appointment with 'Signor Spada' was a handsome two-storey baroque *palazzo* with widely spaced windows, ornate cornices and shallow balconies protected by metal railings. The main entrance seemed to be on Via Gesuiti itself, but the address to which Zen had been directed was a door about half-way along the left-hand side. Rather to

Zen's surprise, it was open. He knocked tactfully but without result, then stepped inside. The light from the lamp strung on a wire at first-floor level across the street revealed a set of stone steps leading down to another door about a metre lower down.

Leaving the street door open, Zen made his way down. The lower door was not locked. With a very faint creak, it opened into an unlit but acoustically larger space beyond. Zen stood still, sniffing the musty air and trying to decipher a faint sound which he thought at first might be the echoes of the creaking door, amplified by the resonant chamber beyond. The interior seemed at first completely dark, but as Zen's eyes began to adjust he became aware of a tepid luminescence which seemed to emanate from . . .

From whatever they were, those rows and ranks of massive structures, identical in shape and height, which ran the length and breadth of the room. Except for their size, they might almost have been old-fashioned school desks, with sloping tops which caught what little light there was and reflected it. Only they didn't reflect it, he soon realized, they radiated it. By now, his night vision was good enough for him to make out some other features of the place, such as two hulking human forms each about three metres tall standing against the wall at the far end of the room. A warehouse of glowing furniture managed by giants? Well, he had no problem with that. That was just *fine*! He could deal with it. Now what?

The answer was a scream. Well, no, not quite. A keening wail, more like. A lengthy, throaty squawk. It took Zen a long and very uncomfortable moment to match it tentatively in his auditory database with one of those scarily humanoid sounds that cats emit when involved in sexual or territorial disputes. In which case the eerie ululation he had heard earlier had presumably not been the echoes of the door squeaking, but the two mogs tuning up. He wondered idly how large the pets were around here. About the size of ocelots, to judge by the figures at the end of the room and the school desks which filled it.

Only they weren't desks, he realized. His vision was slowly filling in all the time, like a computer downloading a complex graphic screen. He could now make out that the giants lounging against the end wall were in fact statues mounted on plinths. Between them, a broad staircase led up into gloom. On the side walls, the dark patches which he had taken to be windows revealed themselves to be a series of oil paintings. At which point the files of desks shamefacedly removed their carnival masks and were transformed into rows of display cabinets lit internally by a low-wattage bulb. He was in a museum.

A brief investigation confirmed this hypothesis. Beneath a thick layer of glass, each cabinet contained a selection of coins, jewellery, amulets and similar objects of antiquity, each identified by a label with a number and a description such as 'Greek, late 2nd century BC(?)'. It was one of those provincial museums which are open to the public for a few inconvenient hours on various randomly chosen days every month, always assuming that Spada's relative didn't have something more important to do.

So now only the noises remained unexplained. They had diminished in volume, but were still there, troubling and exciting the silence like fingernails raked lightly across skin. His sight satisfied, Zen tuned in to his hearing. The sounds seemed to be coming from the end of the room, where the staircase led up, presumably to the next floor of the building. He walked cautiously down the aisle between the lit display cases and started up the steps at the far end.

They were handsome steps, broad and shallow and as solid as the rock from which they had been carved, flanked to either side by elaborate stone balustrades. It occurred to Zen that this must have been the original ground floor of the *palazzo*, before subsequent infill or volcanic activity had raised the street level. After a considerable fetch, the stairs reached a landing and doubled back the way they had come, giving access to a room of the same dimensions and much the same appearance as the one below, but with a much higher ceiling. This would have been the reception quarters of the original design, the *piano nobile*. All this was quite clear, because the lights were on.

A light, rather: a clear steady beam illuminating what looked at first sight like a sexual act involving two men. One was standing, his back to the stairs where Zen stood watching. From time to time his body jerked spasmodically, each spasm accompanied by a satisfied though effortful grunt. The other man, who was on his knees before the other, was meanwhile emitting a continuous series of weak mewling sounds which were, Zen now realized, the source of the noises he had heard earlier. It took him another moment or two to understand that the distended and discoloured features of the kneeling man were those of the man known as Spada, and that he was not engaged in fellatio but being strangled.

The light wavered to one side, revealing itself as the beam of a powerful torch concealed behind the wall to Zen's right.

'Come on, Alfredo!' said a bored voice. 'It's done, for Christ's sake. Let's go.'

Zen pulled out Sinico's revolver and loosed off a shot towards the ceiling.

'Police!' he yelled as the appalling reverberations died away. 'Drop your weapons and lie down on the floor with your hands above your heads.'

The strangler released his victim and turned slowly to Zen with an imposing yet slightly incredulous look. A moment later a pistol appeared in his hand.

Zen would undoubtedly have died then and there if the late Signor Spada had not intervened, slumping forward into the back of the gunman's knees and throwing him off balance. At such close range, even a marksman as out of practice as Zen could not miss. He fired once, hitting his opponent in the upper chest. The victim, as his status now was, absorbed the shot with an expression which mingled astonishment and resignation, as if he had always known that it would end like this but – stupidly, as he now realized – hadn't expected it just yet. Then the light went out.

Dependent now upon his hearing alone, Zen found that sense perking up just as his sight had earlier. Most of the time, we were functionally deaf, he realized. What we thought of as silence was a constant substratum of noises mentally censored as being insignificant. He recalled a camping holiday up in the Dolomites, years ago, with a friend from university. There, by night, it had been utterly silent, and yet that silence had registered not as an absence but as a massive and disturbing presence. Now that his life was at stake and every sound significant, he found himself bombarded by a barrage of aural data, some potentially identifiable – traffic, televisions, voices in the street –

but all previously classified as irrelevant and therefore inaudible. Within the room in front of him, there was that intimidating silence he had experienced in the Alps all those years ago.

Then, like some unidentified animal stumbling into that remembered campsite, came three distinct sounds: a click, a creak, and a loud metallic snap. They were related both by position and by distance, but above all by the concurrent appearance of a brilliant glow within the room. Unnerved, Zen fired blind. Immediately two other sounds joined the former intruders: a tinkle of glass and a raucous clanging with a whooping siren to back it up. He ran up the remaining steps, just in time to see a young man wearing a baseball cap sitting on the exterior ledge of one of the windows, which he had evidently opened along with its corresponding shutter. He was lit from behind by the streetlamp strung on a wire almost level with the window. His face was in shadow, but he turned briefly to Zen and seemed to pause for a moment, as if in recognition. Then he abruptly disappeared.

A dull thud and the sound of running footsteps told the rest of the tale. The narrator could still prove to be lethally unreliable, however, so Zen endured another minute or so of the hellish racket of the security alarm before he ventured out into the upper room. The torch used to illuminate the execution lay on the floor near the two bodies. Switching it on, Zen quickly ascertained that he was alone, and that both Spada and his killer were dead. Zen recognized the latter as one of the two ROS agents who, together with Baccio Sinico, had tried to take him into 'protective custody' earlier that evening. A quick search of his jacket turned up a wallet, which identified him as Alfredo Ferraro.

By now, the shrieks of the alarm system were intolerable. Looking around, Zen realized that it had been set off by the second shot that he had fired, which had apparently struck one of the display cases. Dipping his hand in amongst the priceless relics there, he selected an object at random and headed quickly back downstairs.

It was almost midnight when the surly staff of the ferry finally deigned to allow passengers to board. The blue and white hulk had been moored to the dock for over three hours by that time, at this latest stop on its leisurely and much-delayed passage from Naples to Tunis. Needless to say, no one had bothered to explain the reason for this further delay, still less to apologize. The employees of the Tirrenia ferry company had an attitude as charmless, peremptory and inflexible as tax inspectors or prison guards – or policemen, for that matter.

But why should they care? Their jobs were state-funded sinecures, hard to obtain but virtually impossible to lose. If the passengers had had any power and money, they would have gone by air. So if you were here, pacing up and down the dock at almost one in the morning at the mercy of a bunch of incompetent slackers like them, then you evidently had neither money nor power. In which case, who cared?

The passengers' only consolation was that if they had to wait out in the open for hours on end, this was the perfect night for it; pleasantly cool, with an almost imperceptible onshore breeze scented with a subtle briny tang, an appetizer for the voyage to come. The scene would have been almost idyllic, in fact, if it hadn't been for the banks of floodlights mounted on tall masts, mercilessly baring the concrete and steel austerities all around. And then, of course, there were the foreigners.

These last represented a majority of the thirty or so people waiting to board the ferry, but the noise they were creating made them seem even more numerous and obnoxious. They were all in their twenties, the sexes roughly evenly represented. The males were all wearing red T-shirts with the word ARSENAL printed in large white letters, while their mates were in various stages of undress, revealing large quantities of sun-burned thigh, shoulder and midriff.

One of the men, who seemed to be in charge, to the extent that anyone was, sat at the bottom of the gang-way perched on four cases of Peroni beer cans. From time to time he reached down and produced a fresh can from a partially dismantled fifth case lying open in front of him. The others all had beers in their hands, except for a separate group who were sharing a bottle of whisky, and one girl who had apparently passed out. From time to time, one of the men would start what sounded like a war chant, and pretty soon they all joined in, even the women. One of the whisky drinkers yelled at someone in the main pack, and Zen was surprised to catch what sounded like the words 'Norman' and 'beer'.

So, the Normans have returned, he thought, lurking in the shadows created by a stack of metal cargo containers and trying not to look up the collapsed girl's dress, which had ridden up over her hips in a fascinating manner. He remembered being taught at school how the people of Normandy, themselves originally invaders from Norway, had conquered Sicily in the Middle Ages and ruled the island for over a hundred years. He remembered it because, as with the increasingly few things he remembered these days, it came with a story.

The story, Zen now realized, was almost certainly apocryphal, but this knowledge did not diminish its mythic charm and power. One fine day, his teacher had told the class, a group of Norman soldiers on their way home from the crusades stopped off at a port in Sicily, quite possibly Catania. Being hard-drinking northerners, they consumed the local wine without regard to its high alcohol content, and soon got very merry indeed.

At this point a fleet of Moorish corsair ships appeared in the harbour, striking terror into the hearts of the inhabitants, who had been collectively raped, plundered, shipped into slavery and put to the fire and the sword for as long as anyone could remember. It was like the plague. It came and went. Some people survived, others succumbed. There was nothing to be done.

Within minutes, the bells of the city's churches started tolling out the bad news, and incidentally deafening the Normans, who grabbed a passing waiter and told him in no uncertain terms to turn off those fucking bells or else. The trembling native explained the reason for this tocsin, and advised his clients to flee immediately – 'presumably after settling the bill', the teacher interpolated with a sly wink at the class – since the Moors were about to rape and plunder, ship people into slavery, and generally put the city to the fire and the sword as usual.

The Normans looked at one another *and smiled*.

The teacher now broke off the story to give a brief lecture on physiognomical changes over the past centuries, their dietary causes, and why this meant you should eat your greens, just to show that this narrative digression had by no means extinguished his capacity for tedious pedantry. The Normans, he pointed out, would have been slightly less than the average height of Italians today, benefiting as the latter were from the 'economic miracle' of post-war reconstruction, but they would still have been a good head taller and proportionally broader than the Saracen marauders.

Imagine, he said, that you are one of the latter, out for a pleasant day's looting and pillaging in an undefended town at the very toe of Italy. The inhabitants have all fled or are in hiding. The place is yours for the taking, you think. Then you round a corner to confront a horde of gigantic blond beings, completely drunk and utterly fearless, shrieking berserker battle cries and wielding their enormous swords and maces like children's toys.

It wasn't a question of courage, the teacher explained. The Arabs had never seen such creatures before. To them, they must have seemed like extraterrestrial aliens gifted with incomprehensible, superhuman powers. To try to fight against them would be mere folly. So they ran back to their boats, those who survived, and the local townspeople asked the Normans how much they would charge to stay around and provide this sort of service on future occasions. Not very much, was the answer. 'But then,' the teacher ended with a sly smile, 'wine in Sicily is cheap.'

And now the Normans had returned, Zen reflected as the waiting passengers started to make their way up the gangplank, whose sullen Cerberus had finally consented, after a lengthy discussion on a two-way radio, to open to public access. The sleeping girl had been shaken into semi-consciousness and was helped along by a couple of the red-shirted men. Arsenal, thought

Zen. He knew what the word meant, of course: the naval yard in his native city where the fleets of galleys which had built and maintained the Venetian empire had been constructed. But why were these drunken barbarians advertising it on their beefy chests? It was all a mystery. All he knew was that the Normans had returned, and that he was going to have to spend the next seven hours with them in the spartan public lounge of the ferry, since the cabins were apparently fully booked.

Apart from the latter-day Normans, the passengers consisted of a few dauntless young backpackers, and a selection of elderly Sicilian, Maltese and Tunisian persons, none of whom aroused any suspicion in Zen's mind. Once on the ferry, he took up a position near the head of the gangplank, lest anyone else should board before they left. No one did. Ten minutes later, the mooring lines were cast off and they were steaming quietly off into the Ionian Sea, past the glowing lights of the refineries at Augusta and the twin headlands encircling the harbour of Syracuse, rumbling quietly south. Zen left his post and went down to the saloon. He was safe. He'd made it. They would never be able to find him here.

Down in the saloon, a major crisis had erupted, sparked by the Tirrenia line employee in charge, who was attempting to close the bar. This decision was being vigorously contested by the neo-Normans, one of whom, it turned out, spoke some Italian. But the barman was paying no attention to his protests and pleas. Closing time was closing time and that was that. The metal grille covering the bar came rattling down with the finality of a guillotine.

It was at this point that Zen intervened. He couldn't care less about the foreigners, but he wanted a drink himself – thought he deserved one, in fact – and also wanted to throw his bureaucratic weight about a little in return for all the aggravation which he and everyone else had been treated to by the ferry company's staff so far. Flashing his police identification card at the barman, he told him to reopen the bar immediately, lest his actions provoke a breach of the peace given the presence of a large number of evidently unhappy barbarians from the north, which might easily lead to actions of assault and affray likely to endanger the safety of the ferry, her crew and passengers.

The barman made the mistake of sneering at him.

'I don't know if you've noticed, but we're in international waters now. Back in Italy, you're the law. Out here, what I say goes. And I say the bar closes.'

'Where is this vessel registered?' asked Zen.

The barman didn't know. Zen took him by the arm and led him over to a framed certificate on the

275

bulkhead, which showed that the motor-vessel *Omero*, built in 1956, was registered at Naples, Italy, with a stamp from the relevant authorities to prove it.

'So?' the barman responded.

'So wherever we may be geographically, from a legal point of view we're on Italian soil, and Italian laws therefore apply.'

Zen gave him an avuncular smile and an encouraging pat on the shoulder.

'Think of this ship as a little island,' he said in accents borrowed wholesale from the history teacher who had retailed the story about the Norman occupation of Sicily all those years ago. 'An island temporarily mobile and detached from its home, but still subject to all the rules and regulations which apply in that state, of which I am an official representative. I therefore order you to reopen the bar *sine die*, on the aforementioned grounds of provoking a possibly injurious if not fatal breach of the peace.'

The barman gave a defeated snarl.

'You sons of bitches really enjoy this, don't you?' he said, sliding the grille back up with a loud racket.

'Damn right we do,' Zen replied.

The Italian-speaking Norman materialized at Zen's side.

'Is it open again?' he asked.

Zen nodded.

'It's open. And it'll stay open until I give permission to close it.'

The foreigner yelled something to his companions, who immediately surged forward to the bar.

'How did you do it?' the Italo-Norman asked Zen.

'How do you do this?'

'Do what?'

'Speak Italian.'

'My grandmother was one of yous. I'm from Glasgow myself. In Scotland,' he added, nothing Zen's troubled frown. 'Came over in the twenties, never went back. But she brought me mam up to speak the lingo a bit, and she passed it on to me.'

'And why do all your shirts have that word on them?' asked Zen.

'Arsenal? It's a football club. We won a competition at this place where we all work, in Croydon, just outside London. Know where London is? Best sales team in the company. Free week's holiday in Malta. Came over to Italy on a day trip, had one too many, missed the hydrofoil back. One of the lads is an Arsenal supporter. I'm a Celtic man myself, but he bought the shirts for all of us, so we sort of have to wear them. Would look a bit thankless else. Can I get you a drink?'

'That's very kind of you. A grappa, please.'

Zen stood there amid the swirling alien mass while the other man fought his way to the bar. He already felt very foreign, and very reassured. *They* – whoever they might be – certainly couldn't get him here. In the centre of the saloon, the girl who had earlier been asleep on the quay was now dancing alone to some inaudible music. Her breasts, Zen noted with some interest, were even better than her legs.

The Glaswegian returned with Zen's grappa and one for himself.

'Never tried this stuff before,' he said. 'Not bad, and cheap too.'

'Are you Norman?' asked Zen.

'No, Norman's the one sitting on the beer supply. I'm Andy.'

'Why is that girl dancing all alone?'

'Stephanie? Well, you know how it is on trips like this. Couples form and couples fall apart. Hers fell apart.'

He looked sharply at Zen.

'Do you want to meet her?'

Zen shrugged.

'Why not?'

After that, one thing led to another with astonishing rapidity. Eventually they all ended up on the afterdeck of the ferry, under a clear sky and an almost full moon, surrounded by the benign vastness of the sea. Zen was getting on very nicely with Stephanie, who seemed both easy to please and also quite intrigued by this distinguished-looking foreign gent who kept trying out his incomprehensible English on her while peeking down her cleavage in a sexy but respectful way. Wit flowed like wine, and the wine – well, grappa, beer and whisky, actually – flowed like the softly enveloping air of the Mediterranean night.

The other noise, when it first became apparent, seemed at first just a slight annoyance, a minor case of interference which might disturb but could not obliterate the experience they were all sharing. But it persisted, and at last someone went to the stern rail to see what was going on.

'It's a boat,' he reported. 'Got writing on the side. C, A, R, A, B, I, N . . .'

Zen dragged himself away from Stephanie's side and went to look. It was true. A dark-blue Carabinieri launch was closing rapidly with the ferry, its searchlight scorching the gentle wavelets between them. A few moments later, it was alongside. A rope ladder was thrown down, and a man swarmed up it from the launch.

Zen felt himself sobering up rapidly. He knew who had come aboard, and why he was there. Reluctantly he got Baccio Sinico's revolver out of his pocket and hurled it into the sea. Then he returned to Stephanie. She said something which, like all the things she had said, he did not understand. He shook his head and clutched her hand tightly. She looked alarmed. He forced a smile.

Then he remembered the other piece of incriminating evidence. He searched in his pockets until he found the object he had stolen from the museum. It was a silver cross, with forked ends and intricate engraving on the surface. Zen pressed it into the palm of the hand he had been holding.

'For you,' he said.

Stephanie looked down at the cross, turning it this way and that so that it gleamed gently in the moonlight. Then her face suddenly crumpled, she turned away and burst into tears. Panicked, Zen looked around for the Italian-speaking man.

'What did I do wrong?' he demanded. 'I didn't mean to insult her! Christ, can't I get anything right?'

The Glaswegian came over and spoke rapidly to Stephanie, then turned her back to face Zen. The girl was still weeping and making little sniffing noises as she spoke.

'It's not what you think,' Andy told Zen.

The girl started to talk, seemingly not to the two men but to the silver cross cradled in the palm of her hand.

'She says it's the most beautiful thing she's ever seen,' Andy translated. 'She says she didn't know that such beauty existed in the world. She says she feels ashamed because she doesn't deserve to have it.'

At the end of the deck, adjoining the superstructure, a man appeared.

'Tell her that no one deserves such beauty,' Zen said quickly. 'Tell her that it is indeed very precious, but no more than she is. Tell her to care for it, and for herself.'

He stood up as the ROS agent appeared in front of him.

'Aurelio Zen,' he said. 'You evaded our plan of preventative detention and are therefore officially considered to be at risk. I am are here to accompany you back to Catania.'

Zen gestured defeatedly.

'And if I say no?'

Roberto Lessi tossed his head contemptuously.

'Let's go. The boat's waiting.'

And there indeed was the Carabinieri launch, lying about ten metres off to port, wallowing slightly in the softly bloated seas.

'Excuse me,' said Andy, in Italian. 'He's a friend of ours.'

Lessi gave him a hard glance.

'So?' he replied.

The Glaswegian smiled.

'*So*, if you want to take him, you're going to have to take all of us. And I'm not sure that we'd fit on that wee boat of yours. That's always supposing that you were able to get us on board in the first place, which personally speaking I wouldn't be inclined to place a bet on.'

The ROS agent turned furiously to Zen.

'Tell this little prick to fuck off before I break his balls!' he spat out.

'What did he say?' asked Andy. 'I can't understand when they speak so quick.'

Zen racked his brains. What was the name of that other English team? Leaver, Leever . . . And what was the phrase that taxi driver in Rome, the vociferous Lazio supporter, had used?

'He said that Arsenal supporters are a clan of degenerate wankers and marginal know-nothings,' Zen confided to Andy. 'According to him, the only half-decent English team is Liverpool, and compared to Lazio they suck too.'

The Glaswegian spoke loudly and rapidly to his red-shirted companions, who dropped whatever they were doing and clustered tightly around the ROS man. The latter pulled out and displayed a police identity card embedded in his wallet.

'*I am a police!*' he declared in cracked English.

'Is that right?' Andy replied, plucking the wallet from the Carabiniere's hand and tossing it over-board. 'Awful hard job, they say.'

The Carabiniere looked around at the towering Arsenal supporters with a furious but cornered expression.

'You are all under arrest!' he screamed. 'Outrage to a public official! Surrender your papers immediately! You are all . . .'

At which point a whisky bottle slammed into his skull.

'Liverpool, my arse,' said Norman.

Stephanie giggled.

WHEN THIEVES FALL OUT read a sub-headline in the copy of the newspaper *La Sicilia* which Zen bought the next morning in Valletta. 'A brutal strangulation concludes a successful break-in to the Civic Museum of Catania. The presumed killer makes a daring escape by leaping from a window and remains at large. A twelfth-century Norman crucifix "of inestimable value" is missing.'

Zen smiled sourly. So that's how they had decided to pitch the story. But why was there no mention of Alfredo Ferraro, the ROS agent whom he had shot? And why hadn't he been named as the 'presumed killer'? He was sure that Roberto Lessi, the other ROS man, had identified him in that final moment before he leapt from the window, but there was no mention of this in the article. This was both good news and bad. Good, because it meant that they were not going to be coming after him openly, with arrest warrants and extradition orders. Bad, because it meant that he didn't have the slightest idea what they *were* going to do.

The ferry had docked in Valletta at just after six o'clock that morning, following a night which from Zen's point of view had been extremely eventful. Following the intervention of the English football supporters, the ROS agent had been placed in one of the lifeboats hanging from cradles along both sides of the main deck. At Zen's suggestion, Norman had moved his beer supply to a nearby bench, and when the supposed Liverpool supporter finally regained consciousness, it had been made clear to him that the alternative to lying low and keeping quiet was another dose of whisky.

'And, frankly, I'm not at all sure that whisky should really be your drink of choice, Roberto,' Norman had added, brandishing the bottle as if unaware that it was in his hand at the time. 'To be perfectly honest, I don't think you can handle it. I'm not sure you've got the bottle to deal with the hard stuff. Seems to go straight to your head. Personally speaking – and this is just my opinion, with which you may well disagree, as is your right – but *personally*, for what it's worth, I think you should stick to beer.' With which he split open another can of Nastro Azzurro and handed it to the still only partially conscious ROS agent with a significant grin.

Meanwhile the Carabinieri launch had come alongside, and two of its crew, armed with machine-guns, were searching the ferry for their missing colleague.

Aurelio Zen was in a feigned clinch with Stephanie at the time, having explained the realities of the situation through the Italian-speaking Glaswegian. Stephanie clearly didn't believe a single word of this rigmarole, assuming that this Italian was just trying to get into her pants. But she was prepared to play along, up to a point, and so when the Carabinieri officers passed through on their sweep of the boat, all they saw was a horde of drunken English football hooligans, two of whom were necking.

Had they persisted, the truth would no doubt have emerged in time, but by then dawn was breaking and Malta was in sight. A coastguard cutter closed in on the ferry and its escort, and over a very powerful loudspeaker demanded to know just what the Italian police thought they were doing, trespassing in Maltese waters. At this point the Carabinieri acknowledged defeat, withdrew to their launch and sped off northwards. Unfortunately Norman had also passed out, exhausted by the stresses and strains of the night's adventures, and when Zen reluctantly disentangled himself from Stephanie's embraces and went to inspect the lifeboat where the ROS agent had been stowed away, he found it empty.

Nor did Lessi put in an appearance when the passengers disembarked in the imposing harbour at Valletta, but this was hardly surprising. He could not arrest Zen on foreign soil, and since his identification papers were now at the bottom of the Mediterranean, he was not in a position to enlist the help of the Maltese authorities either, even if they had been disposed to be helpful.

On the quayside, Zen said goodbye to his seriously hung-over British friends and kissed Stephanie, who surprised him by putting her tongue in his mouth and then starting to weep again. He then changed some money and, after a discussion in very fractured Italian with a taxi driver, had himself driven to a small hotel at the top of the old town.

For a moment he thought he had hired a suicidal maniac, since the driver proceeded to turn out of the port area and start driving on the *left*-hand side of the road. But if he was mad, everyone else seemed to share his madness, and the short journey passed uneventually. At the hotel, Zen took the one remaining room, a small single at the rear of the premises, overlooking what had once been a small internal courtyard and was now a deep, dank shaft filled with air-conditioning ducts, rubbish and cooking smells.

There had been no obvious sign that his taxi had been followed, but he knew that it wouldn't take them long to find him. His Italian identity card had been enough to get him through passport control, but he had to fill out an entry card which would now be on file. He was officially registered as having entered the country, and it was far too small a country to hide in, particularly for someone with no friends and who didn't speak the language.

His best hope, he reckoned, lay in that entry card. Persons leaving Malta legally would have to complete a similar exit card, which would also be filed. If a search for 'Zen, Aurelio' turned up no such card, it would naturally be assumed that he was still in the country. The resulting confusion might just be enough to buy him the time he needed. But first he had to find a way to leave the country illegally. With a heavy heart, he lifted the phone and dialled a number in Rome.

There was no answer, so he left a message.

'Gilberto, it's Aurelio. I'm in it up to here, and I don't even know who with, but they don't mess about. I can't say any more on the phone, and I can't give you my number, but I need help desperately, and after what happened in Naples you owe me, you son of a bitch. I'll call again every thirty minutes until I get you. Don't let me down, Gilberto, and none of your stupid jokes. This is deadly serious. And I mean that literally.'

He took his shoes off and lay down on the bed, but with his head and shoulders propped against the wall. After a sleepless night on the ferry, exhaustion was starting to overcome the adrenalin which had kept him going thus far, but he could not afford to sleep until his arrangements were made. He turned on the television and watched a documentary about tree frogs until the thirty minutes had elapsed.

There was still no answer from Gilberto's home phone. Since his recent legal problems, the Sardinian no longer had an office number, and Zen was wary of calling him on his cellphone, knowing how easily such calls can be intercepted. In the end he tried anyway, only to discover that Gilberto's *telefonino* was either switched off or out of range. Back on TV, the tree frogs were mating.

It was another two hours before Gilberto finally responded, and he when he did he initially sounded distinctly flippant.

'I thought you weren't speaking to me, Aurelio.'

'I'm speaking to you now.'

'So what's the story this time?'

'I don't trust stories any more. I'm too old.'

'It's no fun growing old. But as someone said, the only alternative is dying young.'

'Can we stop pissing around, Gilberto? I'm in serious trouble.'

'What kind of trouble?'

'I can't tell you over the phone. We must do this on a strict need-to-know basis.'

'All right, what do I need to know?'

'First, I'm in Malta.'

'Never been there. Are those Knights still around? I seem to remember that you had trouble with them some years back.'

'Will you please shut the fuck up and listen, Gilberto?'

'Sorry.'

'Second, I need to leave as soon as possible, ideally this evening.'

'I'm not a travel agent.'

'Yes, you are, because the third thing is that I need to travel clandestinely. No tickets, no passport control.'

Gilberto whistled.

'That's a tall order, Aurelio. What did you have in mind?'

'Preferably a light plane owned and flown by someone with a shady reputation. Take-off and landing at private airstrips.'

'I don't know anyone like that.'

'But you have friends, and they have friends. Somewhere in that pyramid-selling scam you call your social life, there may be someone who knows the contact I need. Your job is to locate him.'

'How can you know that such a contact even exists?'

'Because Malta is, among other things, a notorious staging-post for a whole range of illegal import–export operations between North Africa, the Middle East, and Europe. Arms, drugs, you name it. And those people don't fly Alitalia.'

'I don't blame them.'

'This is not a joking matter, Gilberto!'

'All right, all right, calm down.'

A distant sigh.

'I'll see what I can do, but it's going to take some time.'

'Time is of the essence. How long?'

'I don't know. I'll drop everything else and get to work right away. Call me on my *telefonino* at noon and then every hour on the hour after that.'

'We can't discuss this stuff over a cellular link.'

'Oh, I heard a great story the other day! There's this guy on a train, making life hell for everyone around with an endless series of calls on his cellphone, right?'

'Gilberto!'

'Then this woman across from him has a seizure of some kind, and all the other passengers say, "Please, we need to call an ambulance at the next station, lend us your phone." Only he won't, see? Absolutely refuses to let anyone else use his cellphone. And . . .'

'And in the end it turns out that it was one of those fakes. Yes, I've heard that story, Gilberto. Now can we get back to the point?'

'Of course. Here's the deal. If I come up with something, I'll tell you so. Then you phone me about thirty minutes later on that landline number we used before, when I was having those legal problems. Do you still have it?'

'I never throw anything away, Gilberto.'

'Except your friends.'

'I'm sorry about that. I probably over-reacted. I apologize.'

'Don't grovel, Aurelio. It's not your style.'

The line went dead. With a yawn of immense weariness, Zen set the alarm on the clock-radio, took off his clothing and slid in between the sheets. Seconds later he was asleep.

At a quarter to twelve, he was woken peremptorily by the alarm, which sounded as though it had been triggered by a fire or a burglary rather than the clock. He took a quick shower and then dialled the twenty-one-digit number of Gilberto's cellphone.

'Nothing yet, but I've turned up some possible leads,' was the curt reply.

Zen grunted and hung up. He felt refreshed but starving, having had nothing to eat since a ham roll on the ferry the night before. He was strongly tempted to go out and forage, but the risks of running into Roberto Lessi or one of his associates – a back-up team could well have been flown in by now – were too great, so he called the front desk. The hotel didn't serve lunch, but the manager offered to send someone out to get Zen a snack.

This duly arrived fifteen minutes later, in the form of two pasties made with filo pastry and a filling of soft cheese or meat sauce. They were stodgy, greasy and almost completely tasteless, but they were certainly filling, in a depressing way. Zen seemed to recall that the British had owned Malta for several hundred years. The local cuisine had apparently been one of their legacies to the island's culture.

Satiated but unsatisfied, Zen turned the television back on and watched an American thriller dubbed into Maltese. This was an interesting experience, since the rhythm and cadence of the language sounded wholly Italian, while the noise it made was one which Zen associated with the Tunisian and Libyan street traders who sold jewellery and accessories out of suitcases on the streets of Rome. To make matters worse, an entire Italian word such as *grazie* or *signore* would suddenly flash by, casting its brief, deceitful light on the prevailing obscurity.

At one o'clock, Gilberto reported no further progress. At two, 'I think I may be starting to narrow it down, but don't get your hopes up.' At three, 'Why in the name of God did I let you sucker me into this, Aurelio? I should have just let you go on not speaking to me. I should have *encouraged* you! Friends like you I can do without.'

And then, at four o'clock: 'Done it.'

The next thirty minutes seemed to last several hours. Zen had been asked to show his documents at the desk, and had therefore had no possibility of registering under an alias. And there weren't that many hotels in Valletta. If Lessi had taken the number of Zen's taxi, established that it had not left the city, then visited each in turn asking after his good friend Aurelio Zen, he could be knocking on his door at any moment. If he had called in back-up, they could cover the whole island by evening. And if they or their patrons in Rome had persuaded the Maltese authorities to cooperate, they might already have found him and be waiting for him to emerge, so as not to cause problems at the hotel, which could damage the island's lavishly promoted tourist image.

When Zen finally called, he was told that Gilberto hadn't arrived yet, although they were expecting him, because the traffic in Rome was a disaster, what with all the roadworks, renovation and construction designed to equip the city for the twenty-six million pilgrims expected for the forthcoming millennial Jubilee year. Try later, he was told.

Zen hung up, yelled an obscenity and smashed his fist into the wall, leaving a dent in the flimsy plasterboard. Then he told himself not to be stupid, lit a cigarette to calm himself down, and called again.

This time, Gilberto answered.

'You're on, Aurelio,' he said. 'It's going to cost you, though.'

'I wasn't planning this trip, Gilberto. I have precisely fifty-eight thousand lire on me.'

'I don't mean *now*, you polenta brain. The bill will be presented in due course after your return. I just wanted you to know that it will be in the region of five million lire.'

'Jesus!'

'This sort of thing doesn't come cheap. I've had to grease a lot of palms and to buy a lot of silence.'

'And then, of course, there's your cut.'

There was a long pause.

'I don't think I deserve that, Aurelio.'

'I'm sorry. I'm really sorry. It's just with all this stress and strain I'm under . . .'

'You're grovelling again. Let's get back to the point, which is that I've booked your flight.'

'How did you do it?'

'You lectured me about need-to-know. The same applies here. Briefly, a friend of a friend of a friend knows someone who has been planning just such a trip as the one you mentioned, to visit some friends of his in Sicily.'

'What a lot of friendship! I'm moved.'

'To quote an ex-friend of mine, "Can we stop pissing around?"'

'Sorry. To quote a true and valued and shamefully misused friend of *mine*, "What do I need to know?" '

'Have you got a pen? These people are likely to be extremely nervous. The person concerned had originally been planning to leave at the weekend. For a consideration, partly in cash and partly in kind, he agreed to contact his Sicilian friends and rearrange the trip for tonight. But if you get any part of this even slightly wrong, he simply won't show up.'

'Go ahead.'

'In the centre of Valletta, there's a road called Old Bakery Street. Towards the bottom of the hill, it crosses St Christopher Street. Just after the crossing, there's a set of steep steps leading down to the left. About halfway down there is a bar called Piju. Be there at seven o'clock this evening. Go to the barman and ask, in Italian, for a Beck's beer. He'll tell you that they don't have any. You say, "Just give me a beer." He'll ask if you want Maltese or imported, and you reply, "Maltese is fine with me." Got that?'

'What happens after that?'

'I don't need to know, so I wasn't told. One more thing. If these people find out that you're a policeman, you're dead meat. Understand?'

'Only too well.'

'All right, that's it. Good luck, Aurelio. If you make it, give me a call as soon as you arrive. I've been missing you, you old shit. I don't want anything to happen to you now you've finally got over our little misunderstanding.'

'I've missed you too, Gilberto. I'll try not to do anything stupid and I'll call as soon as I can. Meanwhile, thanks for everything.'

It was only when he saw the tiny single-engined aeroplane that Zen realized that flying back to Sicily was going to mean . . . well, *flying*. He had been so preoccupied with other problems in the hours leading up to this moment that this basic point had completely failed to register. The moment it did, he also realized that the state of comatose indifference induced by the news of his mother's imminent death, which had protected him through the turbulent flight to Rome, was no longer operative. He was sane again, and the only sane way to look at flying was to be utterly terrified.

'What happens if the propeller falls off?' he asked in a tone of forced jocularity as they taxied to the end of the baked-earth runway.

'It won't.'

'But suppose you have a heart attack or something?'

The pilot stroked his black moustache.

'Well, we'll be flying low, to keep off the radar screens, so you'll have about fifteen seconds to put your worldly and spiritual affairs in order. Not enough, probably.'

A moment later, the plane was lined up, the pilot pulled back the throttle, and all talk became impossible.

By then it was past eleven o'clock at night. Zen had spent most of the intervening hours locked up in a stuffy apartment whose windows were covered by exterior grooved metal shutters which he had been strictly ordered not to open.

Shortly after half-past six, he had gone down to the reception of his hotel, settled the bill and ascertained that the bar Piju was no more than a ten-minute walk away. He then seated himself in a corner of the lounge from where he had a clear view of the entrance and lobby. If the ROS men did come looking for him, there was just a chance that he would be able to slip out while they were upstairs hammering on the door of his room.

In the event, no one came in except couples, evidently tourists, but he was still nervous about showing himself on the street. There was nothing to be done, however, and after studying a map of Valletta displayed in the lobby and determining his route, he pushed open the glass door and turned sharp left down a narrow, steeply inclined alley. It had occurred to him that the telephone line of Gilberto's Sardinian friends might be under surveillance, and possibly that of the hotel as well. Of course, 'they' could grab him at the bar if they wanted to, but it had also occurred to him that they might prefer not to act so publicly. He had therefore located the steps where the bar was situated on the map, and then planned an alternative way to get there. This was not difficult, since the city was built on a grid plan.

And a very handsome city it was too, he thought, as he made his way along St Mark Street and turned left on to a long straight paved thoroughfare swooping downhill and then up again like a carnival ride. The buildings to either side were of pleasant proportions, the architecture sober and restrained, the material a golden sandstone which glowed in the late-afternoon sunlight like warmed honey. The balconies were enclosed with wooden walls painted green or left bare, which made a charming contrast with the stonework. There could hardly have been a more complete contrast with the tortuous baroque excesses of Catania, executed in the black solidified lava which had so many times overwhelmed the city. Although he was hundreds of kilometres south of Sicily, almost half-way to Africa, Zen felt quite at home with this form of urban planning, where all was calm, functional and restful.

At the bottom of the street he turned left and then immediately right, and walked up the steps to the bar. It was a small, poky place, obviously designed to appeal to a circle of regulars and to repel anyone else. Zen strode up to the bar and ran through his ritual exchange with the owner, whose jolly, tubby physique was belied by a pair of startlingly direct black eyes. Once their dialogue was completed, the man served Zen the beer, picked up the phone and spoke a few phrases in the guttural false-Italian of the island.

It was another half hour before his contact showed up. At first, Zen paid him no attention. Various people, all men, had come in and gone out while he waited, and this skinny, pimply, gangly youth seemed an unlikely candidate for a mission of this presumed importance. It was only later that Zen realized that this had been precisely the point. They were not yet sure of Zen, so they had left him to stew while they checked the comings and goings in the neighbourhood. Then, once they felt reasonably sure that he had come alone, they'd sent this expendable kid to make the first approach, just in case they were wrong.

The owner of the bar had appeared to speak, or at least be able to pronounce, some Italian, but the youth gave no sign of having any use for language at all. He appeared at Zen's side, standing close enough in the uncrowded bar to draw attention to himself, then jerked his head sharply back and to one side and walked out. Zen duly followed. Under the circumstances, he didn't bother paying for his beer. They could take it out of the five million.

They walked down through a warren of steps and alleys to a dock on the waterfront, where they boarded a small ferry. During the crossing to the other shore of the harbour inlet, the youth closely inspected each of the other half dozen passengers, but made no eye contact with Zen and still did not speak. When they disembarked after the short crossing, he took up a pose of stoic resignation near the top of the gangplank and remained there until all the other passengers had dispersed. Then he gave Zen another of his violent head gestures, like someone slinging water out of a bucket, and crossed the street to a blue Renault saloon. He opened the passenger door for Zen, who noted that the car had been left unlocked. Either Malta was an incredibly crime-free country, or these people enjoyed a level of respect which made such routine security precautions unnecessary.

They drove at what seemed to Zen a remarkably sober and steady pace – considering that his chauffeur was not only about twenty-two, but presumably also a gang member – up a wide street leading from the harbour to a sprawling development of apartment blocks with a vaguely Arab air: clusters of white cubes of different heights and sizes all jammed together in apparent disorder like a residential souk. The youth drew up by one of the entrances to this labyrinth, gave Zen another of his patented cranial swipes, and led him inside.

Despite the folkloristic appearance of the complex, the interior was completely modern and remarkably luxurious. They rode in a lift up to the fifth floor, where the youth opened a door – once again, unlocked – and gesturally jerked Zen through to a room to the left. He switched on the light, pointed to the shutters over the window and made a savage slicing motion with his right hand, looking Zen in the eye for the first time.

Zen nodded.

'I won't open them,' he said.

The youth looked at him in astonishment, as though his dog had just given voice to a political opinion. Then he walked out, closing the door behind him. A moment later, Zen heard the lock engage.

The room was minimally furnished with a sofa, a chair and a table, all in what appeared to Zen to be execrable taste. There was no telephone, radio or television, and the walls were bare. It was as neutral and impersonal as some hutch at a cut-price hotel on the *autostrada*.

Zen had long ago decided not to concern himself too much about those aspects of life which he could not control, and he certainly could not hope to control or influence his fate in this situation. Gilberto had come up with a solution to his problems, Zen had accepted it, and now it was out of his hands. He was still very tired after his night on the ferry and all that had preceded and followed it, so he lay down on the sofa, covered in some garish acrylic material. He closed his eyes, thought about Stephanie and wondered where she was now, and so fell asleep.

He awoke, sensing that there was someone in the room. It was the gangly youth, standing over him where he lay on the sofa. Half asleep as he was, Zen knew what was going to happen next, and indeed the head-jerk was duly performed. Zen staggered groggily to his feet and followed the kid out of the apartment and down to the street. He glanced at his watch. It was half-past nine.

They got into the car and drove out of the city along narrow, gently winding roads. There was little other traffic, and what there was proceeded, like them, at a moderate pace, giving way to other drivers where necessary and never using the horn or flashing headlamps. The light was fading fast, but Zen could just make out a crooked grid of dry-stone walling all around, enclosing small fields with the occasional isolated house.

The drive lasted another hour, broken by regular stops when the youth got out and scanned the road behind them, and then made a cellphone call in his incomprehensible dialect. So he *could* talk, thought Zen, lying back in his seat and smoking cigarette after cigarette. He had always had a good innate sense of direction, and by reference to his internal compass, the glow in the west and the rising moon, he soon worked out that they were taking an extremely circuitous route to their destination.

In the end, though, they arrived, bouncing off the tarred road on to a dirt track which they followed for another kilometre or so, before pulling into a large field with a metal barn of recent construction at one end. In front of it stood the tiny single-engined plane, and beside it a short, stocky man with a moustache, wearing a pair of blue overalls and an old-fashioned flying cap with flaps over the ears.

Without waiting for another head-jerk, Zen got out of the car. The man in overalls walked over to him.

'Signor Zen!' he said. 'Pleased to meet you. I apologize for the delay, but we needed to wait for dark and also make sure that you were unaccompanied.'

Zen held out his hand, then retracted it, noticing no equivalent gesture from the other man.

'Of course,' he said. 'No problem.'

The man smiled roguishly.

'I will be your pilot tonight, as they say on the commercial airlines. If you care to step up here, I'll start the engine and we'll be off.'

That had been almost an hour ago. Since then there had been nothing except the racket of the engine and the occasional lights of a ship passing so close beneath them that Zen felt sure they must rip off their wings against its masts. But the flight passed without incident, until the pilot spoke over the radio microphone he wore under his flying helmet and produced a spectacular display below: plumes of reddish light spaced equally to form two converging lines in the darkness.

The plane immediately started manoeuvring, turning this way and that until it was centred on the strip of dark between the beacons. It dipped dramatically, causing Zen's stomach to rise and his panic to return, and then floated down as effortlessly as a feather past a group of cars and a panel van and touched down lightly on a smooth surface. Well before they reached the last flare, the plane had stopped, circled around and begun to taxi back towards the waiting vehicles.

'But that's not your real problem,' the pilot said once the clamour of the engine had died down again.

'What?' demanded Zen, stunned by this *non sequitur*.

'The propeller falling off, or me getting a heart attack,' the pilot replied. 'Your real problem was arriving safely. And I'm afraid we have.'

'What do you mean?'

The pilot grinned.

'I'll be straight with you, Signor Zen, since you've been straight with me. Well, not quite straight. For instance, you didn't tell us that you're a policeman.'

Zen felt the adrenalin rush like walking into a wall.

'I didn't think it was relevant,' he mumbled.

'It isn't. It doesn't matter at all, because in a few hours from now you won't be in a position to tell anyone anything. When I asked our Sicilian friends if it would be possible to move the delivery date because I had been asked to transport a certain Aurelio Zen, they got very excited indeed. It seems that some friends of theirs are anxious to meet you to discuss the recent death of a friend of theirs. Name of Spada. My friends here were of course only too happy to be able to do their friends a favour.'

The plane drew to a halt beside the cars and the van. Figures emerged from the darkness. The door was opened and Zen told roughly to descend. He stepped down on to a surface which felt like tarmac. On each side, the lines of flares stretched away into the darkness of the night, illuminating the scene in garish hues. The van had backed up to the rear door of the plane, which was open. A team of about five men were lifting out large, plastic-wrapped packages and stowing them away in the back of the van.

That was all that Zen had time to see before he was hustled over to one of the waiting cars. A man of about thirty with shiny ribbons of thick black hair and a notable nose got out of the driver's seat and approached Zen and his handler.

'Search him, Nello,' he said to the latter.

Hands patted him down.

'No gun,' Nello reported.

'Give me your mobile,' the other man told Zen.

'I don't have one.'

The man stared at Zen in total disbelief.

'Well, actually I do,' Zen went on, realizing that he was cutting a poor figure. 'But I left it at home. I never use it, to be honest. The last thing I want is people being able to get in touch with me day or night, wherever I may be. I'm suppose I'm old-fashioned.'

Nello laughed.

'You're not just old-fashioned, *Papà*. You're extinct!'

He grabbed Zen by the arm, pushed him into the back of the car and got in beside him. The other man got behind the wheel and gunned the engine. They drove off along the runway, which looked suspiciously like an *autostrada*, then turned right on to a steep dirt track down which they bumped and bounced. When they reached the bottom, Zen saw that the landing strip behind them was indeed a portion of a two-lane highway, elevated on concrete stilts and breaking off abruptly just beyond the earthen ramp which they had just descended.

'What's going on?' he demanded in an indignant tone.

Nello laughed.

'You're a VIP, *Papà*! You get met at the airport.'

The car turned left on to a minor paved road and accelerated away.

They drove in silence for almost two hours. Zen saw signs to Santa Croce, Ragusa, Módica, Noto, Avola, Siracusa, Augusta, Lentini . . . The fact that his captors hadn't bothered to blindfold him almost certainly meant that he was going to be killed. Quite apart from anything else, he now knew the approximate location of the section of uncompleted motorway which the local clan used as a landing strip for its drug shipments. Yes, they were going to have to kill him, no question about that.

'How do you light up the runway?' he asked.

Rather to his surprise, the answer came at once.

'Sets of distress flares hooked up to an electrical cable,' Nello replied with a certain technological eagerness. 'We rig it all in advance, powered by a car battery, then when the pilot calls in on the radio we switch on the current.'

'Shut up, Nello,' said the driver.

'What did I . . .?'

'Just shut up!'

A large commercial aircraft flew overhead, its powerful landing lights seemingly vacuuming up the clouds scattered low in the sky. Then Zen saw the signs for Catania, and had a surge of hope. In the city, there would be traffic lights and, even at this time of night, traffic jams. He might be able to make a run for it, get away from these Mafia thugs and throw himself on the mercy of the authorities whose protection he had so arrogantly spurned. They wouldn't be too happy about his disappearance, of course, and still less about what had happened to Alfredo Ferraro. He would have to be patient, penitent and remorseful, like an adulterous husband, but in the end they'd have to take him back. After all, he was one of them.

Unfortunately for this pleasing scenario, the signs to Catania rapidly died out, to be succeeded by ones to Misterbianco, Paternò, and a host of other places which Zen had never heard of. The car was labouring like a boat in a broken sea, the road rearing up and spinning round. Apart from that, there was nothing but fleeting glimpses of the small towns through which they drove at speed, the two men now apparently more tense than before.

At length they reached another town, more or less identical in appearance to all the others. The driver drove through the back-streets to the main piazza and drew up next to a gravel-covered park dotted with trees. At the end, next to them, stood one of those imposing but uninspiring civic statues which dot the minor towns of Italy, commemorating some local celebrity who had the misfortune to be born there. This one was of a man in vaguely nineteenth-century garb, his right hand clutching a book to his chest and his left outstretched in greeting or appeal. Zen read the name on the plinth by the light of one of the few streetlamps which adorned the piazza. It meant nothing to him.

Meanwhile the driver had taken out his *telefonino* and was now speaking rapidly in dialect. If he and Nello were indeed 'only too glad to be able to do their friends a favour' by handing over Zen, they were doing a good job of concealing the fact. So far from being happy, they looked as though they were scared to death.

About a minute later a car appeared at the other end of the piazza and swooped down towards them. Nello nudged Zen.

'Out,' he said.

Zen opened his door and stood up. The air smelt fresh and cool. The other car screeched to a halt alongside the first, its engine still running. The driver got out and shook hands with Zen's captor and they spoke quietly for a while. Then the other man stretched out his arms and exposed his palms like a saint displaying his stigmata. His chin was slightly raised and pushed forward, his lips turned down. The gesture, typically Sicilian, meant, 'I couldn't care less.'

This sealed Zen's fate. They couldn't care less about him. They didn't even glance in his direction. If they weren't bothering to guard or even watch him, it was for the same reason that the ancient Romans did not build walls around their cities. It would have been redundant. They already controlled the whole place.

The two men concluded their discussion with a handshake and Nello turned to Zen.

'You're to go with him,' he said, indicating the new-comer.

Zen nodded and started to walk over to the other car. Without a word, the driver opened the back door for him, as though this were a taxi which Zen had summoned. His nonchalant confidence confirmed Zen's worst fears.

Then, just as Zen was about to get into the car, his head lowered like an animal entering an abattoir stall, the planet suddenly went into labour. All four men shuddered where they stood, as though suffering sympathetic but lesser convulsions. There was a deep groaning which seemed to come from nowhere, the cobblestones beneath them trembled and the trees shook their branches in the windless air. Finally, just as these symptoms began to subside, the statue of the local celebrity turned towards them, its left arm apparently waving goodbye. Slowly, but with utter inevitability, it tumbled forward off its plinth and crashed to the ground.

Panic-stricken, the four men started to run, each in a different direction. Where was not important: the essential was to get away. After a fifty-metre sprint, Zen found himself all alone in a darkened alley, facing a tall, elderly man wearing a dressing-gown and slippers, and carrying a walking-stick.

'Is everything all right?' the man said in heavily accented Italian. Not in dialect, *in Italian*.

'Help me!' said Zen. 'Please help me.'

The man inspected him.

'Are you hurt?'

'Get me out of here.'

'Out of where?'

'Look, you've got to help! The Mafia is after me. They kidnapped me. I'm a police officer. I need to make a phone call, that's all. The authorities will be here in no time with helicopters and armoured vehicles. They'll have the whole place surrounded in less than an hour, but first I must make that call!'

The man looked at Zen.

'Who are you?' he asked.

Zen produced his police identification card, which the other man inspected by the flame of a lighter.

'Please!' said Zen as his wallet was handed back. 'I just need to make one phone call and then a place to hide until my colleagues arrive.'

'I think what you need is a drink,' the other man replied.

313

'So that's where they landed you! Of course, of course. The project for that motorway has been in the pipeline for twenty years or more, and will doubtless stay there for another twenty. In theory, it's supposed to run along the south coast, connecting Catania with Géla. At present it only exists on paper, but various people who own or have bought bits of land along the route will have been able to persuade the regional government to get a compulsory purchase order, buy them out, and then build that particular stretch to justify the purchase in the budget.'

'But most of that land must surely be worthless?'

Zen's host picked up the packet of *Nazionali* which Zen had left on the table, having chainsmoked three immediately after arrival.

'How much is this worth?' he asked.

'There's about half a pack left . . . Two thousand lire?'

'I'll pay you four thousand.'

'Why would you do that?'

'Why should you care? Let's say I'm desperate for a cigarette. At any rate, if you agree, this pack is now

314

worth twice what it was a moment ago. Now then, let's suppose that you suddenly realize that you don't have any more cigarettes, so you offer to buy one back from me. At four thousand for ten, it's worth four hundred, but I want to make a profit on the deal, so I'll charge six. That makes the remaining packet worth five thousand four hundred lire. We've almost tripled the value of these cigarettes in twenty seconds, without any money changing hands.'

They were sitting in a small room on the first floor of a house which might have been anywhere from a hundred to a thousand years old. Facing them was an empty fireplace. At one end of the room, by the stairs leading up from the street, was a cubby-hole kitchen. At the other, a window open to the balmy night air, and another set of steps leading to the next floor. The other furnishings consisted of an oil painting showing a young man in military uniform, cases of books in four languages, and a stereo system from which emerged the mellifluent sounds of a wind ensemble. Zen took another sip of the whisky which he had been offered and tried to drag himself back to reality.

'Listen, I really must make that phone call.'

His host shook his head.

'I used to have a telephone, but no one ever called me, and on the rare occasions when I wanted to place a call, the thing always seemed to be out of order.'

Zen slammed his fist against his forehead. Why hadn't he brought his mobile with him? *You're not just old-fashioned, Papà. You're extinct.*

'Anyway, the point is that what applies to our hypothetical deal on your cigarettes also applies to land,' the elderly gentleman went on. 'Even more so, because they aren't making any more land. So what there is is worth just as much as people will pay for it. And I imagine that the stretch where they built the section of motorway where you landed was sold at a very high price indeed. The buyer will have had friends in the regional government who informed him about the route of the proposed motorway. He buys the requisite fields, then resells them at twice the price to another friend, who then sells them back to him at twice that. Depending on how long they keep it up, they can then show legal bills of sale to the government agents, proving that that particular patch of parched scrub is now worth twenty or forty or a hundred times what the patch of parched scrub next to it is worth. And of course our friends' friends in the regional government will ensure that, instead of rerouting the motorway, that price is paid.'

The whole house quivered briefly, setting the ceiling lamp swaying gently to and fro, shifting the shadows about.

'An aftershock,' Zen's host said calmly. 'There may be more. But what we really worry about here is that

316

this could be the prelude to an eruption. The last time, in 1992, the molten lava almost reached the village. And that was just a leak, a dribble. If Etna were to blow as it did in 1169, 1381 or 1669, or in 475 BC for that matter, everyone in this village would be dead within seconds.'

'So why do you choose to live here?' asked Zen. 'You're not Sicilian, I take it.'

'No, I'm not Sicilian.'

There was a long silence.

'I will answer your questions in due course, if you wish,' Zen's host said at last. 'But first we need to resolve your own problems.'

'There must be a phone box in the village,' suggested Zen. 'Could you go down and make a call to a number I will give you and explain the situation?'

The other man again shook his head.

'The only public phone is in the bar, which will have closed by now. I could go to a neighbour's house, but this would be so unusual that they would almost certainly listen in on the call. I am eighty years old, *dottore*. Very soon now I shall move house for the last time, so to speak, but I do not want to have to do so until then. If it becomes known that I gave you refuge and then called the authorities, life here would become impossible for me.'

'Can you drive me somewhere else?'

'I have no car.'

'So what are we to do?' demanded Zen in a tone of desperation.

'First strategy, then tactics, as my commanding officer used to say. I need to know a little more about the situation. For example, you say this light aeroplane which flew you from Malta landed somewhere near a town called Santa Croce, is that right?'

Zen nodded.

'That was the first sign I remember seeing.'

'In that case, the reception committee was almost certainly composed of members of the Dominante clan, which controls the Ragusa area, or of one of the splinter groups which is trying to take it over, such as the D'Agosta family.'

Zen looked sharply at him.

'You seem very well informed on these matters.'

'Village gossip. What football league ratings are to other cultures, Mafia family ups and downs are to us. You also said that the pilot told you that they were doing a favour to some people here who want to talk to you. That would be Don Gaspare Limina. This is his home village, and although almost all his operations are conducted in Catania, this remains his power base and the refuge to which he retreats when things get too hot for him in the city.'

'He's here now?' asked Zen.

'He's here now. Can you think of any reason why he should want to meet you?'

Zen lit another cigarette and sat silently for a time.

'Even better, I can think of a reason why I want to meet him,' he said finally.

'Excellent. But it may be dangerous, you understand. I can set up such a meeting, but I am not in a position to guarantee your safety.'

'I understand. I'll take my chances.'

His host got up and poured them both another shot of whisky.

'They may well be better than you fear,' he said. 'You asked me why I live here. Well, one reason is that the people of whom we've been speaking remind me to some extent of myself and my comrades, many years ago. Contrary to popular belief, they are not sadistic thugs with a taste for violence. They do only what they need to do. If they need you dead, then they will kill you. If not, you will be safe. I've been living here for over forty years, and no one has ever bothered me. I'm not worth bothering about, you see.'

He raised his glass.

'*Gesundheit.*'

'You're German?' asked Zen.

The other man just looked at him.

Zen gestured in a relaxed way. The whisky was starting to have its effect.

'I did my "hardship years", as we call them in the police, up in the Alto Adige – what you call the Südtirol – and I learned a few words of the language.'

The other man smiled.

'Yes, I'm German. From a city called Bremen. My name is Klaus Genzler.'

Zen bowed slightly.

'I can't thank you enough for your hospitality, Herr Genzler. If you hadn't taken me in, I would have been dead by now, and all for nothing. I didn't know where I was, you see. I had no idea who these people were. But now I do, and I look forward to meeting them.'

'And why would that be?'

'Because I think they killed my daughter, and I want to find out.'

'Your daughter?'

'Carla Arduini. She died along with a judge, Corinna Nunziatella. You may have read about it in the papers. They machine-gunned the car and then threw in a stick of plastic explosive, just outside Taormina.'

Klaus Genzler smiled reminiscently.

'Ah, Taormina! I haven't been there in over fifty years.'

He's gaga, thought Zen.

'Kesselring based his headquarters in Taormina, in the old Dominican convent. I had the good fortune to be summoned there several times. Wonderful buildings, stunning views. Did himself well, the *Feldmarschall*. But I don't think the Limina clan killed your daughter.'

Or maybe he's not.

'You don't?'

Genzler shook his head.

'I remember when the news of that atrocity arrived. There was a sense of fear and confusion. People here are used to terrible things happening, but they expect Don Gaspare to know who did them and why, even if he didn't order them himself. They're like children. As long as Daddy seems to know what's going on, and not be bothered by it, then the children won't be troubled either, even though they don't personally understand.'

He took another sip of whisky and unwrapped a short cigar.

'But the day that news arrived, there was a sense of panic in the village. I knew at once what must have happened, and subsequent enquiries have proved me right. Not only did Don Gaspà not order that operation, but he has no idea who did.'

Genzler lit the cigar and stared at Zen.

'Do you know what that means, in the circles in which he moves? It means that you're finished. Taormina is part of the Liminas' territory. If something happens on your territory which you didn't order, and you can't find out and punish whoever did it, then you

321

might as well retire and open a grocery store, because no one will ever take you seriously again.'

Zen nodded quickly. A mass of thoughts were stirring in his brain like a school of porpoises creasing the surface of the sea and then vanishing. He wanted to let this process work itself out before trying to assess the consequences.

'So you were here in the war?' he asked Genzler.

'I was indeed. This village was our main forward position in 1943, after the Allied invasion. Many of my friends fell here. Most were not buried.'

He took a long draw at his cigar.

'We – the Germans – held this part of the island against the invading forces. Our Italian allies were responsible for the north side. We were up against the British, they against the Americans, who had a secret weapon called Lucky Luciano. You may have heard of him. An expatriate *mafioso* whom they released from prison, where he was serving a fifty-year sentence, to persuade the Italians not to resist the invasion. And it was successful. Luciano got Calogero Vizzini, the *capo dei capi* at the time, to guarantee Mafia support for the Allies in return for the release of all their friends from the Fascist prisons where they had been languishing since Mussolini cracked down on them. As a result, we were quickly outflanked, despite having put up a vigorous defence, and forced to withdraw to the mainland.'

He smiled bitterly at Zen.

'The rest, as they say, is history.'

Zen finished his whisky.

'That doesn't explain why you're living here.'

'Doesn't it? Well, that would perhaps take too long. At any rate, I was captured later, during the battle for Anzio, and spent the rest of the war in a prison camp. When I got back to Germany and learned exactly what we'd all been fighting so bravely to defend, I realized that I wouldn't be able to live there again. I gathered up what little money I had, added a little more left me by my parents, who were killed in a bombing raid, sold what was left of our family home and moved here. In 1950, this house cost me thirty thousand lire, including legal fees. I have been living here on the remnants of my meagre fortune ever since.'

'Doing what?' asked Zen incredulously.

Klaus Genzler shrugged.

'Trying to remember. Trying to forget. Trying to understand.'

He threw his cigar butt into the fireplace.

'Now then, shall I contact our friends and tell them you're here?'

Zen took a hundred-lire coin from his pocket and spun it up into the air. Grabbing at it clumsily, he managed only to send it flying across the floor into the vast shadows at the back of the room, where it ended up underneath an ancient leather sofa the size of a car. Both men laughed.

Zen shrugged wearily.

'Do it,' he said.

The German went to the end of the room and leaned out. Taking hold of the metal clothesline strung across the alley, he jerked it hard three times, so that it clanked in its socket at the other side. After a moment, the shutters on the house across the road opened and a man's head appeared.

'*Buona sera, Pippo*,' said Genzler. 'Yes, wasn't it? No, no damage here. And you? The statue fell? Well, I'm sure the mayor can get a grant from his friends in the regional government to have it put back up again. He's very good at that sort of thing. Listen, I happen to know of someone who wishes to talk to Don Gaspà, and I am informed that the Don is equally anxious to talk to him. The person's name is Aurelio Zen. Do you think you could make enquiries and . . . He'll be out here in the street, in about five minutes. Very good, we'll expect them soon.'

He closed the shutters and turned to Zen.

'They're on their way. Have you a gun?'

Zen shook his head.

'Good,' said Genzler. 'I'll see you to the door.'

'I can find my own way.'

'No, I'll accompany you.'

324

'That's very kind of you, Herr Genzler.'

'It's not a question of kindness. Like this, they will know that I know that you are in their hands. So if they kill you, they will have to kill me too. As I said, I can't guarantee anything, but it may improve your chances of survival.'

Zen stared at him.

'But you don't even know me! Why would you risk your life like that?'

Genzler's gaze was an abyss of pride and anguish.

'Because I am a German officer,' he said.

Zen pondered the implications of this statement until his thoughts were cut short by the sound of several cars outside. Then came the knock at the door.

This time he was blindfolded: a thick band of fabric over the eyes, taped to his forehead and cheeks. He tried to make himself believe that this was reassuring.

They drove for about twenty minutes along roads which reared up and down and roiled about without sense or reason. No one spoke. There were at least three of them with him in the car, the ones who had come to the door and taken him away. No one had said anything then, either, even when the German had extended his hand and said, '*Buona notte, dottore.*' They didn't seem interested. Zen was just a piece of merchandise which they had to deliver, like those plastic-wrapped packages transferred from the plane to the van on the strip of motorway where he had landed, many hours ago.

At last the car made one final lurch to the right and came to a halt. There was a brief exchange in dialect, then Zen was shoved out of the car and hustled across a paved surface, up a set of steps, where he stumbled twice, and into a building. It smelt musty and disused. His escort marched him along a bare board floor, turned him to the left, positioned him and told him to sit down. Oddly, he was more afraid of doing this blind-folded than of anything else that had happened so far, perhaps because of some memory of a childhood prank where the chair is removed at the last moment and you land on your silly bottom, hurt and humiliated.

But these people were not playing such games. He touched down on a chair to which his ankles and wrists were immediately bound with what felt like nylon cord. The men then withdrew, leaving Zen alone in the room.

It was perhaps half an hour later that he heard the car pull up outside. Being unable to see seemed to have disoriented him to a point where it was difficult to judge time. Cut off from external distractions, how-ever, the rest of his brain had been working much more efficiently than usual. By the time the clomping of footsteps on the wooden floor announced the return of his captors, he had reviewed everything he knew or could infer about what had happened in the past weeks.

He had also decided how to handle the interroga-tion which he was about to undergo. He would be respectful, and demand respect in return. 'Don't grovel,' Gilberto had told him. Grovelling to these people, even though he was totally in their power, would be fatal. If they were planning to kill him, no amount of pleading would stop them. But if they came to despise him, they might well kill him anyway, out of sheer contempt.

The broken rhythm of footsteps came to a stop near and in front of him. It was as if the room had suddenly become smaller. There were at least six of them, Zen estimated. Silence fell. He sensed that someone was inspecting him, sizing him up, gauging whom he had to deal with.

'So, Signor Zen, why did you kill our friend Spada?'

Zen noted the epithet *signore*, itself a form of insult in Sicily, implying as it did that the person concerned had no right to a title of more weight.

'Why did you kill my daughter, Don Gaspare?' he replied.

'We didn't.'

'Well, that makes us quits, because I didn't kill Spada.'

There was a brief sardonic laugh.

'Spada's brother-in-law is the caretaker at that museum. He lives in an apartment which is part of the building. When he got home later that evening, he noticed a window open on the first floor. When he went to investigate, he found Spada lying on the floor, his hands bound behind him. He had been strangled. That was at ten o'clock. He had been dead approximately two hours. You had an appointment to meet Spada there at eight o'clock. I understand that you're a

328

policeman, Signor Zen. What conclusion would you draw from these facts?'

The voice was deep, the accent strong, the man perhaps about fifty.

'Is that all that Spada's brother discovered?' demanded Zen.

'Isn't it enough?'

'No, it isn't.'

'There was some damage to some of the exhibits, and the opened window.'

Zen deliberately paused before replying.

'You asked what conclusion I would draw from what you've just told me, Don Gaspare. The answer is that I would have come to the same conclusion as you, if I hadn't been assured by an eye-witness that another man had also been killed in the museum that evening.'

Several men laughed this time, even more sardonically.

'I'm afraid we're not in a position to call this eyewitness of yours, Signor Zen, even supposing that he existed.'

'You don't need to call him. And he does exist. He's sitting in front of you.'

'So you admit you were there.'

'Certainly I was there. But so were two other men. One of them was strangling Spada when I surprised them. He drew a gun and I shot him dead. His partner escaped through the window. Evidently he returned later, turned off the burglar alarm which I had tripped, and removed his accomplice's body.'

Another laugh, slightly less assured this time.

'Why should we believe this?'

'Don Gaspare, Spada was strangled by a professional. Not the clumsy two-handed grip you see at the movies, but with one hand gripping the windpipe and the other pressed into the back of the neck. It's hard work. Look at my hands. I'm a bureaucrat, I work at a desk. Spada was strong, vigorous and at least ten years younger than me. There's no way I could have strangled him like that, still less tied him up before.'

A dense silence formed.

'So you're saying that another clan killed Spada? Who, the Corleonesi?'

'They didn't kill Spada. And I don't think they killed Tonino either.'

The blow came first as an outrageous surprise. It was only when he hit the floor that Zen began to feel pain, and to taste the dense salty blood in his mouth. Hands picked him up with the chair he was bound to and set him upright again.

'Don't you *dare* mention my son's name again!' the voice said, very close to Zen's face now.

Zen spat some bloody saliva on the floor and took a few deep breaths.

'As you mentioned, Don Gaspare, I'm a policeman. I know how interrogations are conducted. I know all the moves and all the methods, hard and soft. If you want to go hard, there's nothing I can do to stop you. But if you want the truth, we're going to have to cooperate. You know things that I don't know, and I know things that you don't know. If you beat me up every time I mention one of them, we're not going to get very far.'

A sound of shuffling feet.

'All right, then! Tell me something I don't know.'

'Spada was killed by an agent of the Carabinieri's Special Operations Group, the one I shot. His name was Alfredo Ferraro. His partner, who got away, is called Roberto Lessi. They wanted to dispose of Spada before he could talk to me, but they wanted to do so in a way which would make it look like a classic Mafia execution.'

He paused.

'That's how you do it, isn't it? If you're going to kill me, later tonight, you'll strangle me.'

'We might,' the voice conceded lightly. 'You seem very calm about the prospect.'

'Don Gaspare, in the past week my daughter has been murdered and my mother has died. My own life no longer seems as important as it once did.'

There was a brief whisper of indrawn breath.

'I had heard about your daughter's death, of course, but not about your mother's. I offer my sincere condolences.'

'I appreciate it, Don Gaspare. Now let's get back to the death of your son. You won't hit me if I call him that?'

'Go on.'

'Before she died, Judge Corinna Nunziatella made a photocopy of her file on the so-called Limina affair. She evidently feared that the papers would be officially "disappeared", as indeed happened. A hand-written note at the end of the copy mentions the names of the two ROS agents who murdered Spada. Apparently they took possession of the original file. The copy, however, was left in my safe-keeping, and after Nunziatella's death I opened it. The evidence it contains is indirect, and at first sight not very striking, but taken in conjunction with the other recent events, I think it indicates quite clearly who killed Ton . . . who killed your son.'

A raucous guffaw.

'We already know that! It was those bastards in Corleone, and we've already returned the compliment. We sent them a gift of some nice fresh meat from Catania! Right, lads?'

The other men all laughed loudly.

'The Corleonesi didn't kill your son,' said Zen stolidly.

'That's ridiculous!' snapped the other man. 'We all know that they control Palermo – or like to think they do, at least. Tonino was found in a wagon of a train which had come from Palermo, with our family name written on the waybill. The message is clear.'

'That train never existed.'

'This is totally absurd! You of all people should know that! Your colleagues had it under investigation at the marshalling yard in Catania for weeks. For all I know it's still there.'

'*A* train existed,' Zen replied, 'and it certainly originated in Palermo. But the wagon in which your son was found was never part of it. All the indications are that it had been sitting on the siding where it was found for at least a month and possibly much longer. Your son was kidnapped in Milan on his way to Costa Rica. He was then brought back to Sicily and locked in that wagon, to which a fake waybill was attached. Once he was dead, a goods train from Palermo was stopped and backed briefly into the siding where the wagon was parked, precisely to make you and everyone else believe that this was indeed a message from Palermo.'

'But if it wasn't the Corleonesi, then who? And why?'

The voice was almost imploring now. Zen had gained the upper hand.

'We'll come to that in a minute,' he said in a slightly condescending tone. 'First, I'd like to discuss something else. We've talked about your son, Don Gaspare. What about my daughter?'

'I already told you that that had nothing to do with us. We had no interest in killing that judge. I was informed that the DIA had closed the case, having accepted our declaration that the body on the train was not Tonino. It was, of course, but we prefer to settle our accounts in our way and in our own good time, without interference from the authorities. Anyway, they believed us. Why should we bother killing a judge who had been taken off a case which was no longer active?'

'Nunziatella must have had other active cases, perhaps involving other clans. Maybe one of them killed her.'

'No!'

'How can you be sure?'

'*You don't understand!*'

The words were like another fist in the face.

'Nothing happens on my territory unless I have either ordered or connived at it, understand? I run Catania. The port, construction projects, kickbacks, protection rackets, hiring and firing, everything! And most certainly any killings that occur. I wouldn't be who I am if I didn't. And I'm telling you that neither I nor any of my friends had anything whatsoever to do with the murder of that judge.'

'You *used* to run Catania,' Zen said quietly.

An enormous silence.

'Maybe I'll have Rosario cut your throat,' hissed the other man. 'If only to show that I still have some fucking say about what goes on around here!'

'Of course you do, Don Gaspare,' Zen replied soothingly. 'But killing me wouldn't prove that. Just the opposite, in fact. I'm just a common policeman, not even a DIA operative. You would actually lose respect by killing someone like me. It would be like mugging an old lady.'

There was a low laugh.

'You've got balls, Zen, I'll give you that.'

'I'm not a fool either. I think I know who killed Corinna Nunziatella, but I don't have conclusive proof and so I had to make absolutely sure that you and your friends were not involved. But there was no need to get so angry. You could simply have given me your word as a *uomo d'onore*. I would have accepted that without question.'

'So who did kill that judge?' the voice asked in a mollified tone.

'The same people who killed Spada. The same people who killed your Tonino.'

He braced himself for the blow, but it did not come.

'The ROS agents?'

'Either them, or someone very much like them.'

'But why would they kill one of their own?'

'Well, they might have done so because Nunziatella had stumbled on evidence undermining the official line on your son's death. If one of the clans had wanted to kidnap Tonino, they wouldn't have waited until he was in transit at the international airport in Milan to do it. And diverting a train is much easier if you've got the power of a state organization behind you. But as a matter of fact I don't think that killing the judge was their primary intention. She was just an extra, a little ham on the bread, as they say. But it was very helpful to them, because it enabled them to make the operation look like a typical Mafia hit, and so disguise the identity of the real target.'

'And who was that?'

'My daughter.'

This time, the ensuing silence felt thin, diffuse and frail.

'You're making me feel old and out of touch,' the voice said.

Zen smiled for the first time.

'Welcome to the club. I've only worked it out myself in the last day or two. There's nothing like being on the run to concentrate the mind. My daughter was installing the new computer network for the DIA offices in Catania, designed to link them to each other and their colleagues in Palermo and elsewhere. She told me that she had discovered an anomaly in the system, someone coming in from outside and spying on the status of the work in progress. She had also identified the "fingerprint" of the computer being used to access the system. That meant that it could be traced.'

He broke off.

'Could someone give me a smoke?'

After a brief pause, a lighted cigarette was pushed between his lips. He inhaled urgently. It was a *bionda*, by the taste of it, probably American. That made sense. The Mafia would smoke the cigarettes they smuggled, and these wouldn't be the low-cost, low-profit *Nazionali*. He took two or three puffs, then spat the cigarette out to one side.

'Carla naturally assumed that the intruder was someone working for Cosa Nostra, so she informed the director of the DIA in Catania about her discoveries. Unfortunately, her assumption was almost certainly mistaken. For one thing, you and your friends don't strike me as being any more computer-literate than I am. No doubt you could hire someone to try to hack into the DIA server, but I doubt that such an idea would even occur to you. More to the point, according to Carla, the DIA network hadn't been forcibly entered. The access which the intruder was using had been planted in the system from the start. Well, we know who specified the system to be used by an élite judicial and law-enforcement department, and it wasn't you or your friends.'

Zen tried to loosen slightly the bonds on his wrists and ankles, which were beginning to ache intolerably. To his surprise, the voice barked an order in dialect, and the cords were untied.

'Thank you, Don Gaspare,' he said.

'So they kill your daughter because she knows that they exist. But who are they, and what are their aims?'

Zen rubbed his wrists, trying to get the circulation going again.

'The short answer, of course, is that we'll never know. But on the basis of the events we *do* know about, I think we can make a pretty accurate guess. Are you familiar with that famous trick picture, Don Gaspare? You can see it either as a vase or as the profile of two faces in silhouette. I think that this affair has been a similar trick. Everybody assumes that the Corleonesi killed your son, that you or some other clan killed Judge Nunziatella, and that some equally shadowy party *di stampo mafioso* strangled Spada.'

'Well, it certainly looks like that's what happened, doesn't it?'

Zen smiled again.

'But what would it look like, if it looked like my version of events? What would it look like if someone had an interest in promoting violence between the clans here in Sicily, and in showing that they are still capable of killing heavily protected DIA judges? What would it look like if that someone had ordered your son to be kidnapped and then left to die in that wagon, in such a way as to make the killing appear to be a message from Palermo? What would it look like if they had discovered that my daughter had unearthed evidence which would identify this someone, and that Spada was about to give me further details when we met that evening? What would it look like if all this were the case, Don Gaspare?'

There was a pause, then a low cough.

'It would look the same as it does in fact look,' the voice replied.

'My point precisely.'

'But who is this "someone"?'

'Who knows? There must be plenty of people in Rome who regret the good old days of the Red Brigades and the Mafia wars. Too much stability is the last thing a politician wants. Who needs a strong government when everything is going well? Politicians have a vested interest in problems, crises and general unease. And if those things don't happen to exist at a given moment, then they have to invent them. And that's what this whole bloody business has been from start to finish – an invention.'

'You don't need to lecture me about the *terzo livello*,' the other man replied drily. 'But believe me, it's dead.

All our contacts are either in prison, in exile, or politically disgraced and powerless.'

'The *old* Third Level, perhaps,' Zen replied. 'But there may be levels that you don't even know about. The fact is, Don Gaspare, and I say this with all due respect, I get the impression that neither you nor the Corleonesi are quite at the cutting edge of organized crime here in Sicily these days.'

Footsteps sounded out loudly, stomping towards him. The voice said loudly, '*No!*' The steps ceased in a sigh of mute frustration.

'Forgive me, Don Gaspare,' Zen went on. 'I'm simply repeating what I've heard. And I'm all the more inclined to believe it, because it would explain why these people in Rome chose your two clans as subjects for their destabilization project. You both still have a high profile, which will guarantee lots of publicity in the event of another Mafia war breaking out, but the truth of the matter is that you're both finished as major players. The real action now is in smaller places like Cáccamo and Belmonte Mezzagno, and above all in Ragusa, where I was "met at the airport" tonight. Those are the people that the politicians will be courting. You and your friends are yesterday's men, just like me. We're all expendable, counters in whatever game they're playing.'

He paused significantly.

'And if you kill me, you'll be playing their game.'

There was a mutter of voices, a subdued argument, a sense of suppressed dissension. Then the voice returned, quite close to Zen, and slightly to his right.

'We're not going to kill you, Dottor Zen. You have treated me with respect, and I shall accord you the same treatment. You have never set eyes on me, and the place where we are is nowhere near my home. You therefore pose no threat to us, although those pushy little squirts in Ragusa could be in trouble if you reveal the location of the landing strip they use for their drug runs. But fuck them!'

A wave of laughter enveloped the room.

'It has been a privilege meeting you,' the voice went on, 'but for both our sakes I hope that our paths do not cross again. You cannot be my friend, and I would hate to have you as my enemy. We shall be leaving now. Your wrists and ankles have been freed. In your own interests, I ask you not to remove your blindfold for at least five minutes after we leave. If you do, and any of us are still here, we shall have no compunction about killing you. Once we are clear of this area, one of my men will place a call to the authorities in Catania and report your whereabouts. Goodbye, Dottor Zen.'

'Goodbye, Don Gaspare.'

The herd of footsteps trooped out, and then Zen heard the roar of car engines. Soon they faded, and a perfect silence formed.

It was not broken for another three hours, much longer than Zen had reckoned on. He spent the time sitting on the steps of the abandoned farmhouse in which he had been questioned. The moon was up, but the only other light to be seen was a curved stripe of glowing red in the night sky, as vivid and troubling as an open wound. He finally realized that it must be the molten lava flowing down one of the many flanks of Etna after the eruption which had been signalled by the earlier tremors.

Then, at long last, other lights appeared: mere points at first, two fixed, the other mobile, weaving from side to side and up and down and sometimes disappearing for minutes at a time. Eventually sound was added to the spectacle, a low thrumming and a slightly higher and more abrasive grating. All these phenomena increased in intensity, until a car and an accompanying motorcycle swept into the farmyard and came to a stop at the foot of the steps. The man seated astride the bright red motorbike started talking into a two-way radio, and Baccio Sinico leapt out of the car.

'Thank God you're safe!' he exclaimed as Zen stood up. 'I'm sorry it took us so long to get here, but our colleagues in the Carabinieri were worried that it might be a trap and wanted to make certain preparations, all of which took some time. Then, to cap it all, their car got separated from us somehow on the drive up. They must have taken a wrong turning, I suppose. But, oh, *dottore*! Why did you run off like that? Look how it turned out! All we were trying to do was protect you. As it is, you're lucky to be alive.'

'We're all lucky to be alive, Baccio,' Zen remarked sententiously. 'The problem is that we often forget it.'

They walked down the steps and over to the waiting car. As they passed the man on the motorcycle, he removed his helmet and put away his radio.

'We're cleared to go,' he told Baccio Sinico. 'We'll be taking a slightly different route, via Belpasso. I'll stay about fifty metres ahead. Keep my tail-light in view at all times.'

Sinico turned to Zen.

'This is our colleague from the Carabinieri, Roberto Lessi. I think you've met before.'

The ROS agent stared silently at Zen, who nodded slowly.

'Yes,' he said. 'We've met before.'

Lessi replaced his helmet and revved up his engine. Sinico was holding the back door of the car open, but Zen got into the one in front.

'Do you mind if I sit here?' he asked. 'They tied me up for a long time and I'd like to be able to stretch my legs.'

'Of course, *dottore*,' said Sinico. Then, to the driver, 'Let's go, Renato! Follow the bike.'

Zen lit a cigarette with trembling fingers.

'But how on earth did you manage to talk the Limina clan into letting you go?' Sinico demanded, leaning forward from the back seat. 'They have a reputation for cruelty second to none. Their speciality is slow drowning in a bath of water followed by disposal of the corpse in one of the side vents of Etna.'

Zen opened the window to clear the smoke from his cigarette.

'Oh, I told them a pack of lies,' he said dully.

'What sort of lies?'

'I turned the facts of the affair inside out and suggested that some secret government agency in Rome was behind the whole thing. A campaign of destabilization and so on.'

Sinico gave an incredulous laugh.

'And they believed you?'

'I don't know if they believed me, but they let me go.'

Sinico leaned forward between the two front seats and spoke quietly into Zen's ear.

'But *you* don't believe this conspiracy theory, do you?'

'Of course not.'

They hurtled along the twisting road, following the tail-light of the Moto Guzzi.

'By the way, do you have my revolver?' asked Sinico.

'I'm afraid I lost it. I'll take full responsibility. Fill out a docket for a replacement and I'll sign it.'

'Only there's a problem, you see. One of Roberto's colleagues has been killed. I think you met him too. Alfredo Ferraro.'

'I seem to remember the name.'

'Well, he was shot. Late last night, in that rough area just north of Piazza San Placido, where the whores and the *extracommunitari* hang out.'

Zen took another drag at his cigarette and tossed it out of the window.

'That's where they found the body?'

'Yes, at about midnight. And the problem is that it seems that he was almost certainly shot with my revolver. As you know, we have to perform test firings whose ballistic characteristics are kept on file. They found one of the bullets fired at the scene, and forensic tests show that the characteristics of my revolver are identical to those of the murder weapon.'

Zen nodded.

'Unfortunately I can't help you, because the gun was taken from me much earlier that evening, just an hour or so after I left you.'

'Taken? How?'

'A pickpocket. You know that Catania is notorious for petty crime. I was walking down a street near San Nicolò when a woman stopped me and asked me for a light. While I was holding it out to her, a man pushed into me from behind. The next thing I knew, they had both disappeared down an alley. Your gun and my wallet had disappeared with them.'

'Yes, I see,' said Sinico doubtfully.

'This Alfredo Ferraro probably saw the couple trying something similar in the Via San Orsola area. He challenged them, and the man pulled out your gun and shot him.'

'I suppose so. All the same, it's awkward.'

'Don't worry, Baccio, I'll sort it all out. We're alive, that's the main thing. The rest is just details.'

Ahead of them, the red light had turned brilliant white, shining straight back at them from the other side of a small valley where the road curved down across a seasonal *torrente*, now a bone-dry mass of lava boulders.

'Get a move on, Renato!' Sinico told the driver. 'We're getting left behind.'

'This is a dangerous road,' the man grumbled.

Nevertheless, he jammed his foot to the floor and the car shot forward on to the low concrete bridge across the river-bed. At the top of the hillside opposite, the man on the motorcycle flashed his headlight on and off. An answering flash of light appeared in the darkness above. A moment later, the bridge exploded.

The motorcycle rider replaced his helmet and turned his machine around. It had been an impressive blast, even though they'd had very little time. The quantity of explosives used was only a fraction of the amount which the Mafia had used to kill the judges Paolo Falcone and Giovanni Borsellino. But this too would be perceived as a message. After all, Zen was just a policeman.

Acknowledgements

Like so much of Italian public and political life, this is a work of fiction. It is however based to some extent on fact, and could not have been written without the help of many friends and contacts in Sicily and elsewhere, some of whom asked not to be named. I would particularly like to thank Dottore Domenico Percolla of the *Questura di Catania*, Karen Bass, Livia Borghese, Michael Burgoyne, Kirk Peterson, Jonathan Raban, Guido Ruotolo, Alexander Stille, and above all my wife Kathrine.

Catania – Seattle – Rome
February 1999

The Zen Series from Michael Dibdin

Ratking
Zen is unexpectedly transferred to Perugia to take
over an explosive kidnapping case involving one of
Italy's most powerful families.

Vendetta
An impossible murder in a top-security Sardinian
fortress leads Zen to a menacing and violent world
where his own life is soon at risk.

Cabal
When a man falls to his death in a chapel in St Peter's,
Zen must crack the secret of the Vatican to solve the
crime.

Dead Lagoon
Zen returns to his native Venice to investigate the
disappearance of a rich American resident, while
confronting disturbing revelations about his own
life.

Così Fan Tutti
Zen finds himself in Naples, a city trying to clean up its act – perhaps too literally, as politicians, businessmen and mafiosi begin to disappear off the streets.

A Long Finish
Back in Rome, Zen is given an unorthodox assignment: to release the jailed scion of an important wine-growing family who is accused of a brutal murder.

Blood Rain
The gruesome discovery of an unidentified corpse in a railway carriage in Sicily marks the beginning of Zen's most difficult and dangerous case.

And Then You Die
After months in hospital recovering from a bomb attack on his car, Zen is trying to lie low at a beach resort on the Tuscan coast, but an alarming number of people are dropping dead around him.

Medusa
When human remains are found in abandoned military tunnels, the case leads Zen back into the murky history of post-war Italy.

Back to Bologna
Zen is called to Bologna to investigate the murder of
the shady industrialist who owns the local football
team.

End Games
After a brutal murder in the heart of a tight-knit
traditional community in Calabria, Zen is determined
to find a way to penetrate the code of silence and
uncover the truth.